WHAT READERS SAY ABOUT **ALIEN LOG**

"I don't usually enjoy works of fiction dealing with UFOs, but Alien Log is very much the exception. Lots of solid info and an interesting story. I can't wait for the next volume. Robert Farrell has done his homework."
Stanton Friedman, Nuclear Physicist –Lecturer

"A great read! It was out of this world. Full of thought provoking fact and a good plot too."
A. Forest Jones III, Journalist, Miami, FL

"The book is an interesting and exciting novel approach to current UFO theory. It brings together many diverse scientific, engineering, and educational aspects wrapped in an eminently readable text. A delightful read to say the least."
Dr. Paul Koch, Professor of Engineering, Erie, PA

"It was a great book. I could not put it down."
Melissa Garthwaite, Seattle, WA

"Great book! It did a great job of incorporating factual info into an interesting story line. It was so good, it made me do further research into solar systems, crop circles, and the Sumerians."
Carol Meadows, Houston, TX

"Completely enjoyable and believable. Due to Dr. Farrell's educational background and professional experience, he does a great job of explaining the existence of UFOs in our world today."
Cynthia E. Braden, Memphis, TN

Nick,

It was nice meeting you at Barnes & Nobles. I hope you enjoy this book and the sequel that will follow.

Bob Farrell 22 July 05

ALIEN LOG

By

Robert E. Farrell

Published by: **R. E. FARRELLBOOKS, LLC**
Peoria, Arizona

R. E. FARRELLBOOKS, LLC
P.O. Box 6507
Peoria, Arizona 85385 - 6507
www.refarrellbooks.com

EDITED BY: Sandi Frederick
www.sandilayne.com

ISBN 0-9759116-0-0

Library of Congress Control Number: 2004108232

Printed in the United States of America

ACKNOWLEDGMENTS

This book never would have happened had it not been for the help of many people.

First and foremost, I wish to thank my wife, Linda, who stood by me patiently during the years of research and writing that went into this book. This says nothing of the countless hours she spent proofreading the many versions of this book as it evolved. Many thanks to my daughter, Wendy, who has worked diligently to get this book to market.

I would like to thank Barry Atkinson for the use of the alien head photo. It was taken of a sculpture he did for The Bear Den, Ltd.. It is a composite of information Barry got from over one hundred drawings made by people who claim to have been abducted. The final sculpture was the one that "passed the test" with the "eye witnesses." Copies of his bust can be purchased through: www.realalien.com.

Also, I would like to thank Steve Alexander and Karen Douglas, Temporary Temple Press Ltd, UK, for the crop circle photo taken in 1996 near Stonehenge. Both Steve and Karen are well known for the hundreds of photos they have taken over the years of the crop circle phenomenon in England. Copies of their work can be purchased through: www.temporarytemples.co.uk .

I owe a special debt of gratitude to the Writers Round Table of Phoenix for their time and patience in critiquing my efforts. Thanks, too, to Sandi Frederick for her superb job of editing.

I especially want to thank John Safin (The Grand **Pooh Bah**) for his help in laying out the cover as well as helping me get this book published.

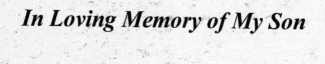

In Loving Memory of My Son

INTRODUCTION

It has been said that good science fiction is based on good science. I have tried to follow that rule in writing this book. As you might well appreciate, it is difficult to find good science in the field of UFOs and ETs. The hard evidence is lacking, at least in the public domain. It is difficult to say how much evidence exists in government warehouses and at top secret bases; they aren't talking.

Once you conclude that the UFO phenomenon is real, you are forced to rethink the entire fabric of your belief system. It now has to be reconciled with the realities of UFOs. This book may cause the reader to do just that.

PROLOGUE

Washington, DC
The Oval Office
Thursday, May 1st
8:23 pm

Colonel Mitchell's face paled as he stared into the briefcase the President had just opened. The President's voice seemed to fade into the background as Mitchell became mesmerized by what he saw.

The President forcefully cleared his throat to get Mitchell's attention. "Colonel … there are only *three* people on this planet who know that this thing exists: you, the retired general who found it back in 1953, and me. As I explained earlier, the general, who's dying of cancer, brought *that* to me only two days ago. After he told me his story, I immediately began the search for the best person I could find to head up an investigating team. You're that person.

"I believe that device you're looking at is a key, not only to our national security but, perhaps, to the survival of humanity as we know it. I want you to know, I will bring to bear all the powers of the President's office to help you with this project. You have carte blanche to assemble the best team you can to unlock the secrets hidden in that device. Of course, security will be of utmost importance; I don't want to set off a world-wide panic. Do you understand what I'm saying, Colonel?"

When Mitchell looked up, the President's eyes were bearing down on him. Mitchell hadn't taken a breath since he set eyes on the device. He almost hissed as the air escaped from his lungs. The room around him came back into focus as he sucked air. His voice quivered, "Yes Sir … I … I'll begin immediately." He closed the briefcase, clasping it tightly as he left the office, his face still pale.

Alone now, the President looked out of his window and stared across the White House lawn. Life on Pennsylvania Avenue still appeared normal. The usual assortment of protesters was there, pushing their causes by marching in circles and brandishing their pickets. As usual, the press cameras were there too, trying to catch whatever human interest stories they might find. The President was deep in thought, *I have a real human interest story to tell, if only I could. I wonder how much time we have? Perhaps it's already too late? Perhaps the general's the lucky one; he'll be dead in three months.*

Chapter 1
The Retrieval

1953
Indian Springs, Nevada
Tuesday, May 21
5:20 PM

Jim Wilcox was busy checking calculations on his slide rule when a shadow came over his desk. He looked up to find his supervisor, Jack Lance, staring down at him with a smile on his face. Jim recognized this smile. Jack used it when he was about to ask a favor. At six-foot-three, Jack was an imposing middle- aged man who generally had no problem extracting favors, especially when he turned on the charm.

"How ya do'n Jim? Looks like you have your project almost finished."

Jim adjusted his bow tie as he gazed up at Jack through his heavy, horned-rimmed glasses. Jim had worked for Jack for over six years. "Yeah, I'm just rechecking my calculations before I turn them in."

"Well, that's what separates you from the rest of the pack; your thoroughness. I think that's why they requested you by name."

"What do you mean?"

"I just got a call from the top brass asking me to get you on a plane to Phoenix as soon as possible. They said they need you there *yesterday*. Don't even pack your toothbrush. They said you would be gone for only one to two days and they would take care of everything you need. I've called the base and they have a plane standing by."

"What's this all about? Did a plane crash?" Jim asked.

"Don't know. They said it was super top secret and you are one of the few people with high enough clearance plus the ability to do the job. That's all they would tell me. They were quite emphatic that you get there now, Jim. The report on your analysis can wait until you get back. Hit the road."

"Okay, I'm off to the 'wild blue yonder.' Can I call Jenny?" Jim asked.

"Nope. They said you were to talk to no one. Just get down there and they'll have someone waiting for you at the Phoenix airport. I'll call Jenny and explain you were called out on an emergency case. Now get mov'n, Jim."

"Should I take my slide rule?" Jim asked, as he was closing his desk.

"Nope, just get yourself down there."

Jim frequently got called out to help investigate crashes. He had developed an expertise in reconstructing crashes. Since getting his master's degree in structural analysis from Purdue, he worked for the Air Force as a civilian technician. Most of his routine work was in assessing damage to vehicles that were bombed by new types of bombs the Air Force was developing. They wanted to know the bomb's effectiveness.

More and more though, Jim had been called in on plane crashes. He often thought of quitting because of the trauma he went through every time he probed though a plane wreck and discovered body parts. Jim kept rationalizing that his investigations would eventually make planes safer.

The flight to Phoenix took about an hour. This was one of the most boring flights Jim could remember. Normally, he had someone to talk to, but this flight was arranged hastily, just for him. During the flight Jim kept wondering, *Why the urgency?* In the past, when he was called out to investigate a crash, he would either fly commercial or catch the next military 'hop.' *This crash must be different,* he thought, as the plane was making its final approach to Luke Air Force Base. *I wonder why such secrecy? It must be a research plane.*

There was only about an hour of sunlight left as the C-54 rolled to a stop near one end of the tarmac. Within seconds, a boarding ladder was docked next to the door. Jim felt like a VIP, getting all of this attention. As he exited the plane and began going down the stairs he noticed two Air Force captains waiting at the bottom.

"Mr. Wilcox, would you follow us please?" The officers motioned for him to follow as they headed off toward a waiting military bus parked a few hundred feet away.

Jim found himself almost running to keep up with the men. When they got to the bus, they motioned for him to enter.

"As you go in," said one of the captains, "enter the special compartment at the end of the bus, please. Don't talk to anyone, and *do not* mention your name to anyone, Sir. You will find a soldier and four other civilians in the compartment. *Do not* talk to them." The soldier has orders to take extreme measures if you violate my orders. *Do you understand?*"

"Yes." said Jim as he opened the door to the rear compartment.

"This is where we leave you, Sir. Good luck," said one of the captains as the both turned away.

Jim entered the rear compartment that comprised the last half of the bus. All of the windows were painted over so no one could see out. As promised, there were four other civilians sitting silently in their seats. A military policeman sat facing the four men. He looked like a wrestler. His biceps were bigger than Jim's leg and he had an ugly scar running from the base of his left eye to the corner of his mouth.

The policeman looked at Jim and pointed to a fifth seat across from him. "Sir, sit down over there, please, so the driver can get started. This trip will take over three hours. I suggest you try to sleep. *Do not* talk with any of these other passengers. If you need to use the john during our trip, use the one in the back of the bus," he said, in a firm voice. He had one hand resting on his sidearm.

Jim followed orders. *This crash must involve the most top secret craft in the military*, he thought. The bus began rolling.

Even though it was night, he found it hard to relax. Eventually, sheer boredom put Jim to sleep. During the last twenty minutes of the trip, the bus began to pitch and roll as it headed up an incline, on what felt like a rocky road. Everyone was awake by the time the bus came to a stop.

"Okay, gentlemen, we have arrived!"

Jim was still groggy as the soldier announced their arrival to the big mystery site.

"Now gentlemen," said the soldier, "I want to remind you to talk to no one except the military personnel who will seek you out as you exit the bus. That officer will direct you to your tent and explain what you are to do. This mission is top secret and I am ordered to shoot if you fail to follow orders. *Do you all understand*?"

"Yes!" said the five nervous civilians as they began to exit the bus. The other four were each escorted away and were out of sight by the time Jim's feet touched the ground.

He peered into the night and saw his escort approach in the darkness. Even though it was dark, he could tell that they were in desert country and in the foothills of a mountain.

"No need for introductions, I know who you are. Please follow me, Sir," a stern looking captain said. Although formidable, he was far less threatening than the man on the bus had been. The captain looked to be in his late twenties or early thirties. Even though they were in the middle of the desert, the captain's uniform was neatly creased in all the right places. He was obviously a career officer.

Jim followed the captain over to a private tent a hundred feet from the bus and equally far from each of the other tents to which the other civilians were being led. It was obvious to him that this was to be his separate briefing. As they entered the tent, the captain motioned for him to sit at a table provided for him.

"Is there anything you need, Sir? Do you need to hit the latrine or do you want anything to drink after your trip?" The captain spoke in a very polite tone.

"No, thank you, but as you can imagine, I am extremely curious about all of this cloak-n-dagger stuff."

"I do apologize for your treatment but it was necessary. You are about to see what few people on Earth have ever seen. With your top secret clearance, you've probably seen things most civilians haven't, but to see what you are about to see requires the highest clearance. It will be considered *treason* if you *ever* mention what you will see here tonight. We are at war. Do you know the penalty for treason in wartime, Mr. Wilcox?"

Jim wasn't aware the Korean Conflict had been upgraded to a war, but he wasn't going to argue. This man truly meant business. "Yes, I do," said Jim. He was feeling very intimidated again.

"Good! In a few minutes I'll take you out to the crash site and you will have thirty minutes to view the wreckage. On that table before you are all the tools I believe you will need to make any measurements you require. Also, I have provided you with a slide rule and writing paper. Your mission is to determine force of impact, impact velocities, and any other information about the structure you can gather in half an hour. You will be given six hours to do your calculations and write your report. At oh-seven-hundred hours the bus will leave, to take you and the others back to Phoenix."

Jim surveyed the instruments and slide rule on the table before him.

"Is everything in order?" the captain asked.

"I guess this will do."

"Good. Then let's go out to the site. If any of the other civilians are at the scene, you are not to talk to them. Understand?"

"Yes." Jim was beginning to get tired of this constant reminding. He wasn't an idiot!

The captain led him out of the back entrance of the tent and into the darkness. By the time Jim's eyes began to adjust to the darkness, he could see a larger tent in the distance about a hundred yards ahead. The tent looked like it was about forty by sixty feet and had red lights shining on all sides. "Is the total crash site contained inside that tent?" Jim asked.

"Yes."

Very unusual, Jim thought. *Normally, wreckage is spewed over the area of one or two football fields. This plane must have come straight down.*

Armed guards were stationed around the perimeter of the tent. They were spaced about twenty feet apart and stood facing away from the tent. These guards meant business. They were well armed and had fixed bayonets. There were also several canine police circling the area.

As Jim and the captain approached the entrance to the tent, one of the guards challenged the captain for authorization. After the captain did the proper identification, the guard pulled the tent flap back so they could enter.

What Jim saw was difficult for him to believe! Even though the tent was dimly lit, he could see, before him, a lens-shaped craft about thirty feet in diameter and ten feet thick. "It has no wings!" Jim blurted out to the captain. He looked at the captain with embarrassment for his lack of composure.

The captain didn't respond right away but then followed with, "If you need any help taking measurements, let me know."

"Thanks, I may need help holding this tape measure from time to time."

The craft was tipped up at an angle of twenty to thirty degrees. One end was buried two feet into the ground. It was a dull gray metallic color. The captain motioned Jim to follow him around to the "rear" of the craft. Rear had little meaning on this craft since it was round. As they got to the rear, he could see a small hatch on the underside that had been removed.

"It's a bit of a squeeze but you can crawl in here," the captain remarked. "I'll follow you. Watch your head, please."

As Jim squeezed in, he found the interior dimly lit by some makeshift lights. The interior was only about twenty feet in diameter and about five and a half feet high, not enough room for an average man to stand upright. There was a small hatch in the floor that appeared to lead to a lower compartment.

On this 'deck' Jim could see a small console with four small seats along one side. Some of the seats were smudged with what looked like blood stains. His heart began to throb as he scanned the room for body parts. There were none. *Thank God!* Jim turned his attention again to the four small seats. *These seats are really strange. No pilot I ever saw could fit in those. They would have to be midgets*, he thought.

Jim looked toward the captain, "Is this craft one of ours?" He already knew the answer.

"You *do not* have the need to know," the captain responded tersely, "Let's get on with the measurements. You only have a limited time here."

After measuring the interior, the captain took him outside for further measurements. For the next few minutes, he and the captain worked their way around the craft, taking various measurements. At the buried end of the craft, Jim bent over to brush sand away from the craft. Almost simultaneously, he and the captain noticed a small shiny black object next to the hull. It was almost completely buried. "What's this?" Jim said as he pulled it out of the sand and held it in front of the captain.

The captain's face grew pale. "Let me have that!" he barked. "You did not see this. Do not mention to anyone that you saw this. *No one.* Do you understand?" The captain unbuttoned two buttons of his shirt and slid the object in. He looked at Jim and buttoned his shirt with a glare. "If you mention this to *anyone*, I'll have you shot," he hissed.

They returned to the tent assigned to Jim and he began to do the required calculations for his report. By oh-seven-hundred, Jim had finished his report and was placed aboard the waiting bus.

The captain shook Jim's hand as he boarded the bus. He gave Jim a piercing stare. "Don't forget, *do not* tell anyone what you saw or did here. *No one*, not even your supervisor!"

Chapter 2
Do Your Duty

Present year
Boston, Massachusetts
Wednesday, May 7th
8:45 AM

The visitor exited Massachusetts Avenue onto the tree-lined drive that wends its way through the corporate grounds that resembled a well groomed college campus. He pulled into the visitor's parking area and parked under the shade of a tree.

Opening the briefcase on the seat next to him, he extracted one of the manila folders and leafed through its contents. Satisfied, he took the folder, got out of his car and began the long walk up the winding, shrub-lined sidewalk toward the entrance of the imposing building in front of him.

This twenty-story stainless-steel-and-glass structure dominated the landscape. The mirrored glass surface reflected the skyline of downtown Boston, just six miles to the southeast. Emblazoned along the top of the building, in two-story high letters, was the word GraviDyne.

The visitor entered the building and paused just inside the cavernous lobby. Slightly overwhelmed, he looked around to get his bearings. He spotted the reception desk thirty yards to his left and headed towards it. As he walked through the empty lobby, his hard leather heels beat out a cacophony that echoed through the marbled, four-story canyon.

"May I help you, Sir?" said the beautiful, middle-aged woman sitting at a console behind the counter. She was wearing an earpiece that had a small microphone projecting along her cheek towards the corner of her mouth.

"Yes, thank you," the visitor said as he handed her his business card. "I'm Mr. Allison and I have a nine o'clock appointment with Dr. Fox."

"Just one moment, please, and I'll see if he's in his office." She glanced at his business card.

"Thank you," said the visitor as he scanned the lobby. Marble columns straddled oak paneling that was accented with heavy oak cornices. This felt like a bank. There was no doubt that he was near Boston. The stodgy New England atmosphere permeated throughout every detail of the lobby. It was the clean, graceful lines of the building's exterior, along with the campus-like landscape, that indicated this might be a research facility. Indeed, research was being done on a grand scale within these walls. With MIT and Harvard only four miles down the road, there was an endless supply of brilliant minds ready to take on the latest scientific challenges.

"Dr. Fox is ready to see you now," she said as she held out a plastic badge. "Here you are, Mr. Allison, please wear this visitor's badge at all times while you're in this building. The elevator to your right will take you to Dr. Fox's office." She pointed toward the elevator. "Use that express elevator. It takes you straight up to the executive suites on the eighteenth floor. When you get off the elevator, turn left and you'll see Dr. Fox's executive assistant. She'll be waiting for you. Have a nice day," she said, with a smile.

"Thank you," he said and headed towards the elevator.

_ _ _ _ _ _ _ _ _ _ _

On the second floor, Dr. Corey Newton was deep in thought as he eased his tall well-built frame through the narrow aisles separating the rows of books in the company's library. In this seven-thousand-square-foot room were publications representing the world's body of knowledge on the physics of gravity. Corey continued down one row after another. Suddenly, he stopped in front of one particular volume, bound in brown, with gold printing along its binding. He stared for a moment and then removed it from the shelf.

"Let me see," he said softly as he opened the book— "I think this is it. Yes ... *The Quantum Aspect of Gravity Waves*. Yes, this should have what I need." As he began thumbing through the pages of the Doctoral dissertation, a squeaky voice from behind called out.

"There you are, Corey. Dr. Fox is looking for you."

Corey knew who it was without turning around: the one person with whom he always hated to make even the most remote contact.

"Hi, James," Corey said, forcing himself to be pleasant. He turned to face the squeaky voice. At six-two, Corey was at least six inches taller than James. Looking down on him, Corey smiled and said, "What does Dr. Fox want?"

"How should I know? He probably got another call from someone complaining about your articles on flying saucers," responded James Atherton III, Ph.D., as he stood well inside Corey's comfort zone. He was staring up at him through thick, horned rimmed, glasses that were taped in the center. Corey didn't know why they were taped, nor did he care.

"I do those papers on my own time. No one has any right to complain," Corey responded with a hiss of contempt. "You know, James, I know that since you have a Ph.D. from MIT, you consider yourself a scientist. But ... you give science a bad name by not keeping an open mind. If you would only take the time to read even one of my papers," Corey shrugged, "perhaps even you might understand the potential advantages of the technology I discuss."

In Corey's mind, James was full of unguided intelligence; unencumbered by any hint of wisdom and completely lacking social graces. To Corey, James epitomized a mousy, brown-nosing nerd.

With another annoying squeak, James said, "Well, *those* papers make us all look like crazy geeks and give our company a bad name. Even if your UFOs do exist, what do they have to do with the study of gravity? So ... why *shouldn't* Dr. Fox be upset?"

"Did Dr. Fox say that's the reason he wants to see me?" Corey asked, with restraint.

"No, I'm just guessing. Judith was down looking for you at your cubbyhole and said to find you and send you to Dr. Fox's office, *right away*. So you better go now," James commanded. Without giving Corey a chance to respond, he continued his attack. "I know, just because all the females around here swoon when you walk down the aisle, you think you're better than I am. Well, you may be better looking, but I'll match my brains against yours any day."

Corey felt compelled to tell James about another part of his anatomy that would better match his brains, but decided not to go to his level. He hesitated for a moment as James, arms folded, continued to look up at him with a sneer. Corey studied him for a moment. It was time to end this conversation. "Perhaps we'll do that on another day, James. I need to go now."

Before James could respond, Corey turned and headed out of the library.

It was true; most of the women at GraviDyne did give Corey a second look. What made him even more attractive was that he was not aware of his appeal. Ever since the tragic loss of his fiancé, he kept to himself.

Corey had a unique enthusiasm for life. In many ways, he was like a young child whose mind is like a sponge, absorbing everything around him. Every rock is hiding a new adventure, if only it were overturned.

It took only minutes for Corey to make his way up to the executive suites. He entered the outer office and approached Dr. Fox's assistant. "Hi, Judith, James said Dr. Fox is—"

"Hi, Corey," Judith interrupted with a smile. "I'm sorry." She shrugged apologetically. "I had to send James out to find you because he was the only one not busy." Judith understood the chemistry between Corey and James.

"Why am I not surprised that James was not busy?" Corey asked as he rolled his eyes in disgust.

"Dr. Fox has a visitor with him, but he told me to interrupt as soon as you arrived. I'll tell him you're here." Judith pressed a button on the intercom. "Dr. Fox, excuse me, Dr. Newton is here."

The voice on the other end said, "Thanks, Judith. Send him in."

As with all of the offices on the eighteenth floor, Dr. Fox's office was plush. The entire six hundred square feet was covered with plush light-blue carpeting. The walls were covered with conservative gold-striped wallpaper and a rich, cherry, wainscoting. The entire twenty feet of the rear wall was glass that looked southeast over Spy Pond towards downtown Boston. Four miles in the distance, along Massachusetts Avenue, was Harvard University. Farther down the avenue was a domed building that marked the MIT campus. Two fireside chairs graced the front corners of Dr. Fox's large, uncluttered desk.

Dr. Tom Fox was Corey's senior by twenty-five years. He had served on Corey's dissertation committee as he completed his Doctorate in astrophysics at MIT. Tom had been so impressed with Corey's work on quantum gravity that he hired him full time, even before he received his degree. Their working relationship had grown to become a strong, personal one. Even though Corey was three inches taller than Tom, he always said he 'looked up to' Tom as his mentor.

As Corey entered the inner sanctum, he noticed a middle-aged man with graying temples and a conservative blue suit, sitting in one of the chairs across from Dr. Fox's desk. "Come in, Corey, I'd like to introduce you to Mr. Allison. Have a seat," he gestured to a chair. "I've been telling Mr. Allison about your work here."

Mr. Allison rose and shook his hand.

Corey took the seat next to him. "I hope you've been telling him only the good stuff," he said with a nervous smile on his face. The visitor had a sweaty handshake; perhaps James was right. Perhaps this man was a stockholder.

"Certainly, only the good stuff." Tom was not in his usual relaxed mood. His voice was tense as he continued … he knew Corey wouldn't be happy with what he had to say; this wouldn't be easy. "Corey, Mr. Allison is here from Washington. He wants to talk to you about becoming an important part of a special project."

"Yes, Corey, that's right," Mr. Allison added, in a calming voice. He could see that Tom was struggling.

"The project is one of extreme importance to our government."

"What sort of project? Why do you want me?" Corey was more relaxed now. The man was not a stockholder.

"Perhaps I should start by telling you that it's not my project. I work for a government recruiting agency. We recruit for other agencies to fill their needs. Usually, as is the case now, I'm not given the details of the position or the project. As to why you were selected … I don't know. Perhaps they chose you for your expertise in physics. I was not part of the reviewing process. My client just directed me to recruit you.

"How did they get my name?"

"I don't know."

Corey looked at Tom. "Would this be a temporary assignment from GraviDyne?"

"Yes," said Tom. "You'll only be on loan for the duration of the project.

Corey looked at Mr. Allison. "Where is this project site located?"

"I don't know," said Mr. Allison.

"I see," said Corey.

Tom studied Corey's face for signs of acceptance. He could tell by the way Corey kept studying Mr. Allison that he had deep reservations about his credentials. "I just called a general I know at the Pentagon. The general said that Mr. Allison has helped him many times in staffing issues."

"Mr. Allison, how long will I be gone?" Corey probed for a way out of this situation.

"I don't know. They said they needed you until the job is done. I really don't know how long that will take and I don't want to mislead either you or Dr. Fox."

"When do I have to leave?"

"As soon as possible; Saturday, at the latest." Mr. Allison's cell phone began to ring. "Could you two excuse me for a moment while I take this call?" he said as he rose to step outside the office.

"Sure, it's no problem. Why don't you take your call in the conference room next door," Tom said.

"Thanks. I'll just be a moment," Mr. Allison said as he left.

Corey scratched his chin. His project was just getting exciting and now was not the time to leave on temporary duty. "Tom, I didn't want to say this in front of Mr. Allison, but I don't think I can be ready to leave that soon. It'll take at least another month to get to the point where I can set our project aside." Corey took on a more relaxed expression; the government would have to find someone else.

"Believe me, Corey, this transfer is not something I want. I'm only going along with it because Mr. Allison assured me that the project is of vital importance to our national security."

"Maybe he just said that so he could complete his assignment in recruiting me."

"No. He's telling the truth. There's a great deal of urgency. When I questioned him about that, he had me call someone else … the President."

"How would the president of GraviDyne know about that?"

"No, I mean the President of United States!

"Are you kidding?"

"No, I'm not! I really did talk to the President of the United States. Trust me Corey, they want you for this project and they want you now."

Corey sat back against his seat, in disbelief. "The President of The United States wants me? I can't believe that. I've never done anything important— not yet anyway. Why would he want *me*?"

"They do want you," Tom insisted. "The President convinced me that it was important for our national security to loan you to the government ... *as soon as possible*. What could I do? I agreed. Truthfully, the President made me feel like this project is so important, that both of our careers will somehow take a nosedive if you don't sign on. It's very difficult to say no to the President. So you see, the choice is really not yours. "

Corey looked at Tom with a blank expression. "How long will I be gone?" He was trying to buy time to regroup his defense.

"I don't know. Neither Mr. Allison or the President could answer that question."

"Do you think we're talking a month, six months, a year or what?" Corey's face was now distorted. He was out of options and losing this battle.

Tom could see Corey becoming frustrated. "I really don't know. I don't know what agency you'll be working for or what you'll be doing. This is not unusual, especially in high security projects."

Corey looked at Tom with pleading eyes. "Tom, who will run my project while I'm gone?"

"We'll just have to work around your absence. We have no choice here. You must understand."

"I understand." Corey did understand but he didn't like it. "But, I've been working on project ACCENT for six months now and feel like a father to it."

"I understand, but this is a higher calling. You must let go of your project; at least for a while." Tom paused for more ammunition. "You should be flattered that the President has asked for you ... by name. It's a wonderful honor. I envy you."

"Don't misunderstand me, Tom, I am flattered. And, if Mr. Allison's project is a matter of national security, how can I refuse? Surely, you can understand my apprehension though. I'm being asked to join an unknown agency to do an unknown project in an unknown place for an indefinite time. How would you feel, Tom?"

Tom studied Corey for a moment. He could see that he was going to fall in line but just needed a little more stroking. "The same… but just as I'd go … I know you'll do the right thing and go … right?"

"Of course I will." Corey was beginning to relax. He knew he had lost the battle and now he began to rationalize the benefits of doing what was going to be inevitable. After a few moments of silence: "The President actually mentioned me by name?   I am honored.   It sounds exciting," Corey said with a forced tone of excitement.

Mr. Allison returned in time to hear Corey's last comment.   "It sounds like you've decided to join the project."

"Yes. Yes, I have. It sounds exciting."

"Great!" Mr. Allison was beaming; he had fulfilled his mission here. But just to make sure, "The President will be so pleased."

The tension in the room vanished and Tom, relieved at Corey's decision, smiled at Mr. Allison and said, with a sigh, "That's it, then. It's settled." Tom knew the outcome before Corey ever arrived at his office. This little dance was just a formality. The government wins every time.

"Yes," said Mr. Allison, "I'll begin to set things into motion. Corey, your travel arrangements will be taken care of by my client. Someone from my office will contact you about that. By the way, don't worry about your apartment or any of those details. My client will cover all expenses to hold your apartment. I don't want you to worry about anything. Just get packed." He looked at Tom and then Corey. "You understand, your acceptance of this job must remain confidential. Dr. Fox, you are the only one at this company who will know why Dr. Newton isn't here."

"Corey, our cover story will be that I have temporarily sent you into the field to do some important research for your project."

"That sounds good," said Mr. Allison. "Well, I must leave now so I can get things set into motion. I'll be out of my office for several days, so my assistant, Mr. Johnson, will be contacting you about your travel arrangements. Oh, by the way, pack light. All of your clothes will be provided to you when you arrive at your destination; courtesy of Uncle Sam. Mr. Johnson will also be contacting you, Dr. Fox, to make salary arrangements for Dr. Newton." Mr. Allison rose to leave. "Thanks again, goodbye to both of you."

Corey and Tom rose and shook his hand as he left.

"Corey, stick around for a few minutes so we can iron out some details," Tom said as he returned to his desk and sat down.

"Sure," Corey said as he returned to his seat, "what do you think this project that Mr. Allison discussed, is all about?" Corey was already beginning to become excited.

"I don't know, but they searched you out, so it must have something to do with your expertise on gravity. You seem to be getting excited about this. I'm glad for you."

"Thanks, I am. I don't understand why all of the secrecy, though. The study of gravity and the search for gravity waves is being done by a number of universities and organizations around the world. To my knowledge, none of those projects are top secret."

"Well, you'll know in a few days what they want you to do. Given the high level of secrecy, I guess I'll never know. I envy you. You'll be off doing exciting work and I'll be stuck here shuffling paper around and worrying about schedules and people problems." Tom wanted to reinforce Corey's decision to go.

"I'll keep that in mind the next time you want to promote me into management."

"So ... we have to come up with a cover story. What are you going to tell your parents?"

"I'll tell them that I screwed up and you're placing me in solitary confinement for six months," Corey said with a straight face.

"No, really, we need a plausible story to tell everyone."

"I think that story is plausible. James would be delighted."

"Oh yeah … James. Corey, perhaps, when you come back, you can help me figure out a way to make him disappear," Tom said with a grin. "Don't tell him I said that," he added quickly.

"Only if you promise not to promote me."

"Okay, now let's get serious. What story will we use? Let's say what I told Mr. Allison; I sent you out to do some field work on your project. Let's send you far away where it'll be hard for people to reach you. How about China? There's work being done at the Institute of Theoretical Physics in Beijing. Yes, that's it. We'll say that you discovered a paper by one of their scientists that makes us believe they're on a parallel path to your project."

"That sounds good. China is on the other side of the planet. Other than the moon, that's about as far as you can send me."

"Yes, and the only way you can contact anyone is through me so that we can maintain security on the project. Your visit there will be on the hush-hush so people are not to discuss it. Tell your parents that I'll give them periodic updates on your well-being."

"That sounds good. I think people will buy it." Corey paused for a moment. "Well, I'd better get moving. I have to get some personal arrangements made. You'll have our purchasing people process an order for airline tickets to China, won't you; so we cover our trail?"

"Oh sure, that's a good idea. I'll take care of all the other details with Mr. Allison's agent. Don't worry about a thing. Just go and do your duty."

"I'll do my best," said Corey. He shook Tom's hand and left.

After Mr. Allison got back into his car, he pressed a series of numbers on his cell phone and placed it to his ear. After someone answered, he spoke, "This is Mr. Allison. We got your man and he'll be ready to leave by Saturday morning. I was told that you would take care of his transportation. Is that right?"

"Yes," said the voice on the other end of the line. "Tell him that he'll be picked up at his apartment at oh eight hundred hours on Saturday morning. I'll arrange for the pickup."

"Yes, I'll tell him. By the way, it was very helpful having the President in on this. Well, I'm on my way to get the second person on your list. Wish me luck."

Chapter 3
Join the Team

State College, Pennsylvania
Thursday, May 8th
4:15 PM

Dr. Wendy Ahearn held the pile of bluebooks against the hip of her slim, five-foot, eleven-inch frame with her left hand. With her right, she unlocked and entered her office. The late afternoon sun sent a beam of light through her office window and onto her desk, highlighting the only vacant spot. Wendy set the exams onto the clear spot and maneuvered herself behind the desk, taking her seat as she prepared to grade her last final of the semester.

Frustrated by the cramped space, she picked up one of the piles of folders on her desk and scanned her office for another flat surface. She found one on top of her file cabinet and removed two of the piles from her desk. There were times when Wendy thought she spent more time shuffling piles than doing useful work. By some standards, her cramped ten by twelve office may have looked cluttered. To Wendy, everything was in its place; she could put her hands on any needed book or paper without having to hunt. The piles were organized by either projects or classes. All three piles on the table next to her desk were background information for the book she was writing about the Sumerian civilization. The two piles she had just moved off her desk were for two of the classes she was teaching this semester. And so it went.

Wendy could have made more room in her office by removing the extra chair that was always placed next to her desk. She refused to part with that chair; it was for her students. They needed that chair whenever they visited her for help on homework, for advising issues, or just for having a friendly bull session. She encouraged her students to stop by for a chat anytime.

Wendy put on her glasses and focused on the bluebooks. She hated wearing glasses but found they extended the time she could read before fatigue set in. She had also discovered that half-height, wire-framed reading glasses added some maturity to her face. At twenty-seven, she was only seven years older than most of her students. The glasses made her look more like a professor, she thought.

She began sifting through the pile of bluebooks. This was her last exam for the semester, and she wanted to get her grades turned in early so she could enjoy her weekend.

"Professor Ahearn?"

Wendy hadn't noticed the young girl standing in her doorway. She looked up and, pushing her glasses back up to the bridge of her nose, smiled and said, "Hi Julie, come on in." She pointed toward the extra chair. "Have a seat." Julie was her favorite student and even though only a sophomore, had already taken two classes from Wendy.

"Oh, thanks, but I don't want to keep you from your grading. I just stopped to wish you a pleasant summer. Your final was my last, so I'm heading home now. Your course was really great! Not only did you make it interesting, but I had fun."

"Thanks Julie, I enjoyed having you in my class. It's always a pleasure having students who ask good questions."

Julie beamed. "If you do have a moment, I would like to talk to you about changing majors next fall."

"What will your new major be?"

Julie could hardly contain herself. "I'm thinking about changing my major to linguistics with a minor in antiquities." She walked over to a wall where several plaques were mounted.

Wendy smiled up at Julie. "That's wonderful! I think you'll really enjoy this field. I do. You seem to have a natural bent for linguistics."

"Those lectures you gave on the ancient Sumerian tablets were fascinating and were what really got me thinking about changing my major. They were *so* exciting," Julie said as she read the inscriptions on the plaques. "I never read these plaques before. You've gotten quite a few awards for the papers you've presented. This one here says you won best paper at the Near East Antiquities Conference."

"Yes, that was for a paper I presented two years ago. It was on the Sumerian transcriptions that I had done when I was in Iraq."

"That's right. You mentioned in class that you had spent a summer in Iraq."

"Yes, I did that while working on my dissertation. Actually, I've done a considerable amount of traveling since I got into this profession. That's one thing that you need to consider, especially if you plan to minor in antiquities. You'll do a lot of traveling. My first summer in graduate school was spent in Philadelphia, studying Near Eastern antiquities at the Museum of the University of Pennsylvania."

"Oh, I love to travel. I find it exciting."

"Do you really?" Wendy studied Julie for a moment. "No promises; but perhaps next year, after you finish your junior year, I can arrange for a summer internship in England at either Oxford's Ashmolean Museum or the British Museum. I spent a summer there and have some good contacts. If you're interested in antiquities and Near Eastern culture, both of these museums are repositories for important artifacts from many of the digs in the ancient cities of Nineveh and Ur. You remember; that's the birthplace of Abraham of the Old Testament."

"Yes, I remember. Oh, that would be so cool! I hope you can arrange that."

"I'll sure try."

"When you were lecturing about your work in Iraq, I wondered how you got entry into that country. There's so much political unrest, I'm surprised that the State Department let you go in."

"That's true. I was lucky. After much effort by my congressman and friends at the British Museum, I was finally able to get a student visa. I spent an entire summer studying some of the ancient Sumerian clay tablets held at both the Mosul University and the Baghdad Museum in Iraq.

"The most fortunate part of that trip was that I was able to work under the direction of the famous Dr. Zecharia Sitchin. I helped him translate many of the tens of thousands of Sumerian tablets that have been unearthed. There's still much to be done yet. Perhaps you'll be able to do some work in that area. I'm proud to say that I think our work contributed greatly to the body of knowledge about the Sumerians. In fact, that third plaque just to your right is one that I shared with Dr. Sitchin for our work there."

Julie smiled, "That whole subject is so fascinating."

"Julie, are you sure you won't have a seat?"

"Oh, no thank you, Dr. Ahearn, I really do have to go now. Well, thanks again for your inspiration. I'll see you next fall. Have a great summer."

"Thanks, Julie, and you have a great summer too." Wendy stood and hugged Julie goodbye.

Wendy returned to the task of grading. She was only ten minutes into the process when her office phone rang.

"Hello, Dr. Ahearn here ... Oh. ... Hi Bob! ... Yes, I just finished and have just now started grading. What's up? ... You do? What does he want to see me about? A summer job? That sounds interesting but you know that I am considering an offer from NSF? ... Sure. ... I'll be there in ten minutes. Bye"

Six years ago the School of Linguistics was only a Department within the School of Humanities and Social Studies. It was only through the hard work of Dr. Robert (Bob) Greenwith that it became its own School, financed by several significant endowments he had brought in. Bob had a natural charm, a great power of persuasion and a silver tongue. The word around campus was he could charm a zebra to give up its stripes. Gray haired and slightly pudgy, he was disarming to those who met him.

His ability to attract funding was enough to convince the university to form a separate School and make him its Dean. His strategy for building the prestige of the school was to hire some of the best minds in the field to teach and do research. Wendy was one of the most recent, and most brilliant, of all his acquisitions.

"So, Dr. Greenwith, now that you have talked with the President, are you convinced? You'll let Dr. Ahearn go on leave of absence, won't you?" Mr. Allison said as Bob replaced the receiver on his phone.

"Of course ... the President gave me no choice. But I want you to know, Wendy is my best and most promising faculty member. Had it not been for the President's persuasion, this would be a short meeting. As it is, I now have to use some friendly persuasion of my own on Wendy."

"I appreciate you calling her over to your office while I'm still here. I'm anxious to meet her. Her record intrigues me." Mr. Allison scanned the file he was holding. "While we wait for Wendy, I'd like to get some more information." He looked down at the dossier. "An area is highlighted here. It mentions that she has a unique ability to read inscriptions. The agency that wants her seems to think that's extremely important. Could you elaborate on that that?"

"Yes, she has very unique abilities. She has a natural gift that I'm not sure I can explain." Bob leaned back in his chair. Staring at the ceiling, he smiled and continued, "During her doctoral defense, she demonstrated that she had the ability to decipher any written text. I mean *any*. Such a thing was unheard of until then. Believe me, I know. I've been in this field for over twenty years and I've never encountered anything even close to what she's done.

"I remember," Bob continued with a smile, "how she astounded her dissertation committee by deciphering inscriptions on an artifact found by one of her committee members. Without warning Wendy, this member brought in a tablet he had discovered in a Mayan temple in Paraguay. For ten years he had labored, trying to get it translated, but without success. Wendy looked at the artifact and, in less than ten minutes, she had it translated.

For what seemed like an eternity, her committee fell silent in awe. You can trust me when I say, she does not speak Mayan."

"How did she do that? My understanding is that most major breakthroughs in reading inscriptions require some other inscription that has a known translation. As I recall, the Egyptian hieroglyphics remained a mystery until the Rosetta stone provided the key."

"That's true."

"So, how did she do it?"

Bob stared at Mr. Allison with a blank smile for a moment, blinked his eyes and said, "I don't know."

"Really?"

"Yes, really. That's not all. In just three short years, since earning her Ph. D., she has published seven peer-reviewed papers dealing with translation of ancient texts. Last year, she was an invited speaker at one of the major linguistics conferences. She was the youngest speaker they had ever invited to such a prestigious event. Most of the people in this field are twice her age and have only half her ability. She has quickly become recognized as a world leader in her field.

"Her students love her too. With her record, Wendy will be a shoo-in to pass her fourth year review as she heads down the tenure path." Bob was beaming. "I can't say enough. Whoever picked her for this project, did their homework. They'll be surprised at her youth but they'll quickly find they got the best."

"I gathered that." Mr. Allison was well aware of Wendy's strengths. "I'm curious though, her file says that her parents are both deceased. What do you know about that?"

Bob thought for a moment, to collect his thoughts. He turned and looked out the window. His eyes began to water as he looked into the distance; his eyes were unfocused.

"That's right." His voice quavered. "They both died in a tragic plane crash when Wendy was a junior here. I was her advisor at the time. I was also a *very* close friend of both her parents. They were faculty here. Her father was a professor of engineering and her mother was a professor of musicology. When Wendy was in her junior year, her parents went away for spring break and ... and never came back." Bob took a deep breath and turned to Mr. Allison.

"Fortunately ...Wendy had an undergraduate research paper due right after break and elected not to go with them."

He continued, "I was executor to her parent's estate and made sure she had everything she needed to continue her studies. The insurance settlement from the airline was significant. It paid for the rest of Wendy's education. Six months before she received her Ph. D., I offered her a full time position here. She's been like a daughter to my wife and me. You'll be impressed when you meet her."

"She's an only child?"

"Yes."

"Dr. Greenwith," a voice said on Bob's intercom, "Wendy's here."

"Good, Nancy, send her in."

They both rose to greet her when she came through the door. Anyone who saw her for the first time would have guessed she was a model; Wendy Always walked as though she was modeling the latest outfit from Fifth Avenue. Her graceful sway was echoed by her long, flowing auburn hair. As she came over to shake Mr. Allison's hand, he marveled at her poise and grace.

"Mr. Allison," Bob said, as he beamed with pride. "This is Dr. Wendy Ahearn. And, Wendy, I would like you to meet Mr. Allison."

"I'm very pleased to meet you, Mr. Allison."

"Thank you. Likewise. Forgive me for being so bold, but I feel compelled to comment on your poise. As a recruiter, I've interviewed a number of models for promotional ads. Did you study modeling?"

They both sat down as Mr. Allison waited for her answer.

Wendy was beginning to blush. "Sort of. When I was in high school, my mother enrolled me in a modeling class. She said that if I was going to become a professional pianist, I needed to show poise as I entered and left the stage."

"You were going to be a pianist?"

"I considered it."

Bob knew this was a touchy subject for Wendy and stepped into the conversation. He cut right to the chase. "Wendy, Mr. Allison is a government recruiter. There's a government project that needs a linguistics expert. Surprise, surprise, your name came up. He's here to offer you a temporary job. This sounds to me like a great opportunity for the summer."

"Yes. What sort of job?" She didn't want to mention her other job offer as she looked at Bob and waited for Mr. Allison to answer.

"Well," Mr. Allison hesitated, "I'm afraid I haven't told Dr. Greenwith what the job is. I can't, because it's in an area of high security."

"Bob, you have a security clearance, don't you?" Wendy looked at him quizzically.

"Yes I do, but— "

"Yes, I know he does," interrupted Mr. Allison, "but it's not high enough."

"Well, I don't have any security clearance. So, how can I take a job like that?"

"My client needs you're skills, desperately. We began getting a clearance for you two days ago. I've been instructed to tell you that you're going to be one of the key people on this project."

"So, Bob, you don't know what I will be doing?" She looked at him quizzically.

"That's right," Bob said. "I don't know what the job is but I do know that it's of utmost importance to our national security." Bob looked at Mr. Allison, "Can I tell her about the President?"

"Yes."

"Wendy, Mr. Allison couldn't satisfy me with enough details about this job offer, so he put me on the phone with the President." Bob paused. "He convinced me that your skills are desperately and urgently needed. You'll have to trust me on that." Bob knew it was time to apply pressure.

"I don't understand. Why is the president of our university so concerned about the national security?"

Bob gave a nervous laugh. "Wendy, when I said I talked to the president, I meant the President of the United States: *The President!"*

"The President of the United States?"

"Yes!"

"He wants me?"

"Yes," Bob smiled back. He knew she was sold now.

Wendy hesitated for a moment as she considered what Bob was telling her. She turned to Mr. Allison. "Mr. Allison, you said that this is a summer job. When will I start?"

"Well, I didn't say it was just for the summer. You'll be on the project until it's completed; however long that takes."

Bob knew Wendy did not want to hear that and braced for her next move. He knew he'd have to become more forceful on the next round.

"Bob, that means that I might not be here next fall. Is that right?"

"Yes ... but don't worry about that. I'll put you on a research leave. I'll buy out your teaching load. I've done it before and I know it won't hurt your tenure position. In fact, it will enhance it. Trust me, you should go with this."

Wendy looked at Mr. Allison. "Where is your client located? Do I have to travel out of the country?"

"I don't know."

"Wendy, don't worry about those details," Bob said.

Wendy got the message. "Bob, you know I trust your judgment. I can see that you feel strongly about this but do you suppose that I could have a day to think about it?"

Bob looked over to Mr. Allison who gave his nod of approval. "Yes, sleep on it and we can discuss it some more, tomorrow."

Mr. Allison was beaming. Bob had lived up to his reputation as a smooth talker. "Wendy, I need an answer by noon, tomorrow. There's a great deal of urgency in this project."

"By noon! I guess there is some urgency, indeed. How can I reach you?"

"I'll call you at your apartment tomorrow sharply at noon."

"Do you have my phone number?" Wendy asked with a voice of concern.

"Oh yes, I have all that information," he replied matter-of-factly.

"Well, if I do accept your offer, when do I start?"

"They want you to start now."
Wendy drew tense. "How soon is *now*?"
"They want you there by Monday."
Oh no, here it comes, Bob thought.
"This Monday?"
"Yes."

"Well, that's awfully short notice. Even though I've finished my classes for this semester, I have to get someone to look after my dog and take care of many other details just in case I'm not back by the fall. I don't think I can do all that by this weekend!"

"You don't understand, Dr. Ahearn, this project has the highest urgency. I mean it has the highest urgency of any project for which I've ever been asked to recruit. You must not worry about *any* of those details. I will remove *all* obstacles and take care of *all* details. The government will pay your rent and utilities and you won't have to close down your apartment." He said with firmness. "We will even hire a dog sitter if you want.

"That sounds impressive but you still need to give me time to think.

"Of course, Wendy, you should sleep on it," Bob said

"Okay Bob, I will." Wendy had never felt this much pressure from Bob before.

"That's fine," Mr. Allison said as he got up to leave. "I'll leave now so you can get back to your grading. That's one thing I can't do," he smiled. "Until noon tomorrow," he said as Bob walked him to the door.

Bob returned to his desk. He couldn't look directly into her eyes. Not yet anyway.

Wendy began the conversation. "Bob, as you might expect, I have some concern about taking this offer. I already have that NSF offer to consider and it's pretty well defined. This job offer is different. I don't know whom I'll be working for, or where, what I'll be doing, and how long I'll be gone. The worst part is not returning by this fall. I have students returning who will expect to take classes from me that are part of a three-course sequence. I can't leave them in the lurch."

"Yes, I know, but trust me, the students will survive. If it makes you feel better, I promise that I'll personally watch over them."

"Would you do that for me? That will make my decision easier."

"Look, why don't we continue this discussion tomorrow? Mr. Allison is right, you need to go back to your office and finish grading. I'll free up my calendar for tomorrow so we can get together to discuss this some more. Nine at your place okay? I'll bring the croissants and Brie made with microbial rennet."

Feeling less pressure she turned with a smile and said "I'll make the rainforest friendly Brazilian coffee".

With a calming look, Bob said "Go; finish your grading; and then go home and think about it. Okay?"

Wendy rose to leave. "I'm sure you're right, I'll see you tomorrow."

After Wendy left, Bob turned back to the window and looked at his own reflection. He began to search his conscience. *Are you really doing the right thing?*

It was difficult for Wendy to concentrate on grading. Her conversation with Mr. Allison kept overriding her attempts at doing so. However, by eight p.m. she had finished and left her office for home. Half an hour later she

was at her apartment. She could hear Tigger barking as she
unlocked the door.

"Hi Tigger, did you miss me? Let's go for a walk!"
He jumped excitedly; ready to go. He was a fluffy white
Lhasa Apso and was Wendy's pride and joy.

Within twenty minutes and three bunny chases later,
they were back. After fixing some food for Tigger, Wendy
fed herself and was at her piano. Johann Sebastian Bach
was appropriate, she thought; *Jesus bleibet meine Freude*
was one of her favorites and now seemed to fit the moment.

Music was as important to her as her teaching and
research. She found that playing the piano helped her clear
her mind. Often, her best work came after a session with
the piano. Sometimes she thought that she should have
taken her mother's advice and pursued music as her chosen
career.

But, her dad was right, she did have a gift for
languages and as her parents had shown in their careers,
being a college professor had many rewards. Also, her
career in languages offered more stability and far less
flying than a career in music.

As Wendy continued to play, she thought about this
afternoon's meeting. *Mr. Allison's offer would be a good
opportunity to do some important research; whatever that
might be. National security, Bob did say that this project
was important to the nation. At least that's what the
President had told him. If it was a matter of national
security then it must be very important work. The
President of the United States was involved. It's that
important? On the other hand, life is just beginning to
become comfortable. Why take on some unknown project
that could last months? Mr. Allison did say I would be the
key player. The President of the United States wants me.
What about Tigger?*

Wendy continued to play.

Chapter 4
The Voyage

Friday, May 9th
9:26 AM

"Good morning, Bob." Wendy beamed a smile to him as she opened her door. Bob was late, as usual.

"Good morning yourself" Bob replied as he handed her the cheese and croissants and proceeded into the living area. Tigger was there to greet him.

Wendy lived in a two-floor townhouse. Upstairs she had a full bath and two bedrooms, one of which she used as a study. Downstairs, there was a half bath at the bottom of the stairs. Her kitchen was separated from the rest of the living area by a series of half walls, shelves and cabinets. Between the living area and the kitchen she had a small rectangular table. It seated two comfortably, four if needed, and six if she didn't mind watching her guests knock elbows as they were eating.

Her piano was in the back left corner of her living area, facing a window. She was very protective of her piano and even though the idea of looking out the window while playing, sounded great, she never drew open the curtains. She was afraid the sun would hurt her baby.

Over in the right hand corner of her living room, somewhat hidden from sight, was a sofa and a fully equipped entertainment center.

"I gather from your smile that you've decided to take Mr. Allison's offer," Bob said as he took a seat in the dining area.

Wendy was happy about her decision to take the position. However the smile she gave to Bob was her way of saying to herself, *I told you so*. She had told herself that Bob would be late that day. Even with the best of intentions, in his personal life, he still could not manage to be on time.

After her parents died, Bob and his wife, Lisa, had become like parents to her. In fact, up until she started traveling in grad school, it had become a tradition for the three of them to spend Sunday together, normally at their house. She supposed this tradition had started as a way for them to check up on her fragile mental state. She really needed the support and friendship they offered, and accepted their kindness wholeheartedly. Although the Sunday tradition faded with time, the three of them still had a very close relationship.

"Yes, I have, and you know, the more I think about it, the more excited I get," she said, as she placed the nicely arranged food and coffee on the table and took a seat across from Bob.

"That's great! I thought you might take the offer, so I've been playing around with teaching loads and have a plan for covering your classes." Bob pointed to a worksheet he had taken out of his briefcase and placed in front of him. "If it becomes necessary, I'll teach them myself. You'd let me do that, wouldn't you?" Bob smiled at her.

"Do you think you're qualified?" she teased.

"I trust you have all your class notes in your office," He said with a wink. "Who knows, maybe this will be an opportunity for me to get back into the teaching harness and away from all of this paperwork." Bob looked at her. "I envy you. You have a chance to do some good research and above all else, enjoy yourself."

"Thanks! I will." Wendy said, squirming in her chair. "I have my class notes here, so we can go over them later."

Bob knew that even with the smile on her face, Wendy still felt uneasy about this job. Even though neither one said the words, they both knew he would wait with her until she got the call from Mr. Allison.

"Oh, almost forgot," Bob said, as he took out another folder from his briefcase and opened it. "You need to sign these forms that give you a leave of absence in the event you don't return by fall. I've already filled in my part explaining that I approve. All you have to do is sign here and here," he said, pointing to the bottom lines on the two forms he slid across his desk. "Oh, guess what..., I've found a temporary home for Tigger."

"You have?"

"Well, I spoke to Lisa when I got home last night, and she'd love to have Tigger stay with us while you're gone."

"Oh, that's great! Tigger loves you and Lisa. I still remember the day the two of you gave him to me after Dad and Mom—," Wendy paused and then changed the subject.

"So can you take him today, I think the next three days might be a little hectic and I might not have enough time for him?" Wendy asked in a sad tone. "Of course, I can drop him by the house on my way into work."

Wendy gave Tigger a little kiss on his nose and then turned to Bob and said, "You know, I really am excited about this new job. Thanks for twisting my arm a little," she said as she signed the forms he had given her.

"Well, I hope I didn't twist too much, but the President did make convincing arguments for picking you. I do think you made the right decision."

For the next two and a half hours, Bob and Wendy talked and looked over her class notes. Wendy kept looking at her clock. Noon came and went. It was now 12:06 pm and no call yet. Bob saw her face and knew what she was feeling. Just as he opened his mouth to reassure her, the phone rang.

"You're late Mr. Allison!" Wendy joked as she picked up the phone, trying to hide the anxiety of the last six minutes.

"Judging from your tone, I take it that you've decided to accept my client's offer," Mr. Allison said. He was confident Bob would succeed and wasn't surprised at Wendy's answer.

"Yes, I have."

"That's great!"

"Yes, and I'm really excited. I talked with Dr. Greenwith this morning and he agrees, this would be a wonderful opportunity for me," she said, winking at Bob.

"Good!"

"What should I tell people who ask where I'm going?"

"Just tell them that you've accepted a temporary position with the government and that you have the blessing of the University. This is all true. Tell them that you'll be out of the country and probably only able to communicate once or twice while you're gone."

"So, this job is out of the country?"

"I don't know, but I've been told to tell you that you'll not be allowed to communicate outside of your workgroup until the project is completed. To save a lot of questions, I think it is best just to tell people you'll be out of the country and in an area that doesn't have a good phone system. They'll think you're in some Mid-eastern desert. The truth is; you might be. I just don't know."

"Okay, I understand. Will you pick me up on Monday and how should I pack?"

"No, I won't be picking you up. My job is done here. A government car will pick you up Sunday night at 8:00 sharp and drive you to the university airport."

"Sunday?" Wendy asked with surprise. "I thought you said they wanted me on Monday?"

"Yes, that's true, but you need to leave Sunday night to get there by Monday. I'm sorry. I didn't mean to mislead you."

"How should I pack?"

"Pack only what you can get into carry-on luggage. The agency will provide you with any clothes you may need once you get to your final destination. Tell your landlord that a Mr. Allen will be by to pay for your lease and that they should forward any utility bills to him. He'll tell them where to send them. Have the post office hold your mail until you return. Also, your salary will be paid through the university. Let's see, what else. What about your dog?"

"Oh, Dr. Greenwith and his wife are going to keep Tigger while I'm gone."

"That's great. ...By the way, Dr. Ahearn, I want to tell you what a pleasure it was to meet you yesterday. I'm sure my client will be very happy with you. You'll do a great job for them and I'm sure you'll find the work satisfying."

"Well, thank you. I enjoyed meeting you, too, and am impressed with your ability to get things done quickly. Wow!"

"Thank you. That's my job. Do you have any other questions?"

"No, I think I understand what I need to do," Wendy replied.

"Excellent! That's it then. It's been a pleasure working with you. Good bye for now and good luck"

"Goodbye, Mr. Allison," Wendy said as she hung up.

Wendy's head was spinning. In less than twenty-four hours she went from concern about grading a final exam to concern about how she was going to protect the national security.

Bob saw that she no longer needed him for comfort. After finishing his croissant and coffee, he got up. "Well I think I've got to get back to the office, I don't think Nancy cleared the whole day for me." Wendy looked at him with tears in her eyes as she thought to herself how lucky she was to have Bob and Lisa in her life. "Thanks for everything. See you in a few months," she said and hugged Bob goodbye.

"See you then," Bob said picking up Tigger. "Good luck and don't worry, Wendy. You'll do fine." As Tigger and Bob left her townhouse, Wendy's smile dissapeared.

Her mind began to race about life and love. She wondered to herself, *How much more difficult would this decision have been if I had a husband and kids?*

At times, Wendy worried about her biological clock ticking away; she didn't even have a boyfriend. She discussed this in confidence several times with Bob's wife but was assured by her that there was no rush. "Don't worry, you'll know when you meet the right man," Lisa had told her. So far, the right man had not come along. It was just as well. Wendy wasn't ready to develop a close relationship; not yet anyway.

Sunday, May 11th
8:16 pm EST

Wendy was becoming more nervous each time she looked out of the window of her second story apartment. It was sixteen minutes after eight, growing dark, and no car! This didn't make sense. Just then a light green late model sedan pulled up in front of her apartment. The driver looked her way and got out of the car. He seemed to be checking a paper he was holding. Within less than a minute, Wendy's doorbell rang.

"Who is it?" she yelled, already knowing who it was.

"I'm looking for Dr. Ahearn. Mr. Allison sent me," a strong male voice on the other side or the door answered.

"Just a minute," Wendy called as she made one last sweep of the apartment. She grabbed her over night bag. As instructed, she had packed only a few clothes, toiletries, necessary cosmetics and, of course, a few books and reference papers she thought might be useful. Wendy opened the door to find a casually dressed young man.

"Hi! I'm John and I assume you're Dr. Ahearn?"

"Yes, thanks for waiting. I'm ready," Wendy said.

"Well, if you'll sign these forms, we'll get started," John said as he handed the forms to Wendy. "Can I take your bag?" he said, extending his hand.

"Thanks! What are these forms for?" Wendy asked. She exchanged her bag for the forms.

"They officially put you on the government payroll and prove that I picked you up."

Wendy looked over the forms and after signing, she handed them to John. She made one last look around her apartment. "Goodbye, sweet home," she sighed to herself as she closed the door to her apartment and followed John to the car.

Within twenty minutes they had reached the small airport that served the university and its supporting community. John drove over to a special section reserved for charter flights and parked next to a gate through the fenced-in flight line. A small, unmarked twin-engine jet was waiting just beyond the gate. John, with all the courtesy one might give to a dignitary, rounded the car, opened the door and extended his hand.

"Dr. Ahearn, that's your plane, the Gulfstream 5. I flew in one of those once. They're a dream. A lot of the big movie stars use them. I'll take your bag and check it with the pilot."

"Thanks John," she said. "Do I just walk right over to the plane?"

"Sure. They're waiting for you. Just follow me."

Wendy could see that this was not a large plane. *This is a small plane*, she thought to herself. *Small planes bounce around a lot.* Reluctantly, she followed John through the gate and over to the plane. She was greeted by two young Air Force officers as she boarded the small plane. They were the pilot and co-pilot.

"Welcome aboard Dr. Ahearn, I'm Captain Burns and this is Lieutenant Wilson, my co-pilot," said the elder of the two young men. "You can take any of these seats here in the main compartment. They all recline fully if you want to sleep."

"Thank you," Wendy answered, hoping they hadn't noticed her nervousness. She thought, *He looks younger than me, and he's going to fly this thing! Relax, everything will be okay.*

The interior of the plane was fitted out with fine wood paneling, plush carpeting and soft leather seats. She settled herself into one of the plush seats as the two officers went forward into the cockpit and began their preflight check.

"How—", she began, her voice breaking, "—how long a flight is this going to be?" .

"Oh, about four and a half hours," the captain answered.

"Four and a half hours…that long? How high do we have to go?"

"Relax." Captain Burns answered, sensing Wendy's fear of flying. "You're in one of the smoothest flying planes they make. It's the Rolls Royce of the air. This plane flies like a dream and the air is smooth tonight. This is the plane of choice for most corporate executives. I've been told several entertainers have one just like it."

"Where are we going?" she asked, hoping to get a clue as to who the new employer was going to be.

"West."

"West to where?" Wendy asked more forcefully.

"Dr. Ahearn, this flight is classified top-secret. We have been instructed not to tell you our destination and to have minimum conversation with you. Please don't press the issue. Just sit back and enjoy the flight," the captain said in a very stern and military voice. When he saw Wendy tense up, he knew he had come on much more strongly than he intended.

Unbuckling, he went back into the main cabin. "I'm sorry for snapping like that. I really do apologize. Guess it's my military training. Anyway, we were told of your fear of flying so I'd like to offer you this sedative."

He held out a pill. "Perhaps if you get some sleep, the flight will be easier for you."

He turned and reached into a bar that was built into the front bulkhead. "Here's a bottle of water to go with it."

"Thank you. That's very considerate of you. Is the sedative very strong?"

"No. You can get them at any pharmacy without a prescription."

Wendy downed the pill with water.

Within ten minutes they were airborne and chasing the sun. She watched the sun set in front of the plane as they climbed to altitude. In less than twenty minutes, the plane leveled off. Wendy was asleep.

The sudden jar awoke her as the plane touched down. Except for runway lights, the field was dark. The plane taxied over to within fifty yards of a small, dimly-lit, terminal with a control tower on top. Another twin-engine plane was parked about fifty yards on the other side.

Captain Burns unbuckled and went back to the main cabin. "Dr Ahearn, this concludes this leg of your trip. You have to transfer to that other plane." He pointed to the plane in the shadows. After retrieving Wendy's bag from the stowage compartment, he placed it by the doorway. "I would offer to take your bag, but we've been instructed not to get out of our plane and not to have any contact with the crew of the other plane. I'm sorry, but you'll have to carry your own bag."

"Thanks, it's not heavy." Wendy climbed out and took her bag from Captain Burns.

"Again, I apologize for being so short with you earlier, but we have orders. You understand, don't you?"

"Yes, I do. Don't worry about it." As she walked away from the plane she turned back to face the open door.

"Thanks for the ride."

"Good luck," he hollered after her.

Wendy walked over to the plane parked in the shadows. This one was smaller and propeller-driven. She handed her bag to a tall man standing in the shadows next to the door. As he took her bag, he stared directly into her eyes with the most intense, yet pleasant, stare Wendy had ever seen.

"Dr. Ahearn?"

"Yes, I'm Dr. Ahearn."

"I'm Colonel Mitchell. Welcome aboard. The last leg of your journey will take about an hour. Before we depart, if you would like to use the restroom, there's one inside the terminal here."

"Oh. No thanks. I can survive for another hour."

The colonel extended a hand to help her aboard. "Just strap into that seat in the back," he said, as he climbed into the pilot's seat.

What a dignified gentleman, she thought as the dim light of the cockpit lit his graying temples.

The colonel settled into the pilot's seat in front of her and started the engines. Within minutes they were airborne.

"I don't suppose you could tell me where we are headed?" Wendy asked.

"Sorry Dr. Ahearn, that's classified." After a long pause, "It's after one o'clock your time. I recommend you get some sleep. It'll make the next hour pass more quickly. Don't worry; it'll be a smooth flight. Try to sleep."

Wendy set her seat into a reclined position and tried to follow orders. After they had leveled off, she peered out of the window from time to time. There was nothing; no city lights, no roads, nothing but a slight hint of mountains on the horizon. Except for a few stars, it was pure black outside of the plane. Finally, her eyes grew heavy. She went to sleep.

Colonel Joseph "Pete" Mitchell wondered, as he watched Wendy sleeping, how she would react to the mission that lay ahead of her. *She has no idea what she's getting into*, he thought. *The future of mankind might well depend on her success in this mission.* The colonel knew full well that not only was this mission important to mankind, it was also important to him.

Colonel Mitchell allowed his instincts to take over the routine of flying as he let his mind drift. As his plane carried him and his passenger toward their final destination, he reflected on past events. He was now directing a special project for the President! Surely, this would earn him his general's star. After all, he's had an excellent military record since graduating with high distinction from the Air Force Academy. He was following in his dad's footsteps. Even though his dad got his first star at forty-two, he was only forty-six. If this mission is successful, he should make general. "Working in the Pentagon helps too. That's if you don't screw up," Pete said to himself softly.

He now was attached to the Pentagon with the assignment of a lifetime. He had to be thankful for his dad's political connections at the Pentagon. Since retiring, his father had been a close friend to the Secretary of Defense; playing golf with him twice a week. The Secretary was well aware of Pete's ability for 'getting things done'. His dad saw to that. So, when the President asked the Secretary to pick someone to head an extremely important, but highly secret, mission, Pete's name came up. Not even the Secretary was told what the mission was. It was for PRESIDENTIAL EYES ONLY.

Yes, Pete's career was on track. If only his personal life were as much in order. "If only Sue was still alive," Pete said softly to himself. He desperately missed his wife of more than twenty-two years. Her murder was one of those chance happenings. She was in the wrong place at the wrong time. "Why did you have to wake up when that man, no, animal, broke into our house. I should have been there." Ever since her murder, Pete had been searching for the answer: Why? More and more he had begun to turn to his faith for comfort. There wasn't an evening go by that Pete didn't search his Bible for the answer.

Now, just as he was beginning to accept Sue's death as part of God's plan, he landed this assignment. He knew it was going to test the very fabric of his faith.

Monday, May 12th
2:05 am EST

Wendy was awakened by the jolt of landing. It was still dark outside and she was disoriented for a few moments. She looked quizzically at the colonel. "Where are we?"

"I can't say, but this *is* your destination," the colonel answered as he taxied off the runway.

Even though it was dark, Wendy could make out the silhouette of a large mountain straight ahead. The colonel continued to taxi straight toward the side of the mountain as Wendy watched with growing concern.

"Colonel, there's a mountain straight ahe—!"

"I know," the colonel said, nonchalantly, as he picked up what looked, to Wendy, like a garage door opener and aimed it toward the mountain. As he did this, part of the mountain slid aside exposing a dimly lit cavern inside.

It was a garage door opener! Wendy thought to herself in amazement.

Within seconds, the plane was inside and the huge door closed behind them. As it closed, the cavern became ablaze with lights. For a moment, Wendy blinked and was temporarily blinded. Soon her eyes adjusted and she could make out details around her. The cavern was immense!

When Wendy was young, her father had taken her to the Superdome to see a game. This was much bigger than the Superdome. Numerous tunnels extended in all directions away from the center. Each tunnel looked large enough for a commercial aircraft to pass though. There were many windows and doors located around the perimeter. The plane came to rest near a tunnel in the far wall and the colonel stopped the engines.

"Welcome to your new home-away-from-home," Colonel Mitchell said as he climbed out of his door. He walked around to her side to help her out.

"I don't like to sound repetitive, but where are we?" Wendy asked, knowing the colonel was not going to answer.

"I'm sorry for all the cloak and dagger, Dr. Ahearn, but it is necessary for security," he said apologetically.

Wendy replied sarcastically, "That's okay, I'm getting used to it."

Colonel Mitchell looked at her. "I hope our first hour together didn't get us off to a bad start. We'll be working together for the next few months, and spending a lot of time together as a team."

"Doing what?"

"I'm sorry, but I can't tell you that until we're inside and you've signed some papers," the colonel replied as he walked her to a door in the cavern wall near the plane.

"What if I've changed my mind?" Wendy asked, half joking.

"Then, I'll have to shoot you," the colonel said in his best military tone of voice as he patted his sidearm.

Wendy wasn't sure if he was joking or not. He escorted her into a small office with a window and door that faced out into the hangar. A door in the back wall was marked TOP SECRET.

"Please, sit down," he said and pointed to a small chair across from a desk.

"Thanks," Wendy said as she sat apprehensively across from him.

"Relax," he said with a smile. "My pistol is on safety." After a pause, he continued, "Dr. Ahearn, before I can answer any of the questions that I know you're anxious to have answered, I have to have you take an oath of silence and to sign some documents."

"What documents?"

"Documents that will obligate you to a long prison sentence if you ever reveal what you see and hear at this place. What goes on here is most top-secret."

"What happens if I don't sign?"

"If you wish to withdraw from the project now, you will be sent to another agency where you will twiddle your thumbs, be bored out of your mind and returned home after three months. If you choose to stay, you'll have the opportunity to witness the most fascinating things you can imagine, things you never thought possible. The choice is yours. What do you say?"

"Have you ever thought about selling used cars? You could make a fortune!" Wendy quipped.

"Does that mean you'll stay?" The colonel smiled.

"Yes! I can't wait to find out what I'm going to be doing," she said as her shaky hand reached for a pen.

The colonel called in an aide to witness the administration of the oath and the signing of the documents. After she had signed, he dismissed the aide and placed the signed forms into a briefcase.

"Tomorrow morning you'll meet the other member of the team. I know it's been a long trip for you; it's nearly three in the morning, by your clock. We're both tired, so let me show you to your quarters and you can settle in." He motioned for her to follow and led her through the back door marked TOP SECRET.

They went down a long corridor passed several doors that were each numbered. He stopped in front of the fifth door.

"You will be behind door number five," he jested.

Wendy was beginning to like this man with the dry humor, but she knew that, despite his light-hearted approach to things, he was deadly serious about his mission.

"This is where you'll live as a guest of Uncle Sam until we complete the project," he said as he reached inside the door and turned on the lights.

The room reminded Wendy of a first class hotel suite with a separate sleeping area, lounge area, efficiency kitchen and bathroom. The color scheme was even pleasant, mostly beige and blues.

"You'll find all the clothes you'll need hanging in the bedroom closet. As soon as we were notified of your decision to come, we bought you a wardrobe. Hopefully, you won't be too disappointed. The BX is limited in its choices.

"If there's anything else you need, you've been assigned an aide who will get it for you. Her name is Lieutenant Sandra Gibbs. She's sleeping in room six across the hall. She'll be knocking on your door at oh-eight-hundred hours to make sure you're awake and will take you to the conference room at oh-nine-hundred for a breakfast meeting with the other member of our team. Don't try to pump her for information about the mission. She has no idea what the mission is or who you are. I want to keep it that way.

"You're not to have any conversations with her. I'll explain more tomorrow." The colonel looked directly into Wendy's eyes and smiled. "By the way, I'm really glad you decided to join our team. Welcome aboard."

After he left, Wendy turned to explore her new surroundings. Diagonally opposite her, in the corner of the spacious living area was something she could not believe, a baby-grand piano! "A piano! This is either a wonderful coincidence or the colonel is a miracle worker!" Wendy said to herself in amazement.

The entire wall adjacent to the piano was covered with ceiling-to-floor blue drapes. In addition to the piano, the lounge was well furnished with a tan sofa, oak coffee table, and a beige fireside chair. None of that was of interest to Wendy; she focused on the piano. As she sat down and prepared to play, her curiosity got the best of her and she leaned over to peak behind the drapes. *A blank wall. Why am I not surprised*, she thought as she began to play. The smooth action of the keys and the fine tonal quality impressed her. Chopin's Prelude, Opus 28, seemed appropriate for the moment. She continued playing for over an hour as she unwound from the day's ordeal. Chopin's Nocturne, Opus 9 and Opus 37 brought her session to an end as her eyes grew heavy from the stress of her travels.

Tomorrow, she would continue to explore but for now she was ready to sleep. The sleeping area was separated from the lounge area by double sliding doors. She went into her bedroom, undressed, and took a warm relaxing shower. The bathroom, fully tiled in white, was large with both a shower and a Jacuzzi. A blow-dryer was on the wall. *First class!* Wendy thought as she dried her hair.

After drying, she explored her new wardrobe, trying on a few things to see how well they fit. The slippers and flannel pajamas were very comfortable. She was pleased with the selections. Hanging next to her robe were three uniforms that looked like jump suits. A note was pinned on one saying: "Wear these when on duty." Wendy was beginning to think she had just been drafted. Too tired to complain, she went to bed.

Chapter 5
Introductions

It seemed to Wendy that she had just closed her eyes when she heard someone knocking on the door. "Who is it?"

"Lieutenant Gibbs," the voice answered.

As Wendy opened the door, before her, wearing an Army uniform, was an attractive blue-eyed blonde who looked to be in her mid-twenties. She was as tall as Wendy and their eyes met. Wendy was struck by her intense cobalt blue eyes. They were almost black.

"I'm Lieutenant Gibbs, your aide. I trust you have rested well after your travels."

"Pleased to meet you, I'm Wendy. I am well rested, thank you." Wendy extended her hand.

Gibbs shook Wendy's hand. "The colonel asked me to wake you at oh-eight-hundred hours and escort you to the conference room for a breakfast meeting at oh-nine-hundred hours."

"Okay, I'll be ready by nine. Should I wear one of those uniforms in my closet?"

"Yes, you must wear a uniform whenever you're out of your room. I'll be back in fifty-five minutes." Gibbs turned and left.

Wendy closed her door. *Not much for conversations. Colonel's orders, I guess. Those eyes, they pierced right through me*, Wendy thought as she returned to her bedroom and began dressing. The uniform fit perfectly but was not flattering. It reminded her of an Air Force jump suit. On the left breast was her name, AHEARN, and below that a white insignia resembling a shield contained a simple blue star in its center.

Wendy was ready within half an hour and spent the remaining minutes exploring her apartment. There were separate doors leading from the bathroom into both the bedroom and an efficiency kitchen. A small table with two chairs separated the small kitchen from the living area.

In the living area, across the room from the sofa, was a TV backed by more ceiling-to-floor drapes. Wendy didn't bother to look behind them; she knew the wall was blank. She turned on the TV and scanned the channels. There were only three; CNN, the weather channel, and a reserved channel for local broadcasts from the base. An idea struck her and she began to smile. She selected the weather channel and waited for "local-on-the-eights". Within two minutes the weather in Las Vegas began scrolling on the screen. "I'm near Las Vegas," she said proudly to herself. "I've outsmarted the colonel."

In the corner, nearest to the exit door, was a computer table complete with a laptop computer and a printer. Adjacent to the exit door was a bookshelf with a selection of books and knickknacks that gave the room a homey appearance. On the wall near the computer was a beige phone. She picked up the phone and dialed Bob's office. *"This phone is not authorized for outside calls. Please contact your group director for authorization*," said the recorded voice over the phone. Wendy replaced the receiver, not surprised by what she had heard.

Wendy turned around to inspect her kitchen again. It had all the basics. There was a small stove, refrigerator, microwave, and sink. Next to the sink was a coffee maker.

"This is great! All the comforts of home," Wendy said to herself.

There was a knock at the door. "Yes, who is it?" She knew who it was.

"It's Lieutenant Gibbs. Are you ready?"

"Yes, is it time to go?" Wendy had forgotten to reset her watch. "What time is it?" she asked as she opened the door.

"Oh-eight-fifty hours," Gibbs replied. "The colonel is ready to meet you for breakfast now. Follow me, this way." She turned and led Wendy down the hall.

Gibbs stopped in front of one of the doors. It was labeled CONFERENCE ROOM. The door directly across the hall was labeled DINING ROOM. As they entered the conference room, Wendy could see that they were the first to arrive as the lieutenant led her over to the conference table. In front of her was an oval-shaped conference table and seven chairs; one to her left at the head, and three on either side. At the head of the table, were two phones; one red and one beige.

"Does that red phone connect to the President?" Wendy asked. She was only half serious and did not expect an answer.

"Directly," answered the lieutenant, with a smile. "You can sit next to the colonel. His chair is the one at that head of the table." Gibbs pointed to Wendy's left. "Don't touch the red phone," she said with a grin.

Okay, no more levity, Wendy thought as she took her seat.

Colonel Mitchell entered the room from a door marked PRIVATE, directly behind the head chair. "Hello, Dr.

Ahearn," he said as he sat down. "Did you have a good rest?"

"Yes, thank you," she said as she continued to scan the room.

Across from her was another door labeled RESTRICTED. A keypad was to its right. Around the room, the walls were plain pastel green with drapes hung at various locations to give the illusion of windows. There was a white board and numerous visual aides on the wall to her right.

"Thank you, Lieutenant. You're dismissed now," the colonel said to Gibbs, nodding to the door through which she and Wendy had entered.

"Yes, Sir," she said as she turned and exited the room.

The colonel set the briefcase he had been carrying onto the table in front of him, chained it to a metal loop on the table, and began pressing a few buttons in a small keypad installed on the table next to the red phone. As he did, the room dimmed slightly.

"Whatever's in that briefcase must be important." Wendy was overcome with curiosity.

"We'll be joined momentarily by the third member of our team," the colonel said, sidestepping Wendy's comment.

The door behind Wendy opened just as the colonel spoke. She turned to see an Air Force lieutenant enter. A tall, handsome young man followed. Wendy guessed he was in his early thirties, and his meticulous grooming suggested he was a man who takes pride in his appearance. The lieutenant led him around the table to the side opposite her.

"Thank you, lieutenant, you're dismissed," the colonel said.

"Yes Sir," the lieutenant said, as he turned and left the room.

He turned to the young man. "Take that seat there, Dr. Newton," he said as he pointed to the seat across from, Wendy. "Dr. Newton, this is Dr. Ahearn."

"I'm pleased to meet you, Dr. Ahearn. I'm Corey," he said, ignoring the colonel's signal to sit. Instead, he walked around the table and approached her with his hand extended.

"Hi, I'm Wendy." She stood and took his hand. They both looked directly into each other's eyes. He was at least four inches taller. His pleasant smile and broad chin gave him the air of determination. She noticed he was not wearing a ring.

The colonel lifted the beige phone and keyed in a few numbers. Within a few seconds there was a voice on the phone, and the colonel began to speak. "Colonel Andrews? This is Colonel Mitchell. We're ready for you now. Okay. … Good. … Thank you," the colonel said, and then replace the phone.

After Corey returned to his seat, the colonel continued. "The team is now complete." He paused and the addressed both slowly and deliberately. "We three are perhaps one of the most important teams in the history of mankind." He looked at both of them to measure their reaction. As he expected, they were stunned and remained motionless with their mouths half open.

The silence in the room suddenly was overpowered by the hum of the ventilation system. "We're going to be working together, very closely as a team, over the next few months and I want to begin this operation with proper introductions. I'd like to work on a first name basis and dispense with formality, at least amongst the three of us." Both Wendy and Corey were still trying to come to terms with his first statement and remained frozen in place. "My name is Joseph P. Mitchell, but I want you to call me Pete."

The conference room door opened and a tall middle-aged man entered. He was wearing an Air Force uniform with the insignia of a full colonel. Pete stood up to make introductions. Wendy and Corey followed suit. "Colonel Andrews, these are the remaining members of my team. This is Dr. Wendy Ahearn and this is Dr. Corey Newton. Doctors, this is Colonel Andrews, the base commander."

"Welcome to the base," Colonel Andrews said.

"Thank you," replied Wendy and Corey in unison.

"This may be the only time we see each other." Colonel Andrews shot a glance toward Pete and then back to Wendy and Corey. "I make it my business to meet everyone who comes to this base and try to make their stay pleasant. I hope you enjoy your stay here. It's my job to make sure you have everything you need while you're here. For now, I want to explain more about our operations here. I'm sure you know that you're in a very secure base. It's extremely difficult to enter or leave and, as a result, most people stay on base until their mission is complete. So, maintaining morale is important. It's been my experience that the morale of any base, and especially this one, is directly affected by the quality of food that's served. So, that's my fetish. I make food service one of my prime concerns. The cooks in the cafeteria report directly to me. Periodically, I make my rounds in the kitchens and serving rooms to check on cleanliness and food quality. I want to know if you have any problems with the quality of the food here. Also, if you have any special dietary needs, please let Colonel Mitchell know. I'll make sure we do our best to accommodate you.

"Well, now that you mentioned it, Colonel," Pete interrupted. "Dr. Ahearn is a vegetarian. If you can have the cooks prepare some vegetarian meals, I'm sure she'll appreciate it."

"Yes, that's right," Wendy said. "I wasn't going to mention it, but now that you have, I really would appreciate it if you could serve some vegetarian meals."

"That's no problem. Ovo-lacto or vegan?"

Impressed, Wendy replied, "Ovo-lacto but with restrictions on the cheese. I prefer to have cheese not processed with animal rennet."

"Consider it done," Colonel Andrews responded. "Well, it has been a pleasure to meet you. I'll get out of your hair so you can have your meeting. Colonel Mitchell can brief you on base security regulations. Please do let me know if you need anything else."

"I will. Thank you, Colonel," Pete said. Colonel Andrews shook their hands firmly and left the room.

"Well, let's get back to introductions. Corey, since you arrived a day ahead of Wendy, you've already had a chance to read her bio. You know her expertise is linguistics. For Wendy's benefit, I'd like to give a thumbnail sketch of you, if you don't mind," said the colonel.

"Not at all," Corey replied.

"Wendy, Corey is an astrophysicist. He received a Bachelor's degree in physics from Princeton and went on to MIT to get his Doctorate in astrophysics. His doctoral dissertation was on the interaction of electromagnetic and gravitational fields. After receiving his doctorate, he took a position with a company called GraviDyne. This company is located near Boston and specializes in research dealing with gravity. They're trying to find ways to manipulate gravity."

"That's right," interrupted Corey. "We're trying to leapfrog the transportation industry into a completely unique method of transportation that requires no wheels or roads. Vehicles with our drive system will be able to travel at very high speeds and move through the air like an airplane, but at many times the speed of present aircraft."

Pete interrupted. "Wendy, I'm sure as we go along, you'll find Corey is quite verbal about things for which he has a passion. One of his passions is the study of UFOs, or flying saucers, as some people call them. He believes they exist, and even thinks he knows how they work!" he added with a smile.

"Well, if you military people would stop covering up the evidence, perhaps people would know the truth!" Corey's Irish temper, from his mother's side of the family, was beginning to show as his face began to take on a reddish glow.

"Corey, with the Freedom of Information Act, how can the government hide UFO information? All you have to do is write any agency, and you can get copies of any UFO reports you want. Of course, that assumes there are reports. Right?" Pete was beginning to enjoy pulling Corey's 'chain'.

"That doesn't work. I tried. There's a loophole. It seems that all UFO reports taken by FAA, NASA, CIA, NAS or any government agency, are sent immediately to NORAD in Cheyenne Mountain."

"Well then, why didn't you ask NORAD for the documents?"

"I did. They wrote back and informed me that, since NORAD was a joint organization between the U.S. and Canada, they didn't fall under the jurisdiction of the Freedom of Information Act," Corey replied with a glance toward Wendy.

"Okay. You made your point," Pete said. "We can continue this discussion later, but let me finish discussing your background."

Corey glanced at Wendy, thinking she must already have him pegged as weird.

"Corey's passion got the attention of some important people. When I began to form this team, the government's human resource agency tracked him down through one of the Pentagon's generals who knew his reputation. Word gets around, Corey," said Pete as he gave Corey a smile. "Of all the files they sent me, yours was the best," Pete said with a sincere tone in his voice. "Thanks for agreeing to be part of this project."

"Well, your offer *was* intriguing." Corey smiled as he began to calm down.

Pete laughed. "Before I get into any details about our mission, I must explain certain rules. This project has the very highest level of security, with a security rating of ABOVE TOP SECRET."

"That sounds impressive!" Wendy said.

"Yes, and we three are the only ones at this location who know *anything* about the project. Each of you has an aide to help you with your personal needs, but neither Lieutenant Sandra Gibbs, your aide," he turned to Wendy, "or Lieutenant Marcus Riley, your aide," he turned to Corey, "has any knowledge about our mission and who you two are. Not even the base commander knows, and it must remain that way. It's vitally important that we three be the only ones involved. If news of this project was ever leaked, it could set off world panic. That's why I personally flew each of you here on the final leg of your journeys. I'm the only one at this base who knows who you are and why you're here. I want to make one thing clear. Do not discuss the project in the hallway or cafeteria. However, you two are welcome to have discussions about this project in the privacy of your suites. In fact, I encourage that," said Pete.

"Where *are* we?" Corey asked.

Wendy wanted to volunteer that she knew they were near Las Vegas but decided to wait for Pete's answer.

"If I wanted you to know, I would have told you by now," Pete responded sternly. "Neither of you need to know where you are. It's not important to our mission. The less you know about some things, the better."

Glad I hadn't volunteered that. Wendy thought.

Pete continued. "I chose to have officers serve as your aides because the security of this project demands it. Even with that, never discuss with them what you're doing. You're not to have even a casual conversation with them. They understand and will not feel offended by your lack of conversation. They'll go to the Base Exchange for any personal items you need and do any other errands you request. Once each week, they'll clean your apartment; while you're present. While in your apartment, they are not to see any documents that indicate what you're doing, who you are, or what your background is."

"Why would they take such an assignment?" Wendy asked.

"Trust me. They have a good deal here. They both recently graduated with distinction from military academies and were given promotions to first lieutenant as part of this assignment. Upon the completion of their assignment, they will each advance another grade in rank. That's a significant promotion at such an early time in their careers. In fact, it's nearly unheard of," Pete explained.

"Can you do that?" Corey asked with a tone of amazement.

"I can do almost anything I need to in order to complete this mission. Do you see this red phone? If I pick it up, in less than one minute, I'll be talking to my direct boss, the President of the United States. He will approve *anything* I request. I tell you all of this, not to impress you with my powers, but to impress upon you the importance of this project."

"I'm impressed," said Corey.

"I chose this base for this project because of its resources and its extremely high level of security. In the ten days since I arrived here, I have become extremely impressed with their security procedures. This base is designed so that many concurrent projects can be carried out without any contact occurring between the research teams or their support groups. When we go into the dining area for breakfast, or any meal, talk to no one. The people who work here are used to everyone being tight lipped, so they won't be offended."

"What resources are here?" Corey asked.

"Everything that we need is here." Pete wasn't quite ready to reveal the complete answer to that question; not just yet. "Now, before I continue, let's go to the cafeteria and get some food. I think we're all starved. We'll bring our trays back here so we can continue working."

As they entered the cafeteria, Wendy was struck by how small it was. It had a beverage dispenser and two food vending machines. Between the two machines was an opening which she assumed it was for returning the empty food trays. She could see through the machines into the room beyond.

"The machine on the left is for hot food and the one on the right is for cold. The cooks fill the machines from the rear, so they never need to be in this room. They'll keep them filled with whatever food we specify. The procedure is simple. In your room, you'll find a menu with your room number on it. Just check off the items you want for each of the next seven days' meals. Turn in the slip with your empty trays. On each plate of food will be the room number of the person who ordered it, so if you forget what you ordered, just look for your number. The trays are over there next to the beverage machine. All the condiments you will need are on that table over there." Pete pointed to a small table opposite the vending machines. "Fill your trays and leave. When you're done eating, bring your tray and dishes back and pass them through that opening there in the wall." Pete pointed toward the opening Wendy had suspected was for returns. "This facility is designed to minimize contact between the cooks and the researchers. The cooks have their own entrance to the room behind the vending machines.

"Are we the only ones who use this room?" Wendy asked.

"Yes. This food service is for SECTION G. That's the one assigned to us. We're the only ones who enter here except for Colonel Andrews and, of course, your aides."

In less than ten minutes, they returned to the conference room with their breakfast trays and began to eat.

"Well now, let's continue," Pete said. "I need to explain some security procedures. As you probably have noticed, each door has a security keypad on the wall to the right. To open a door, you need to key in the last six digits of your social security number. That's your personal code. The system is computerized, so, if you are authorized to enter that room, the door will be unlocked. The conference room and the cafeteria are two rooms that are unlocked, by default. However, when we begin our meetings in this room, I will lock the door.

In the event of a security breach, we will go into a lockdown mode. That has two levels that are controlled by the base commander. The speaker system throughout the base will annunciate what level we're at. LEVEL ONE lockdown confines personnel to their sections and prohibits them from leaving the base. LEVEL TWO lockdown locks all doors so you will be trapped in whatever room you're in at the time."

"What about safety?" Wendy asked. "What if there's a fire?"

"Good point. In the event of a fire, a heat sensor will set off an alarm and the sprinkler system. You will be told to evacuate. The computer knows when a room is occupied and will unlock any door required to allow access to the exit doors."

"How does the computer know when a room is occupied?" Corey asked.

"By a combination of motion sensors and by following the doors each of us unlocks."

"Are there hidden cameras or microphones in our rooms?" Wendy asked.

"No. There are only motion detectors in any of the rooms, including this conference room. To make any audio or video recordings in a room would jeopardize the confidentiality required by the various projects. The only exceptions are the hallways. At the end of each hall is a security camera mounted in the ceiling. These cameras record around the clock to monitor the goings and comings of the various personnel."

"Where are the exit doors?" Corey asked.

"For us, the exit door is at the end of the hallway. It leads into the office where you both signed your oath. From that office, you go into the hanger and over to the man-door next to the hanger door. That door will lead you outside. You will not be allowed to re-enter until the all clear is given." Pete looked at both of them. "Do either of you have any questions about how the security system works here?"

"No. I think I understand what to do," Wendy said.

"I understand." Corey hesitated and after glancing at Wendy, decided to probe the colonel's background. "Colonel, you know a lot about the two of us. Can you tell us about yourself and why you were chosen to head up this program?"

"Well, I think I was chosen because, first, I have the proper level of security clearance and second, I have a reputation for getting things done. My training at the War College has taught me how to motivate people." He turned to Wendy and smiled, "Without having to shoot them."

"I feel better now." Wendy turned to Corey and smiled.

"I have a Masters degree in aeronautical engineering. That training will probably be useful in this project. However, I feel that my main function in this team is to lead you two, and to act as a facilitator. It's my job to get you whatever resources you need, so that you can accomplish our mission.   My style in conducting this project is to allow open and free exchange of information. We may be doing a lot of brainstorming in order to get ideas out on the table."

"What *is* our mission and why are we two people, with completely different backgrounds, part of this team?" Corey asked.

"Please be patient," Pete said firmly. "Corey, your role in this team is one of support. You are to provide Wendy with whatever technical assistance she needs in this project." Pete turned to Wendy. "Wendy, you're the key to this mission."

"I don't understand.   My background has no connection with military issues. Does this project involve cryptography?"

"You're close." Pete paused for a moment and then changed the subject. "We're working on a first-name basis because it's extremely important that we be able to brainstorm and have a free exchange of ideas. To help in that, I want to begin by having philosophical discussions and exploring some thoughts together." Pete hesitated and then glanced in Corey's direction.   "Corey, before breakfast, you said that you felt the government was covering up the existence of UFOs. You seem sure of that, even though our government denies it." With a twinkle in his eye, Pete said, "The famous French satirist, philosopher, and historian, Voltaire, once said that it's dangerous to be right when the government is wrong. Why are you so sure flying saucers exist, when the government says they don't? Have you seen one?"

"No. I never have.   But, I find the logic for their existence compelling."

"Perhaps you would share with Wendy and me, what logic led you to that conclusion?"

"Well, it's a rather long explanation. Do you want to hear the whole story?"

"I do." Pete slapped the table and turned to Wendy. "What about you?"

Wendy now had a twinkle in her eyes. "Sure, I'm always curious to know how one can deduce the existence of flying saucers."

Chapter 6
In The Beginning

Corey looked at Wendy and Pete. "Coincidently, only two months ago, I appeared on a call-in radio talk show to discuss my arguments for the existence of aliens."

"How long was that show?" Pete asked.

"It lasted about an hour."

"Oh," Pete said. "I haven't told you yet, but I've scheduled an important tour for the both of you at eleven hundred hours. That gives you only half an hour to give us your explanation."

"In that case, I'll give you an abbreviated version."

"That would be good," Pete said with a smile.

"Yes. I think what I will do first is to give you a summary of my logic that led me to believe. aliens are visiting our planet."

"That sounds logical." Wendy had a sheepish grin. "Then you can fill in the details afterward."

Corey glared at Wendy and then continued. "First, it is a known fact that there are other stars in our galaxy with planets. Of the three hundred billion stars, perhaps thirty billion have planets. These planets were not all created at the same time; the age difference could be billions of years.

"Many of these planets may have liquid water. Most scientists believe it is almost certain that most planets with liquid water have life. Many of the planets with life, may have intelligent life.

"The ages of planets in our galaxy vary by billions of years. As an example, a planet with intelligent life that is only one percent older than the Earth could have a civilization forty *million* years more advanced than ours! Their technology could be so advanced that space travel is easy for them. They most certainly would want to visit our beautiful, blue planet. It's these visitors, in their marvelous flying machines, which people have been seeing for millennia. Now let me expand on all of that."

"That sounds very logical." Wendy was enjoying ragging on Corey.

"Well, when I say the beginning, I mean the very beginning: the beginning of our universe: the beginning of time."

"Are you talking about the Big Bang?" Pete asked.

"Yes."

"Okay, let's start with the Big Bang."

Corey turned toward Wendy. "Wendy, do you understand the Big Bang Theory?"

"I think so. Isn't that the most widely accepted theory about the beginning of the universe?"

"Yes it is."

Wendy's eyes scanned the ceiling as she tried to recall some of the details of that theory. Astronomy 101 was ancient history to her. "What I recall is that several billion years ago, the universe started to expand. At the first split second of its existence it was so small it could fit on the head of a pin. Also, it was so hot that matter could not exist. It was only energy. Then, as it expanded at near the speed of light, it got cooler and matter could begin to exist. I think that the first elements formed were hydrogen, with a small amount of helium. Eventually, this gas formed the stars and planets we have today. Am I right?" Wendy was proud of how much she had remembered.

Corey stared at her for a long moment of disbelief. "I'm truly impressed!"

"Thank you." Wendy placed her finger on her lower lip as she pondered. "Refresh my memory. How long ago was the Big Bang?"

"That's still being debated, but the consensus seems to be that the universe began about 13.7 billion years ago."

Pete leaned toward Corey. "To an outside observer, the Big Bang would have appeared as a bright star just forming, right?"

"Not quite. Not at first. The universe was still so dense that the photons from this vast release of energy could not escape. The universe was still opaque to an outside observer. It took over three hundred thousand years for the expansion of the universe to lower the temperature and density enough for the simplest atoms of hydrogen and helium to form. At that time, the universe became transparent and photons could escape. Then there was light, brilliant light!"

"Then God said: 'Let there be light; and there was light.'" Pete interjected.

"That's right. I've seen many parallels between Genesis and the Big Bang theory." Corey had always marveled at how science and the Bible seemed to be converging.

"So, an observer watching from outside the universe, would not even know the universe had begun, until after three hundred thousand years?" Wendy asked.

"That's right. The universe was in darkness until then."

"In the beginning, was the universe just one giant ball of energy with hydrogen and helium gas?" Pete asked.

"Yes, but the expanding universe was not 'smooth'. There were minute variations in temperature and density, and by about 100 million years, the universe resembled a cotton ball with billions of wisps and strands of higher density gases, intersecting. It was at these intersections, or nodes, that the density eventually became high enough for gravity to take over and form stars."

"As I recall, the gas collapsed at these nodes and the pressure and temperature became high enough for fusion to begin. Hydrogen went through a nuclear fusion process and became helium with a vast release of energy. Stars were formed," Wendy added. *I'm pretty good at this stuff*, she mused.

"Yes, two hundred million years after the big bang, stars were born."

"Was that when our sun formed?" Wendy was on a roll.

"No. As the first stars began to form, they contained only hydrogen and helium. They were hundreds of times larger than our sun and burned fiercely in the blue and ultraviolet light. Astronomers call them blue giants. They burn their fuel so fiercely that they last only a few million years. However, during their lives, the fusion reactions within these blue giants created heavier elements such as carbon and oxygen. When their fuel was exhausted, they collapse and exploded as a supernova, spewing out the heavy elements into the universe. If you've ever seen pictures of the Crab Nebula, then you know what the remnants of one of these explosions looks like."

"The early universe must have resembled fireworks on the Fourth-of-July," Wendy conjectured, as she waved her arms upward in a simulation of the bursting rockets.

"Yes, relatively speaking. If an observer had taken time-lapse photographs over a few million years, it would have looked like the Fourth-of-July. Also, at that time, the universe was much smaller and more crowded. Collisions between stars and even galaxies were much more common than today.

"The energy from the exploding shock waves forged even heavier elements such as iron and some organic compounds. These later became the raw material for living organisms. All of this matter went swirling throughout the universe to join hydrogen and helium that had not yet fused."

"And it was this debris that formed stars like our sun. I remember now." Wendy was amazed at how much detail she could recall.

"Well, about ninety-five percent of the debris and gases are still floating around between the galaxies. However, the shock waves from the exploding stars formed new, dense regions. If the shock wave raised the density high enough, gravity acted to cause it to collapse. If the cloud mass was large enough, the central core eventually reached sufficient temperature and pressure to begin the fusion process again. New, second generation, stars were born.

"The universe was getting larger, and thus, cooler. As a result, many of these second generation stars were smaller and more stable than the original blue giants." Corey looked at Wendy with a smile. "And you are right, intermediate sized stars, like our sun, were formed at this time. They have heavier elements in them that moderate and slow down the fusion reaction. That's why they can burn for billion of years."

"So, our sun is a second generation star?" Pete asked.

"Yes, it's a second or third generation star. It's about half way through its expected life of ten billion years."

"It's been said that there are more stars in the universe than there are grains of sand in all the beaches on Earth. Is that true?" Wendy couldn't remember where she had heard that. Perhaps it was from one of her astronomer friends on campus.

"I've heard that statement too. There are over one hundred billion galaxies in the universe and each galaxy has over two hundred billion stars. Multiply that out, and you get two with twenty-two zeros after it. Our galaxy, the Milky Way, has over three hundred billion stars. Within our galaxy, there are perhaps as many as fifty new sun-like stars born each year."

"How big is the Milky Way?" Pete asked.

"Our galaxy consists of a thin disk about one hundred thousand light years in diameter and only sixteen hundred light years in thickness with a bulge in its center. You can visualize it as two CDs stacked together with a marble at the center. From the center, there are two arms that spiral out to the edge of the disk. Our sun is a little over one half of the distance out from the center and along an edge of one of the arms."

"As these swirling clouds of gas and debris condense into stars, the material that did not get drawn into the star eventually formed the planets. Am I right on that, Corey?" Pete asked.

"Yes, the interactions of all the explosions and collisions between the galaxies caused considerable turbulence within the galaxies. Giant swirling clouds formed and, if sufficiently dense, they collapsed into circular disks of rotating debris. The central region of these disks continued to collapse and, if the mass was large enough, it formed one or more stars. The dust and debris, and some of the gas that was left in the rotating cloud, aggregated out and formed the planets that orbit the star. That's why most planets orbit in the same direction and in nearly the same plane."

"What happened if the mass was too small to form a star?" Pete asked.

"If the cloud of gas and dust was not massive enough, the collapsing core did not have the mass necessary to produce the heat and pressure to start fusion or, if fusion did start, it only lasted briefly. Astronomers call these small stars brown dwarfs."

"I remember that the mass had to be several times larger than Jupiter or a brown dwarf could not form," Wendy added.

"Yes, you're right. It turns out that it takes a mass of at least thirteen times that of Jupiter for a star to form. If the mass is less than this, then the mass stays relatively cool and a planet is formed. Planet may not be the proper name for these bodies since they don't revolve around a star. My preference would be to call them planetoids. By the way, the cloud disk that forms the planetoid could also form smaller bodies. These would be like moons. If the collapsing cloud does not have enough angular momentum, or swirl, then the cloud simply forms a star without planets or a planetoid without moons."

Wendy was becoming intrigued now. "So you mean that, in addition to a universe full of stars, it is also full of rogue planetoids with moons, wandering about without a central star or sun?"

"Yes. There are probably as many rogue planetoids as there are stars."

"Wouldn't we see them?" Pete asked.

"We can't see them because they don't shine or give off enough heat for us to detect, especially through clouds of gas and debris. However, astronomers have recently obtained infrared images of a group of objects beyond our solar system that qualify as planetoids. These objects were seen in the star cluster, sigma Orionis, about twelve hundred light-years away. The reason they can be seen is because they're in an area with very little dust to block the view and because they're young, perhaps only five million years old."

"Why does being young make it easier to see them?" Wendy asked.

"Young planetoids are still relatively hot which makes them visible in the infrared spectrum. Infrared light can more easily penetrate any clouds of gas."

"Could these new planetoids ever wander into our solar system?" Wendy asked. She was beginning to relate to some creation stories of her own— ancient stories.

"Yes. Some rogues probably do wander into a star and planetary system and get captured by that star. Most likely, it would fall into an orbit that is initially out of plane with the natural planets. There is nearly an equal chance that it could orbit in a direction opposite to that of the other planets. Also, the orbit of the planetoid would be elongated. Many of the planets found outside our solar exhibit these elongated orbits and may be captured planetoids. That might explain how gaseous planets like Jupiter are found in very elongated orbits with perigees that are much closer to their star than Earth is to the sun. Such planets could not form that close without evaporating. They had to have formed elsewhere, at a greater distance."

Wendy leaned toward Corey. "Do you think that these planetoids that are wandering through space without a sun could have life on them?" Wendy began searching her memory for the ancient Sumerian creation stories she had studied.

"Most scientists think the key to life is liquid water. If a planetoid has a method of generating internal heat, so that its water is in liquid form, then theoretically, life is possible. If a planetoid has moons whose tidal action can generate enough internal heat within the planetoid to keep water liquid, then life is possible. Europa, one of the moons of Jupiter, has been observed to have a surface covered in ice. Many astronomers now believe the tidal action from Jupiter may generate enough heat to melt the ice below the surface of Europa, and form huge oceans of liquid water. They think there is a possibility of some forms of life on Europa."

"But how can there be life without sunlight?" Pete asked. He had always believed that sunlight was essential for life.

"Scientists used to think that sunlight was required to have life, but that thinking changed. Life was found to thrive near volcanic vents in the floor of our oceans where there is no sunlight. Now, some scientists are proposing that life on this planet may have even originated at these vents, migrated to the surface and then to land. So, sunlight is not a required ingredient for life."

"Would you think that it might be possible for a rogue planetoid to wander into our solar system and have life on it?" Wendy asked. She recalled that the Sumerians believed that.

I think most astronomers would say it could have life as long as there was liquid water present on the planetoid."

Pete got up to stretch his legs. He walked to the other end of the table and looked at Corey. "Our galaxy, the Milky-Way, has stars of various ages. Is that correct?"

"Yes, exactly," said Corey. "There are billions of first, second, and perhaps third generation stars in our galaxy. Most of the older stars are in the central bulge but some are also in our neighborhood. Stars in our region are at various stages of development. Some stars are just now forming; some are dying. A really good example of the star formation process can be seen in Hubble photographs of the Eagle Nebula.

"What would be your guess? How many stars in our galaxy have planets?" Pete asked.

"Right now our technology is very limited. However, astronomers have been able to measure the effects that very massive planets have on their stars. Eventually, we will have the technology to see these massive planets and even smaller, Earth-size planets. Astronomers believe that stars with planets may be more common than stars without. In our own galaxy, there are probably billions of planets in orbit around most of the second and third generation stars. Hundreds of millions of these planets are probably at the right distance from their 'suns' to allow water to exist in liquid form and to support life as we know it. Within our own region of the Milky Way, there may be millions of life-supporting planets. Some are younger than Earth and may have only primitive life. Some are millions of years older than our Earth and may have intelligent life that is far more advanced than ours.

Wendy got up and walked up to the front of the conference room. She found a dry erase marker and drew a large circle on the white board. Then she used the marker to make dots sprinkled uniformly within the circle. "Do you mean that there may be millions of planets with superior intelligence, sprinkled throughout our galaxy?"

"Yes and no. There may be millions of planets with life forms having superior intelligence, but they are not sprinkled throughout the galaxy. They are most likely confined to a belt of stars around the center of the galaxy."

Corey got up and went to the board. He drew a small circle at the center of Wendy's circle. He then drew two more circles. One was about a fourth and the other was about three fourths the diameter of Wendy's circle. "This small circle is the galactic bulge where there is a huge population of stars crowded close together. Between these two other circles is what is known as the Galactic Habitable Zone. About ten percent of the stars in our Galaxy are in this belt. Intelligent life is probably clustered near the center of this belt." He drew two arms that spiraled out from the center. "Because of the high density of stars and dust in these arms, there is a much higher probability of extinctions here and intelligent life may not have a chance to develop where these spirals intersect the GHZ. He placed a mark in the middle of his two circles and near one of the spiral arms. "This is about where our sun is located."

"Why are life-supporting planets confined to that belt? Wendy asked.

"As you approach the center of the galaxy, the stars are so close to each other that radiation and the constant impacts from space debris would kill any life form we know." Corey used the marker to increase the density of dots in the center and moved his hand around to show the many collisions that occur there. He pointed to the region outside of the Galactic Habitable Zone. "Too far away from the galactic center, and the star systems would not have a sufficient quantity of heavier elements to form planets and the building blocks of life."

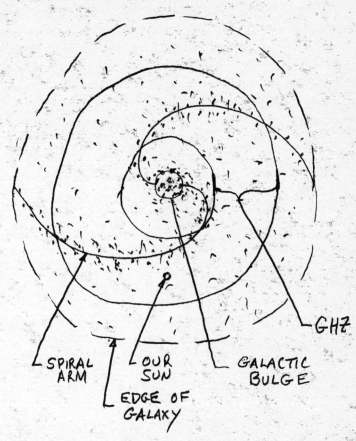

SPIRAL ARM

OUR SUN

EDGE OF GALAXY

GALACTIC BULGE

GHZ

"How close might these planets with intelligent life be to us?" Pete asked.

"The closest star to our sun is just over four light years away. Thus far, even with our limited technology, astronomers have found that ten percent of the stars within one hundred light-years of our sun have planetary systems." Corey drew a small circle around the dot he used to represent Earth. "Astronomers have estimated that there are over a million stars, like our sun, within one thousand light years of our sun. Many of these could have planets with advanced intelligence living on them."

Wendy had returned to her seat. "That is amazing! But, I have one question. Why haven't these aliens in their marvelous flying machines stopped to say hello?" Wendy looked at Corey as if to say, top that one.

"Well, on that note we have to stop, that's a question for another day," Pete said as he looked at his watch. "It's time for our tour. Anyway, my brain is full." Pete pointed toward the door labeled RESTRICTED. "Let's go for a tour. I guarantee, this will knock your socks off."

Chapter 7
The Grays

When Pete reached the door marked RESTRICTED, he began to key in his password. As he did, he cautioned them; "You're going to see why you both had to sign confidentiality papers when you arrived. Also, you're going to find it difficult to believe what you are about to see. You may even experience some discomfort." Pete had a strange smile on his face.

When the green light came on above the keypad, Pete led the two through the door and into a dimly lit corridor. As they walked down the corridor, their footsteps echoed off of the tiled floor and hard walls. Wendy glanced back and noticed a black dome extending from the ceiling. She guessed it concealed the surveillance cameras Pete had mentioned earlier.

Pete began explaining, "What you are about to see are artifacts brought over from Wright Patterson Air Force Base in the late fifties. We only have these rooms scheduled for an hour, so this first visit will be a cursory look. We have to be out by noon. "

"Why do we have a limited time to view this stuff?" Corey guessed that Pete was talking about UFO artifacts. He was getting more excited with each step.

"There are several teams of people who are studying these artifacts. To maintain security, it's important that none of the teams make contact with each other. There is a master schedule for each room, and to gain access we must schedule that room. Admission priority is set by the base commander."

"If our project is as important as you say, why don't we have top priority? Why can't we stay as long as we want?" Corey asked as they rounded a corner in the hallway.

"We do have the highest priority. In our case, the President has intervened to give us top priority. Because of that, any time you want to revisit any room, just let me know, and you'll be scheduled in. I only scheduled an hour for this first visit because I'm not sure how you're going to react to what you see. Anyway, this first visit is just to give you an introduction. After you have a full understanding of our mission, we will return. Are you both okay with that?"

"Yes" they both answered as the team came to a stainless steel door labeled PATHOLOGY G.

Pete keyed in his pass code and waited for the computer to verify that he was authorized entry at that time. The red light over the keypad went out and the green light labeled ENTER came on. Pete pulled on the heavy door. As it began to open, there was a slight hissing sound as air escaped into the hallway.

The team entered a dimly lit room no larger than an elevator. There was another stainless steel door directly in front of them with a small window. Pete closed the door behind them. "This is an airlock," he said. He entered his code again and a stream of strange smelling air blew down over them, passing through a grate in the floor. The

ENTER light came on and Pete opened the second door. Again, there was a slight hiss as air entered the airlock.

"What's that smell?" Wendy asked.

"Ozone," Pete answered.

Pete led the couple into the next room. It was as sterile looking as an operating theater in a teaching hospital.

It's dead quiet in here. Wendy thought. *The ventilation system seems to be whispering something.*

"It smells like a mortuary," Corey said. "There's an antiseptic smell."

"Pete, why is it so chilly in here?" Wendy's hands and ears were beginning to feel the cold.

"It has to be, to keep the bacteria level low." Pete said. "They keep it at only fifty-five and the air is filtered and passed over a corona discharge wire. The electrical discharge creates the ozone that you smell."

Opposite them were, what appeared to be, large aquariums. There were eight, positioned in two rows of four, with eight feet of spacing between each. Each was sitting on heavy metal tables, three feet high. The aquariums were two feet wide by five feet long by four feet high. The room was dimly lit except for floodlights directed to the floor around each aquarium.

Wendy drew closer to the closest tank. "What's in these tanks?" With no light inside the tanks, Wendy could see only her own reflections. "Why can't I see what's in the tanks?"

"They're made with a mirrored glass to reduce the amount of stray room light that enters the tanks. The pathologists are concerned that light can damage the specimens, so they keep each tank dark until the contents are being viewed," Pete explained.

Wendy ran her fingers over the smooth glass surface and felt the coolness within.

"So how do we light the tanks?" Corey asked with excitement. He was sure he knew what was inside.

Pete looked at Corey. He could see that Corey was not going to be held back. "By pressing this button located on the base of each pedestal." Pete pointed to a small green button on the side of the base. "The tank is lit from the inside for only five minutes before automatically turning off. That prevents someone from accidentally leaving the light on."

"What's in the tanks?" Wendy asked again. She was feeling the same sense of excitement as Corey.

"The bodies of the aliens from crashed space ships." Pete looked at both Wendy and Corey to monitor their reaction. "I have to warn you, what you are about to see may shock you. It did me, the first time I saw them. Some of the bodies are not intact, as a result of disintegration, or damage from the impact of their crash. However, this tank has one of the few intact specimens. Are you ready?"

"Yes." Wendy answered, taking a breath.

"Corey?"

"Of course, let's go." Corey looked alternatively between Pete and the tank, in anticipation.

Pete pressed the button on the tank directly in front of them. Immediately, it came to life!

"Oh my God!" Wendy jumped back. She closed her eyes to blank out what was only two feet from her. She needed time to come to terms with it.

"I'm sorry to startle you so, but it is important that you take some time to study the body," Pete said.

Wendy opened her eyes. In front of her was an intact being, person, or whatever one would call it, suspended in a very light blue-green fluid resembling dishwashing detergent. The body looked to her to be about four feet long. It was completely nude.

After a moment, she was able to talk. "The eyes, they're so large. They have a slight slant, and look at how deeply they're set."

Corey moved to behind the tank to get a better view of the head. "Yes, and look at how dark they are. They're jet black."

Wendy began to scan the rest of the body. "The skin looks so soft and shiny. There's no hair anywhere on the body."

Pete stood back from the tank so Wendy and Corey had plenty of room to maneuver. "I found it interesting that there are no genitalia."

"Corey looked at Pete with a puzzled expression. "None of the bodies have any?"

"None."

"My God," Wendy said, "the legs and feet looked like those of a child who died from starvation. Its arms are disproportionately long for its body. The distance from the shoulder to the elbow is longer than the forearm. Pete, is it my imagination, or is the skin green?"

"It's the blue-green fluid that makes it look green." Pete added. "I was told by the pathologist that the skin color is actually a light gray with a brown tinge."

"Look at that." Wendy bent down to have a closer look at the fingers. "The hands have only four fingers. One finger is shorter, almost like our thumb."

"I noticed that too, the first time I looked at it," Pete answered. He moved next to Wendy and pointed to the fingers. "Did you notice this? Look at the fingertips."

"My God, he has four small suction cups on the tip of each of the fingertips!"

Corey came closer to his side of the tank to look at the fingers. "That is interesting." He stood back to get a better perspective of the entire body. "His head seems to be the size of an adult human, but his body is the size of a child."

Wendy was now leaning over, looking at the alien's head. "His neck looks so frail. It reminds me of a chicken's neck."

"I know, it looks like it wouldn't take much of a blow to break his neck. And look, there are no protruding features such as ear lobes or nose," Pete said.

Wendy moved closer.

Pete pointed to the side of the head. "Take a look Wendy. There are almost no ears protruding from the sides. Notice the two ear canals with flaps on each side of the head."

Corey drew closer to check out the ears and the rest of the face. "The nose looks concave, with only two small holes. It hardly has a mouth at all and there are no visible teeth. The mouth resembles more of a crease, or fold, than a mouth. I wonder how they eat."

"They may not have to eat. According to the pathology report, it has no digestive system."

"How does it get nutrients?" Wendy asked.

"The pathologists think that it may absorb the nutrients it needs by transdermal absorption through its skin. They think that it probably has to take a bath in nutrients periodically. It's not known how they metabolize."

"Does he have blood?" Wendy asked.

"Yes, you can see his blood vessels along the top of his head here," Pete said, as he pointed to the top of the creature's head. "His cell structure is vastly different than ours."

"I had heard many stories that portray them as androids. Did he have any life-signs that showed he was a living creature?" Corey asked.

"When this creature was still alive they took measurements of his brain waves. His electronic signature displayed a signal similar to what we would call long, low frequency waves. Also, the creature's brain lobes seem to have been integrated electro-magnetically as well as physiologically and neurologically."

"What does all of that mean?" Wendy asked.

"I'm not sure. Some think they were not really alive but just androids. Others think they were alive but had the ability to act in unison as if they were programmed."

"Where did this alien come from?" Wendy asked.

"This one survived the 1947 crash in the Plains of San Agustin in New Mexico. He died from unknown causes several days after being rescued," Pete explained. "That's why he's intact."

Pete reached into a silver box next to the tank and pulled out an almond shaped piece of thin plastic about the size of an eyeglass lens. His eyes had this covering attached directly to the corneas. At first, the pathologists thought they were a part of his eyes. Then they found that the film could be lifted off."

"Like large contact lenses," Wendy said.

"Yes, or sun glasses without frames." Pete handed it to Wendy

Reluctantly, she reached out and took the eye piece. As she examined it, she noticed how it seemed to amplify the light when she held it up to her eye. "Wow! Even in this dim light, I can clearly see the outline of everything in the room, even those in the shadows."

"Let me see!" Corey was like a child in a toy store.

Wendy handed it to him and he too held it up to his eye. "Yes, and things that move take on a greenish orange glow."

Pete again reached into the silver box and pulled out what looked like a small piece of dull, grayish-silvery cloth that looked almost like silk. "This is a piece of the suit he was wearing." Pete handed it to Wendy.

She crumpled it in her hands and then held her hand open. "Look, it springs back to its unwrinkled shape when I open my hand. This is definitely wrinkle-free."

"None of the other specimens are complete and I suggest you look at them later when you feel your stomach is strong enough," Pete said.

"Okay," Wendy said.

The light in the tank went out as the five-minute timer timed out.

"Can we turn it back on?" Wendy asked.

"Not right now," Pete said. We're on a tight schedule so we need to move to the next room to look at the craft."

"I agree, let's go and look at the craft." Corey couldn't wait.

"Wendy, you and Corey can come back for another look. Just schedule it through me. Now, I want you to see a craft similar to what these guys were riding when they crashed." Pete placed the specimens back into the silver box.

He led Corey and Wendy to the door marked ART C at the far end of the room and entered his code. The green ENTER light lit and he led them into another airlock.

Chapter 8
The Craft

As they exited the airlock, Wendy visually scanned the room. It resembled a small aircraft hangar. Three spotlights in the ceiling shone down on a round craft suspended from the center of the room. It was held at about a ten degree angle to the floor, in a special sling that kept it about four feet above the floor. Three cables attached to the sling, went to three separate winches. By adjusting the three winches, the height and attitude of the craft could be changed. Below the craft were three floodlights that illuminated its bottom surface producing an eerie effect.

"In this room is the craft that crashed in 1953 about fifteen miles north of Kingman, Arizona. It crashed in the foothills of the mountains which are about nine miles north west of the airport," Pete said, as they walked over to the craft.

Corey was so excited he almost tripped over an extension cord feeding one of the floodlights. "This is amazing! It's simply amazing!"

"How did they retrieve it?" Wendy asked.

"Typically, with a craft this size, they use a tank carrier. Even with that, they had to carry it tipped on edge." Pete placed his hand on the edge of the craft.

"Prospectors, who witnessed the crash, reported that it looked like it was trying to land but miscalculated, striking an outcropping." His eyes followed Corey as he raced around the craft. Pete continued to speak. "I've flown over the site myself and it looks pretty rugged. Fortunately, it crashed in a sandy plateau in the foothills of the mountain."

Pete smiled to himself as he recalled a humorous story. "I was told that the craft kept emitting a beeping sound even after they brought it to this base. People who went into the craft got sick to their stomach and had to leave. Finally, after trying for several days to stop the beeping, they had to bring the survivor of the crash back from Wright Patterson. He went in and within seconds he had it stopped."

"Why did they take the alien to Wright Patterson? Why didn't they bring him here?" Wendy asked.

"This base did not have the facilities for a living alien. Initially, the bodies were taken there for analysis. Later, they were brought here after the tanks were installed."

Corey, now in his realm, was trying to soak up every detail of the craft. "This must be at least thirty-five feet in diameter. Wouldn't you agree, Pete?"

"It looks bigger than it actually is. I was told it's just slightly larger than thirty feet in diameter. It's about eleven feet thick in the center."

Corey found a small opening in the bottom. "This must be the access hatch. Other than this, the skin of the craft is seamless." He ran his hand over the surface. "The skin looks and feels like a dull brushed aluminum."

As he continued around the craft, he came to a large portion of one edge that had severe damage. A whole section was missing from the saucer's leading edge, leaving a gaping hole about nine feet wide and three feet high. Corey could see into the craft. "There appears to be a double hull with a bulkhead or deck dividing the craft into two levels. Look at this!" Corey was fingering a portion of the torn skin. "The hull is made of a composite material."

To Wendy, the craft was a marvelous curiosity. She ran around to where Corey was standing, to see what he was talking about. "What's a composite material?"

"See how the hull is made of these two thin layers of metallic material bonded to this quarter-inch-thick core." He bent down closer to the surface to get a closer look. "The core looks like a filled plastic."

"What's this?" Wendy pointed to a strange gray-stranded cable, hanging part way over the opening on one side.

Corey pulled it closer for inspection. "Looks like a bundle of fiber-optic cables. The other end runs up to the flight deck. Look down here!" He pointed into the lower half of the craft. "That's the other half of this cable. See how it branches into three separate cables? They run to each of those hemispheres embedded in the floor of the lower deck."

"Oh," Wendy said as she bent down to look under the craft. "Those hemispheres must be spheres because they extend through the floor and out of the bottom of the craft."

Corey bent down to look. "Damn! I think those spheres are the gravity generators! They're equally spaced around a circle near the bottom edge of the craft. That's exactly where I would place gravity generators to get the most stability. Look! Those cables that run to the upper deck are probably the control cables. The simplicity of the design is awesome!" He looked back inside the lower section of the craft and pointed toward three rectangular box-like structures with doors. "Those are probably lockers of some sort. There's no cabling coming from them so they're not power cabinets or part of the drive system."

"What would they put in those?" Wendy asked.

"I don't know." Corey continued to peer into the lower deck. "Strange, I don't see any evidence of a power source."

Pete came over to the opening. "I couldn't find one either. I even checked the upper deck. The technician who gave me my tour said no one is sure what powers this thing. There's a challenge for you, Corey."

"Perhaps they use some sort of superconducting battery built into the hull of the ship." Corey began to squeeze through the gash in the side of the craft. "I want to try to get inside and to the upper deck."

"Are you sure you won't get stuck?" Wendy's voice was tense. She grabbed onto Corey's pant leg.

"It's okay," Pete said, "I climbed in the same way a few days ago. He won't get stuck."

Ignoring her tugs, Corey managed to leverage his body up onto the deck. He sat up. "Wendy, come up here!" he shouted.

Wendy found it hard to ignore Corey's enthusiasm, but this was something created by a very high intelligence. She felt like there was something sacred about it. Before she could refuse, Corey's hand reached down for her. "Take my hand. You'll be amazed!"

"Okay, but this goes against my better judgment," she said as she began to climb in.

As Corey pulled on one arm, Wendy leveraged herself onto the upper deck. "Boy, it really is cramped up here. I don't think there's room to stand up. The ceiling is way too low."

"Yes, I would guess only slightly more than five feet high at the center," Corey said.

Wendy scanned the room. "Wow! This *is* beautiful! The ceiling, walls and floor are beautifully blended together. There don't seem to be any seams anywhere." She studied the four small seats near a small console. Near each were strange writings that looked almost like hieroglyphics. "And those seats; they look like they came from a child's playhouse." She could see some smudge marks on the floor, seats, and the console. She yelled down to Pete. "Is there blood up here, Pete?"

"Yes, those are blood stains from the aliens who died shortly after the crash. That odor you smell is just the remnants of the disinfectant that was used to kill any foreign bacteria."

She hadn't noticed the smell until Pete mentioned it.

Pete stood outside, near the gash. There was not enough room for three people in the craft. He peered up to the top deck through the hole, watching the two as they explored. "Notice that even though there are no windows, you can see out."

"Yes, that was the first thing I noticed," Corey called down. "The ceiling looks almost transparent and is letting in the light from the hanger. The ceiling didn't look at all transparent from the outside."

"I know. It's pretty amazing, isn't it?" Pete yelled back.

"It almost seems to amplify the light from the ceiling. The material must be similar to the eye pieces we saw earlier," Corey said.

Wendy had pulled herself over the textured floor to the small control console in front of the seats. There were no switches or buttons on the surface, only a strange glassy looking surface with circles, squares, and triangles spaced over the surface. "Look at this control panel, Corey! It has symbols over the entire surface! They look like a mixture of Egyptian hieroglyphics, Sanskrit, and cuneiform. I don't recognize any of them."

"Yeah, I noticed that, too. What do you think all of those depressions are for?"

"They look like buttons in reverse," Wendy said. "I wish I had something on which to take notes, or a camera. This thing is great!"

"Sorry. No camera or notes," Pete called back. He looked at his watch. "Well, believe it or not, we've been here nearly an hour. We have only eight minutes to get out of here and back to the conference room. If we're still here after our hour, all hell breaks loose. So, let's get moving."

Wendy and Corey climbed down out of the craft and followed Pete over to a door in the wall to the right of their original entry point. This door was labeled SECTION G.

Corey scanned the room. In the dim light he could see several other doors around the chamber, each labeled differently. "Where do all those other doors go to?"

Pete was keying in his pass code. "As I mentioned earlier, this installation has several other teams working here, independently of each other. Each team is assigned its own suite of rooms that do not connect to other suites. Our suite is in section G. If you try to go through any of those other doors like the ones marked ART A, ART B, or SECTION F, your code number will not work; at least not today."

"What's behind those doors?" Wendy asked.

"Well, ART is short for ARTIFACTS. You're leaving ART C. The other ART doors lead to chambers similar to this one with artifacts from other crash sites." Pete opened the door and led them into an airlock.

As they exited the airlock, they were in another long corridor. After about sixty feet, it made a sharp right turn and, twenty feet further, ended at another door. Corey guessed this led back into the corridor going to the conference room. He was right. As soon as Pete opened that door, they turned left down another corridor. As Corey looked ahead, he could see CONF. G over the door.

"Pete, I'm used to seeing exit signs in most buildings to help direct people out in case of a fire. I don't see any here," Wendy said, with a concerned tone in her voice.

"Good point. You both must get familiar with the layout of our suite so that you can find your way out in case of an emergency." They stopped in front of the door. "Here, Wendy, try your code on this door."

Wendy keyed in her six digits and, within two seconds, the green ENTER light came on.

"The computer knows who is authorized. Whenever we're having a meeting, I electronically seal all doors in the conference room so we're not disturbed. Also, when we leave, I seal the doors again so nothing is disturbed while we're gone." Pete opened the door and they all entered the conference room.

"It's noon. We'll take a lunch break now. I'm sorry, but I have some details to take care of, so I won't be able to join you. Be back here by thirteen hundred hours so we can discuss what we saw. Also, I'll brief you on our mission."

Chapter 9
The Sumerian Connection

Corey and Wendy returned to Wendy's suite with their lunch trays. Wendy pointed toward the small table in the kitchen area. "Have a seat over there at the table, Corey. I'll grab some salt and pepper."

"Thanks." Corey glanced around Wendy's apartment as he sat down. "Your apartment looks just like mine except I don't have a piano."

"Isn't that great? The piano, I mean," Wendy said. "I was up for at least an hour last night, playing the piano to unwind."

"You'll have to play it for me some time."

"I'd love to." Wendy gave Corey her special smile. "Perhaps if we have time after lunch, I'll play something." She sat down across from Corey and unwrapped her bean and cheese burrito.

"That tour blew my mind! Corey said, shaking his head. "No one would believe me if I told them what I saw this morning." He glanced at Wendy as he put ketchup on his hamburger. "What did you think?"

"It's hard to explain my feelings. It changes everything for me. Now that I know we're not alone in this world, I have to rethink my understanding of our human history, my religion, and who I am." She cocked her head and gave Corey a studied look. "Did it affect you that way?"

"Well, I've always believed that extraterrestrial intelligence existed. I think you know that. But to confirm it, after so many years by actually touching the hardware and seeing a body, is beyond words."

"I agree," Wendy said, as her eyes did an unfocused scan of the ceiling in contemplation. "Corey, as you were explaining the Big Bang and its relationship to Genesis, my mind went back to my studies in antiquities. I brought some notes on the Sumerians with me." Wendy got up and went over to her suitcase and retrieved a bound set of notes.

"You have notes?" Corey stared at Wendy with a shocked expression.

"Yes. Since I didn't know what my mission was, I brought my dissertation and materials that I thought might be helpful for most situations relating to my expertise. As you probably know from my bio, I've spent a considerable amount of time studying the writings of the Sumerians and Akkadians and have even taught courses about them."

"Who were the Sumerians and the Akkadians? Refresh my memory."

"Sumer was an amazing civilization that thrived over six thousand years ago. That was a thousand years before the Egyptian and fifteen hundred years before the Chinese civilizations started. Much of our knowledge of the Sumerians was passed down to us through the Akkadians. They were the later civilization that ruled the northern part of Mesopotamia that is known as Iraq today."

"Amazing? Why?"

"Because. Almost over night, they developed much of our mathematics, medicine, astronomy, laws, and writing. All of these inventions were passed down to subsequent civilizations such as the Greeks and Egyptians. These developments appeared so suddenly that it's as if some other, much higher, civilization handed all of this to the Sumerians."

Corey took a bite from his hamburger. "Perhaps the aliens passed it on to them."

"Based on their writings, and after what we just saw, that is a possibility I can no longer rule out." Wendy began to nibble on her salad.

"What sort of things did they write about?"

Wendy's eyes scanned the ceiling as she searched her memory for the most relevant writing. "Well, their creation story was the basis of the Akkadian and, subsequently, the Hebrew texts on creation. Much of Genesis, in our Old Testament, is an edited and abbreviated version of a more detailed version given in Mesopotamian texts. These can be traced back to the Sumerian texts. You may know that Abraham, the Hebrew patriarch, came from the Sumerian city of Ur in southern Mesopotamia."

"Creation myths ... how did the Sumerians think the universe got started?"

"I'm not aware of their ideas about the universe. However, some of the ancient tablets, which I've translated, deal with their story of the creation of the solar system. I've always considered this story as a myth. That was until today when I heard you talk about rogue planetoids with moons. Then the Sumerian story took on a new reality for me."

"So, how did they think our solar system was formed?"

Wendy thought for a moment. "They believed that, in the beginning, when our solar system was very young and just forming, our Earth was in a position farther out from the sun. One of their tablets showed a diagram of the early solar system and it showed a large planet located between Mars and Jupiter."

Wendy pulled out a drawing of the clay tablet and showed it to Corey. "See here?" She placed her finger on one of the discs shown on the diagram. "They called that planet, Tiamat, their word for 'Maiden of Life.'" She placed her finger on another area of the diagram. "See here, you can see that Pluto was a moon of Saturn, and Neptune and Uranus were shown as twins."

Corey studied the diagram as Wendy continued.

"Other tablets describe them as being watery twins. The Sumerians thought that Neptune was a blue-green, watery planet with patches of swamp-like vegetation. Uranus was also blue-green and was tipped on its axis by ninety degrees. "

"Just a minute." It suddenly dawned on Corey what Wendy was saying. "Did you say that the Sumerians knew about Uranus as well as Neptune?"

"Yes. Why?" Wendy looked at Corey as she took a bite of her salad.

"Because, Uranus and Neptune weren't discovered until after the seventeenth century and Pluto wasn't discovered until 1930! Also, we didn't know Neptune and Uranus were blue-green planets until the fly-by of Voyager 2 in 1986. Before that, they both were thought to be 'gaseous' planets. Data from Voyager also showed that Uranus has a greenish-blue color and lies on its side. I can't believe the Sumerians knew all of that!"

"Well, I wasn't aware of everything you just said but, nevertheless, they did have that knowledge."

"This planet you called Tiamat," Corey said. "It sounds like it's where the present asteroid belt lies. According to Bode's Law, there should be a planet about twice the size of Earth located in that area. The combined mass of the asteroids falls far short of that. Astronomers are still trying to figure out what created the asteroid belt and why it's missing so much of the mass that should be there."

"So you think the Sumerians may have been on to something?" Wendy said with a smile.

"Indeed. So, how do the Sumerians explain the Earth ending up where it is and being smaller than it started out?" Corey asked.

Wendy reviewed her notes to get the sequence of planets correct. "According to the Sumerians in their *Epic of Creation*, there was a great battle. Before the battle, the solar system consisted of the Sun, Mercury, Venus, Mars, Tiamat, Jupiter, Saturn, Pluto, Uranus and Neptune.

"Wait! Why is Pluto just beyond Saturn? Pluto is the farthest planet from the Sun. It should be shown out beyond Neptune." Corey waved his partially eaten hamburger at Wendy.

"Let me finish." She finished chewing her food and swallowed. "A planet, called Nibiru, enters the scene as one of those interloping planetoids you described earlier." Wendy again referred to her notes. "It entered the solar system at a thirty degree angle and in a direction counter to all the other planets." Wendy looked up at Corey. "You said there was a fifty-fifty chance for this."

"That's true." Corey dipped a fry.

Wendy glanced at her notes again. "Nibiru made an extremely close approach to Neptune, forming its moons. Then, it passed Uranus, tipping it on its axis, disturbing it greatly and creating a number of small moons. It then made a close approach to Saturn. At that time, Pluto was a moon of Saturn. Nibiru's close approach deflected Pluto into its present orbit and changed its own path." She glanced at Corey to see his reaction.

He was deep in thought so she continued. "Nibiru, with its seven moons, now headed for Tiamat and its host of eleven moons, headed by Kingu, the largest. Kingu was large enough to be a planet in its own right. As Nibiru with its host of seven, approached Tiamat with its host of eleven, the battle began. The impact of one of Nibiru's moons split Tiamat in half and scattered all of its moons, except Kingu, into new orbits and in the opposite direction. I think you call this retrograde." Wendy looked at Corey with a smile hidden behind a questioning expression.

"That's correct," Corey said as he began to think about a comparison between the Sumerian story and his own knowledge of the solar system.

Wendy continued, "On the second orbit, Nibiru and its remaining moons made a second encounter. The impact shattered one of Tiamat's halves into bits and pieces, forming a bracelet around the sun."

"That would be the Asteroid Belt." Corey dipped another fry into some ketchup as he listened in amazement.

"The other half of Tiamat, plus its remaining moon, Kingu, were deflected into a lower orbit where it is known today as our Earth and Moon." Wendy looked up at Corey. "There you have it."

Corey wiped his chin as he formulated his response. "May I borrow a pencil and some paper?"

"Sure," she said as she retrieved them from her briefcase.

Corey began to sketch. Within a few minutes he finished and turned the sketch around so Wendy could see it. "This sketch is my understanding of how Nibiru made its entry and interacted with Earth and the other planets. I have to say that it all makes sense. It explains some things astronomers have been wrestling with for years."

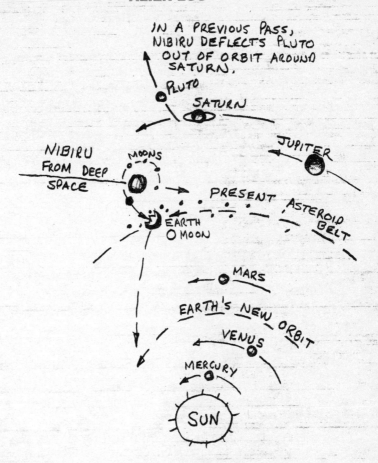

"Like what?" Wendy took another bite of her salad.

"Well, it explains what formed the asteroids and the comets, and why some comets orbit in a retrograde direction. This battle probably occurred over four billion years ago when our solar system was just forming. All of the planets at that time would still be quite hot and plastic, and easily distorted. Rocks brought back from the surface of the moon have been dated to about four and a half billion years. The earliest life forms on Earth have been dated to just over three and a half billion years ago. If the collision occurred after that time, those life forms would probably have been extinguished. What astronomers now think is that the Earth had a collision with a Mars-sized planet. Debris, thrown into orbit around Earth, coalesced to form our moon." Corey scratched his head. "I'm wondering what happened to Nibiru after the second close encounter with the remains of Tiamat? Did it stay in orbit around the Sun or did it escape?"

"The Sumerians believed that it is even now in orbit and revisits the battle scene every thirty-six hundred years."

Corey looked at Wendy. "Do you have a pocket calculator?"

"Yes, I have one in my suitcase." Wendy retrieved it and, with a smile, slid it over to Corey. "If you push the right keys, it gives you all the right answers."

"Very funny," Corey said as he began to work the keys.

"What are you doing?"

"I'm just calculating the size of Nibiru's orbit. I'm curious how the planet Nibiru compares to Sedna."

"What's Sedna?"

"It's the tenth planet that was discovered in March of 2004. It's only about one-eighth the diameter of Earth and has a very elongated orbit with an orbital period of over twelve thousand years."

In less than two minutes, Corey was finished. "Well, I estimate that the orbit has an average distance from the Sun of two hundred and thirty-five AUs. Remember, one AU is equal to the distance the Earth is from the sun."

"Yes, I remember," Wendy smiled back at Corey.

Corey suddenly realized he was being condescending and blushed. "Sorry. Anyway, Nibiru's closest approach to the sun is about three to four AUs where the asteroid belt is located today. Its greatest distance from the sun is four hundred and sixty-six AUs. That puts it ten times as far out as Pluto."

"How does that compare to Sedna's orbit?"

"Sedna never gets closer to the sun than one-and-a-half times the distance to Pluto and goes out almost as far as one thousand AUs, or twenty times as far as Pluto. Also, its orbit is inclined about twelve degrees to the ecliptic as compared to thirty for Nibiru. Sedna is definitely not the planet the Sumerians called Nibiru. If Nibiru's orbit is thirty degrees to the ecliptic, as the Sumerians believed, I think astronomers may not be searching in the right area." Corey winked at Wendy, and bit into another fry. "The whole scenario you've presented about Nibiru explains other questions astronomers are wrestling with."

"Like what?" Wendy leaned over the table, closer to Corey.

"Well, for example, astronomers are wrestling with the question of why the Earth has so much water. A planet that forms at our distance from the sun should not have as much water as it does. Some astronomers propose that much of our water came from impacts by icy asteroids. However, most astronomers feel that only a small part of our water could be from asteroids. If our planet was originally formed in an orbit closer to Jupiter, then the Earth's high water content makes sense."

Wendy was now curious about the window of time in which the Nibirians might interact with Earth. "How many years does Nibiru spend inside Pluto's orbit?"

"About ninety-five percent of the time Nibiru will be outside of Pluto's orbit and difficult to see, even with the Hubbell telescope. It will spend less than two hundred years inside Pluto's orbit."

"So, Corey, do you think the Sumerian creation story has some merit?" Wendy felt that if the Sumerian creation story was true, then perhaps the other Sumerian stories were also true.

"Indeed! It fits very well with what we know today. What has me curious is how they knew all of this. Did the aliens tell them?" He winked at Wendy.

"Well, the story gets even stranger."

"Go ahead, you've got my attention."

"Some of the clay tablets found in Mesopotamia describe the creation tale that is almost identical to that of the Old Testament. These tablets predate the Old Testament by at least a thousand years." Wendy referred to her notes. "According to the Sumerians, the Anunnaki, who the Babylonians called Nefilim, came from the planet Nibiru. They descended to Earth over four hundred and forty-five thousand years ago for the purpose of mining gold and other minerals. Initially, they extracted it from the waters of the Persian Gulf but eventually that gave out, so they transferred their operations to mines in southeastern Africa."

"You're right. That is strange. Go ahead."

"Mining underground was much more difficult for them. So, after nearly two hundred and forty thousand years of toiling, one of their scientists came up with the idea of genetically modifying *Homo erectus*. They took some of their own genetic material and combined it with the *Homo erectus* to create *Homo sapiens*, the humans we are today. By giving them more intelligence and the ability to speak, they could be used as slaves to do the labor required to mine and process the gold. They could also be used to build cities, and whatever else needed to be done."

"So they created us in their image," Corey added, "to be their slaves."

"Yes, I suppose you could put it that way," Wendy said. "According to the Sumerian creation story, this occurred nearly two hundred thousand years ago in a southeastern region of Africa."

"That's really interesting!" Corey said. "Only recently, archeologists have found evidence that *Homo sapiens* evolved in southeastern Africa about two hundred thousand years ago. Somehow, there was a sudden genetic change that resulted in a dramatic increase in brain size. Also, the larynx became located lower in the throat, allowing for speech. Before this, *Homo erectus* could only make grunting sounds and baby talk."

"That's right! I recall seeing a documentary that discussed a study done in 1986 by a group of genetic scientists from California who sampled the mitochondrial DNA from the placenta of hundreds of women from around the world. They were able to trace *Homo sapien's* ancestry back to a single woman who they believed lived in southern Africa two hundred thousand years ago."

"It seems the Sumerians were close on their dates and place for human creation," Corey said.

Wendy continued. "Another part of the puzzle is the Sumerian King List retrieved from a dig in Nenevah where the royal library of King Assurbanipal was uncovered. This list traces the Kings and their cities from the time of the first king, Alulim. He descended from heaven and founded the city of Eridu, near the city known as Ur. This city was in southern Iraq on the northern tip of the Persian Gulf." Wendy reviewed her notes again. "Alulim, ruled in Eridu for eight shars."

"What is a shar?"

"A shar was the unit of time they used. One shar was thirty-six hundred years," Wendy said.

"So, one shar was equal to the time it took Nibiru to complete one orbit. Then the shar was a Nibiruian year."

"Yes."

"What was the longest rule of any king?"

Wendy scanned her notes. "I believe … yes, twelve shars."

"Twelve shars! That would be forty-three thousand Earth years of rule! The Anunnaki had long lives!"

"It seems that way." Wendy was beginning to clean off her tray.

Corey thought for a few minutes. "Well, when you think about it, we live much longer than fruit flies. The total life span of the fruit fly is about fifteen days. The total life span of a human is seventy years." Corey pulled out the calculator and did a quick calculation. "That's a seventeen hundred to one ratio. If the same ratio exists between aliens and humans, then aliens can live for about one hundred and twenty thousand years. It would seem that forty three thousand years of rule for an Anunnaki doesn't sound so unrealistic." Corey shrugged his shoulders. "Who's to say?"

"Eight kings ruled in this region near Baghdad for over two hundred and forty-one thousand years. The Flood came and the Annunaki left."

"Is that the same flood as Noah's?"

"Yes, but the story of Noah was adapted from the Sumerian version."

"Yes, that's right, you said the Sumerian stories predated the Old Testament," Corey said.

"So, according to the Sumerians, after the Flood, the kingships were handed down to men who ruled. They had much shorter reigns. The first king after the Flood was Guar, who ruled twelve hundred years from the city of Kish, just south of Baghdad. The reigns became shorter with each succeeding ruler. Sargon, who ruled from Agade at about 2,300 B.C., ruled for only fifty-six years."

"It seems that in the ancient biblical times, people lived longer the further back you go. As I remember, Methuselah lived to be nine hundred and sixty nine years old."

"Yes, that's true."

"I recall reading that some genetics researchers believe that the process of aging is tied to a particular set of genes that they have yet to identify. They think that someday they will be able to tag these genes and perhaps keep repairing them so we can live as long as we want. An advanced alien civilization might well have discovered that secret."

"From all that you have said, I'm beginning to think the Sumerians really did have a good understanding of the way things were. Perhaps there is a planet, Nibiru, circling the sun every thirty-six hundred years, with intelligent beings, the Anunnaki, living on it. Perhaps they built that craft we saw. Perhaps they were our creators. That creature we saw this morning may just be one of their androids, sent down to keep an eye on us." Wendy sighed. "Who knows?"

"You're right, this is all very strange. I'll be curious to find out from Pete what part we play in all of this. My guess is that your job will be to translate all of those symbols we saw in the craft."

"Perhaps, but why the urgency? That craft has been sitting there for over fifty years. What has happened that makes it imperative to translate now?" Wendy looked at her watch. "We have fifteen minutes before we have to meet with Pete. Would you like me to play the piano?"

"That sounds great!"

Chapter 10
You Must Warn Them!

Walter Reed Army Hospital
2:50 pm E.S.T.

The President sat in a leather armchair and faced his doctor. "So, Doc, am I going to live?"

"Yes, heavens yes. Your health hasn't changed much since your last annual physical. You are about the healthiest sixty-year-old I have ever examined. The only problem is with your cholesterol readings. They're a tad high. Normally, I would tell people to get more exercise and watch their diet. You're already doing that. So, I'm prescribing a statin that you should take once a day at bedtime."

"Well, I think I can live with that." The President smiled and then looked up at the doctor. "I understand General David Wilson is here, at Walter Reed. Is that true?"

The doctor studied the President for a moment. "Yes, he is. Why?"

"I know he is dying of lung cancer. He came to see me two weeks ago. Is it possible to see him in private?"

"Yes. I saw him this morning and he seemed quite coherent. I'm sure he would like to have a visit from you. When would you like to do that?"

"As soon as possible. I am due back at the White House in forty minutes."

"Well then, why don't you come with me and I'll take you to him."

The doctor led the President into the hall where they picked up the secret service entourage. Together, they headed up to the fourth floor to the General's private room.

After reaching the general's room, the doctor tapped on the door and walked in. "General, you have a surprise visitor." He turned and, with a smile, nodded for the President to enter. One of the Secret Service men entered the room first. He quickly scanned the room and checked the bathroom. "All clear," he said.

The President entered. "Hello, David," he said.

The general painfully rolled his body away from the window he had been facing. He grimaced as he looked up at the President, then gave him a faint smile. "Mr. President, I am honored that you took the time to pay me a visit."

"I'm glad to see you're looking so well today." The President could see the general was dying. It was obvious that he was down to his last days. The President turned to the doctor and his Secret Service men. "Gentlemen, would you and Doctor Newman please give me a moment alone with the general?"

The doctor turned and led the men out of the room, closing the door behind them.

The President drew closer to the general so he could speak more softly.

"General, I just wanted to let you know that the project is moving forward. Right after you came to my office, I found a colonel to head up the project. His name is Mitchell, Pete Mitchell. I think you know his dad, General Walter Mitchell."

The general's eyes moved back and forth as he searched his memory, then they brightened. "Yes. I do know him and his son Pete. You picked the right man."

"I'm glad to hear that. Pete has put together a top-notch team. He has someone who is recognized as the top linguistics person in the world. She is supported by an astrophysicist who will give her whatever technical support she needs."

"Sounds like a good team. Are they working in Washington?"

"No. The colonel wanted to have them near other artifacts in case they needed background information."

"Are they at Wright-Pat?" The general's face was tense and his eyes had an urgent look.

"No. Are you familiar with our base in Nevada, near Groom Lake, at S4? You know about that base don't you?"

"Yes. I was stationed there for four years. Please don't tell me they went there!"

"Yes, they are. Why? Is there a problem?"

The general's eyes shut in despair. "Oh, God ... Oh, God. You must warn the colonel."

"About what? That's the most secure base we have. It's run by the CIA, for God's sake! What do I need to warn him about?"

"Mr. President, I spent considerable time at that base. If I had thought it was safe, I would have kept the artifact there, instead of my quarters in Washington. It's not safe!" The general's voice grew weaker.

The President's face flushed with panic. "In what way is it not safe, General?"

The general coughed and winced in pain. "I know you have never been there, but you must have been briefed on the type of things we keep there. You do know?"

"Yes, I have been briefed."

"What we have there are things that were made by an intelligence so advanced ... so advanced." The general coughed. Tears of pain welled up in his eyes. "Do you think for one minute that such an advanced intelligence could not come any time they want and take it all away? *They* don't, because *they* want us to have it. It's one of their ways of spoon-feeding us technology." His voice was barely audible.

The general hissed, "Let me tell you, there are people working at S4 who are not from this planet. I'm sure of it." He sucked in another agonizing breath. "They are there to monitor what we do with the artifacts they've allowed us to keep. There's no way to tell who they are. They look just like us. The general grabbed the President's arm as he fought to overcome the pain.

"But, General, why is *this* project at risk there? They haven't interfered with us up to now."

He looked at the President with pleading eyes. "You must warn Colonel—," The general's mouth froze half open and his eyes glazed over as he let go of the President.

In desperation, the President slapped the general to revive him.

The general blinked and convulsed in pain.

"General, I need to know!"

The general looked up as his mouth began to form words. But they were carried in a whisper.

The President bent down and put his ear closer to the general's mouth. "Please! General, tell me!"

Again, a whisper issued from the general's mouth. The President listened. It was enough.

The President sat up and turned away from the sight of agony. He checked his watch. It was 12:25 in Nevada. He knew what he had to do.

Chapter 11
The Mission

Nevada
1:03 Pacific Time

As Wendy and Corey entered the conference room, Pete was returning the red phone to its cradle. They both took their original seats. Wendy noticed Pete had not touched the food sitting next to him.

Pete was pale and his face was taut. "Are you okay, Pete?" Wendy asked.

"Sure. I'm okay. Thanks. I just received a disturbing call from the President. I'll fill you in later." Pete didn't want to alarm them yet. He took a deep breath and glanced over to Wendy. "What were your impressions of this morning?"

"I'm still in a state of shock." Wendy shut her eyes, clasped her hands on her head and leaned back in her chair. "Today shook the foundations of my whole being, my whole set of beliefs." She opened her eyes and leaned toward Pete. "Yesterday I thought humans were the most intelligent beings in the universe. To me, the Sumerian creation stories were simply myths with no foundation in facts. This morning changed all of that."

"I know what you mean," Pete said, "I had the same reaction the first time I toured this place. What's in those rooms is for real! It's not part of some Hollywood set. Every time I touch that craft, I get chills up my spine." He laid both hands on the table and looked down to avoid eye contact. "I must confess, somehow I have to reconcile my religious beliefs with this knowledge. I'm struggling with it."

"I'm still awestruck by everything I saw. Words are inadequate," Wendy added, as she looked at Corey.

Pete was ready to change the subject and turned to study Corey. "Your dossier mentions that two years ago you were an invited speaker at the Center for UFO Studies in Roswell. It says you gave a talk entitled 'Probable Drive Systems for Alien Spacecraft'. In your talk, you mentioned that you felt UFOs used some sort of gravity drive. Now that you have seen one, do you still believe that?"

"Absolutely!" Corey's face lit up.

"Perhaps you could enlighten both Wendy and me on why you believe that."

"Sure, I'd be glad to." Corey was energized. He was back in his realm. "Over the years, I have tried to reconcile the reported characteristics and behavior of UFOs with the present laws of physics."

Wendy smiled at Corey. "So, this is another one of your deductions?"

Pete looked at Wendy with a half smile. "Wendy, behave. Corey has done very well with his deductions."

"Thank you, Pete." Corey turned to Wendy. "I have always been puzzled when I read reports about the high-G maneuvers the UFOs seem capable of performing. They have been seen to accelerate quickly to very high speeds and then make right angle turns. Some investigators have clocked these craft at acceleration rates of over one hundred Gs."

"Is that a lot?" Wendy asked.

"Yes it is!" Pete chimed in. "Combat pilots often have to make quick changes in direction. That exposes their bodies to many Gs. If the G-force is high enough, it can cause them to black out as their blood is drained from their heads into their legs. Seven or eight Gs is the limit for most pilots, depending on the duration. When I was flying F-16's, my limit was eight and that was with a G-suit."

"How do G-suits work?" Wendy asked.

"The G-suit inflates around the pilot's legs and the pressure keeps the blood from pooling."

Corey looked at Wendy and added, "As far as I know, no G-suits have ever been found in any UFO wrecks. Is that true, Pete?"

"Yes, I asked about that when I first arrived. The tech's here told me that no G-suits have ever been found.

"How do the aliens survive such high G-forces without a G-suit? Do you think that perhaps their anatomy is such that they're not bothered by high Gs?" Wendy asked.

"I asked the pathologist that same question," Pete said. "He told me that an analysis of their tissue showed that it was damaged at twenty-two Gs. There is no way they can survive one hundred Gs."

"The one hundred-G maneuver is one of the characteristics of UFOs that has made many researchers, including me, conclude that the aliens employ some sort of gravity field."

"How does this allow the aliens to survive extremely high G forces?" Wendy asked, with a puzzled expression.

Corey's eyes scanned the ceiling as he composed his explanation. "When astronauts, freefall around the Earth, they experience weightlessness. Actually, they're constantly accelerating towards the Earth's center at one G. That rate cancels the gravitational pull of the Earth. So they feel weightless. If they were in orbit around a planet that is one hundred times the size of Earth such as Jupiter, they would still feel weightless, but they would be accelerating at one hundred Gs."

"I hadn't really thought of it that way before," Wendy said, with a smile of understanding.

"Okay," Corey said. "Now, imagine you're in a craft and you have the ability to project an attractive gravitational field in any direction you want. Suppose you project a one hundred G gravitational field directly in front of your craft. You and your craft would fall in that direction at the acceleration rate of one hundred Gs. However, to all the occupants of the craft, they would have no sensation of accelerating as they are free falling in that direction. They would still be seated, since Earth's gravity continues to pull in the Earth's direction. Even if you projected a one thousand G field, you would still not sense the acceleration. You would be free falling. Thus, you could be traveling at a very high rate of speed and if you suddenly aimed a one thousand G field at right angles to your left, you would instantly 'fall' in the left direction. To an outside observer, you would have made an abrupt right angle turn. You, however, would have no sensation of changing direction and would think you are sitting in a stationary craft."

Wendy gaped. "That's amazing! So, you think they produce a gravitational field that pulls them through space?"

Corey shrugged. "Actually, instead of an attractive gravitational field, I think they produce a negative gravitational field that pushes them through space." Corey paused. "But, the effect will be the same."

"I'm familiar with positive gravity. What's negative gravity? I've never heard of it." Pete asked.

"Negative gravity is repulsive and has never been detected in nature. A quantum physicist might think of it as a negative graviton released by antimatter."

"Why would they go to the trouble of creating negative gravity if they could achieve the same with positive gravity?" Pete wondered. "What evidence do you have for this?"

"Eyewitnesses—people who have been under UFOs when they accelerated upward, felt a force pushing down on them. A positive gravitational field would have pulled them up. This would indicate that the craft had produced a negative gravity field between the craft and the observer that pushed the craft up and the observer down. Also, I have seen photographs of UFOs hovering low over a dusty field. The photo's show dust clouds kicked up as the air beneath the craft is pushed down against the ground."

"That's an interesting explanation, Corey! I would like to talk some more about gravity drive when we go back to see the craft. Now, I think it's time to tell you both about your project," Pete said, as he began to unlock the briefcase. He looked at both of them. "For now, do either of you have anything more specific to add about what you saw?"

Wendy was watching Pete intently.

"I found it curious that for a ship that size, there were no eating or restroom facilities," Corey added. "If they are scout ships, then the missions might be short and those facilities wouldn't be required. However, is it possible that they don't eat?"

"They don't eat," Pete said. "Remember. I told you that the pathologist told me that the grays have no digestive system, as we know it. They think they may absorb nutrients through their skin."

"Yes, I remember now, like our transdermal absorption of medicine?" Wendy asked.

"Yes."

Wendy thought she would push Pete one more time for permission to take notes. "When we were inside the craft, it really would have been helpful to have paper and pencil to make some notes."

"I can't allow note taking," Pete said, firmly. "Please don't push me on that issue again. You can return to the craft for another look whenever you wish."

The room became quiet as Pete finished unlocking the brief case and extracted a jet-black device. It was about the size of a small note pad and about an inch thick. He placed it on the table in front of Wendy and Corey. "This is our mission." He looked at both of them to measure their reactions.

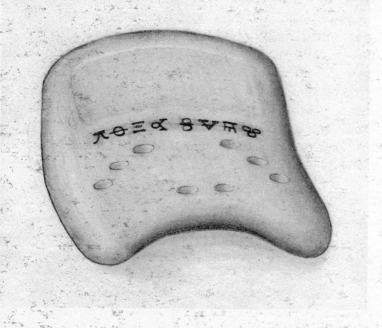

Corey jumped to his feet and bent over the table for a closer look.

Wendy gasped and leaned forward, "What is that thing?"

"We think that is the alien's version of our Palm Pilot. That device before you was one of the artifacts found near the 1953 Kingman, Arizona, crash. We think it might be the ship's log."

"What makes you think that?" Wendy asked.

Pete pointed to the device. "These button-like depressions and inscriptions make it look like a communication or data storage device and since it was with the craft, it seems like a reasonable conclusion. The captain in charge of that investigation had the foresight to recognize what this device is, or at least what we think it is. After retrieving it, he hid it on his person. No one else at the crash sight saw it or knew it existed."

"Why didn't the captain put it with the rest of the debris collected from the site?" Corey asked.

"That's a very good question. I couldn't have answered that an hour ago. However, since talking with the President, I think I now know the answer. He told me, the general felt that if the device was kept with the other artifacts, the aliens would have made an effort to retrieve it."

Corey's face contorted with puzzlement. "I don't understand. Why would that device be any different than the rest of the artifacts? If the aliens haven't tried to retrieve the other artifacts, then why would they single out that?" He pointed toward the device.

"We think this device may be a threat to the aliens because of the information it may contain. It may have information that the aliens consider confidential and vital to their own security."

"Don't you think they're just as concerned about us having their spacecraft, their bodies, and all of the other artifacts?" Corey asked.

"We don't think they care. We think they're allowing us to keep them so we can have a peek at their technology and gradually evolve our own."

Corey thought about what Pete had just hypothesized. "So, they're feeding us technology at their own pace." He turned his attention to the artifact on the table. "Why is it suddenly so important after fifty years?"

"The reason nothing has been done with it all these years is because none of the Presidents knew about it until two weeks ago."

"What made the captain decide to bring it to the President's attention now?" Wendy asked.

"The captain, who is now a retired general, is dying of cancer. His imminent death is one of the main reasons he came forward at this time."

"Okay, that explains why the project is just now getting started, but it doesn't explain why this project is so urgent," Wendy said.

"Over the years, the general has been following the topic of UFOs. Lately, he has become concerned about all of the recent reports by people who claim to have been abducted by them. It seems these people all have similar stories. Under hypnosis, they independently report that something dramatic is about to happen."

Corey looked at Wendy and then back to Pete. "What does the general think is about to happen?"

"The general told the President that he thinks the aliens might be planning some sort of take-over. He feels that whatever the aliens are planning, it is imminent, based on what the abductees report. That's why it's urgent that we learn how to use this device so we can find out what they're up to."

"Pete are you saying that the Earth is about to be attacked by aliens!" Wendy had turned pale.

Corey stared at Pete for a moment. "If they attack, I don't see how we can defend against their technology. Do you think we even have a chance against them? I don't!"

The room was quiet.

Wendy broke the silence. "So, my job is to translate that log so we can find out more about them. Is that right?"

"Yes," Pete said.

"How do we know the information stored in there back in 1953 will be relevant to what's happening today?"

"We don't know, but it's our only hope." Pete slid the device over to her. "Take a look and tell me what you think."

Wendy hesitantly picked up the device and examined it. It felt like a stone that had been worn smooth by thousands of years of exposure to wave and sand action on some seashore. She turned it over several times, admiring the silky smooth finish and beauty of its rounded edges. "Is this made of black onyx?" Wendy asked.

"We don't know what it's made of," Pete answered. "And, I'm not about to let anyone cut into it to find out."

"The surface is covered with purplish-colored glyphs. They appear to be some form of inlay rather than just printed on." She didn't recognize them. "They're beautiful!"

"What do you think of all of those depressions on the surface?" Pete asked.

"They look similar to what I saw on the console in the craft." Wendy studied it for a moment. "You know, now that I've seen their hands, I can imagine them placing their fingers into these depressions. They form two patterns of four, one low and three high in each pattern. I think that would fit their hands since three of the fingers are longer."

"Yes, I thought of that too," Pete said, "but when I placed my fingers into the depressions, nothing happened."

Wendy tried putting her fingers into the depressions. Nothing happened.

"Maybe it's your karma," Corey joked.

"Well, let me try again." She looked at Corey. "I've been told I have good karma." She carefully positioned her fingers into the depressions. Nothing happened. "Maybe my karma is not so good today," she joked. "You try it, Corey."

She slid the device over to Corey. He wrapped his large hands around the object and stroked its silky smooth surface. He then carefully placed his fingers into the depressions. Nothing happened. "My karma is not so good either." He worked his finger as though playing a keyboard and then smiled at Wendy. "See, nothing is happening. Why don't you try again?" He slid the device back over the table.

"What do you make of those glyphs, Wendy? Do they look like anything you've seen before?" Pete asked.

"Some of the characters remind me of the ones in the craft. Other than that, I've never seen characters exactly like these before." She pointed to the area on the device that was slightly recessed. It was a curved rectangle square about six inches across. "This may be the display area." She turned it over. "I don't see any compartment for batteries." Wendy puzzled over the device. "Maybe after I get more familiar with this, I should revisit the craft. Perhaps I can get a correlation to some of the symbols I saw on the control console and get some logical relationship."

"That sounds like a good idea." Pete said. Let me know when you're ready. Also, you may want to visit the Roswell craft. Some of its structural members are showing and are covered with writing. You might find that helpful."

"What's the Roswell craft?" she asked.

"I thought everyone knew about Roswell." Corey smiled at Wendy as he got in his dig.

"I guess I was left out of that loop. Of course I've *heard* of Roswell! I just don't know any details." Wendy smiled back at Corey.

"Let me fill you in on some of the details, then," Pete said. "Shortly after the end of World War II— July 1947 to be exact— two saucers collided during a severe lightning storm. A rancher discovered some wreckage a few miles northwest of a town called Roswell, in New Mexico. The second craft came down, nearly intact, a hundred and fifty miles away, in the Plains of San Agustin. The body we looked at this morning came from that crash. Remember, I told you that when we stood by the tanks?"

"Yes." Wendy looked first at Corey and then at Pete. A thought occurred to her. "The body we saw was not from the Kingman crash. How do we no there is any connection between that body's physiology and shape and the creatures who were flying the Kingman craft?"

"That's an excellent question! We know there is a connection, because the bodies look the same. I didn't want to show you the bodies from the Kingman crash because the ones we have here are badly mutilated."

"Okay. Why don't you continue with your story," Wendy said.

"At first," Pete said, "the Army unit from Roswell went public. News of the recovery of a flying saucer traveled like wildfire, as you can imagine. Only a few hours after the story was released, the Pentagon clamped a lid on it and claimed the 'saucer' was only the remains of a weather balloon. Every civilian in Roswell who came into contact with any of the artifacts was threatened and told to remain silent. They were told it was a matter of national security and they should keep their mouths shut. This was right after the war and the word 'treason' meant a lot to people."

Corey was very familiar with the story, as he had read many accounts of it in his research of UFOs. He had once visited Roswell and spent a day at the UFO Museum and Research Center during one of his fall breaks when he was working on his doctorate.

As Pete told Wendy the Roswell story, Corey picked up the device and examined it for evidence of any power connections. *Strange,* he thought, *there are no ports for connecting power. There are no seams, either. I wonder how you open this thing to replace the batteries or to make repairs. How do they power this thing?* His mind returned to the conference room when he heard Wendy's voice.

"It's scary to know that our government could threaten people in order to do a cover up."

"Yes, but in the government's defense," Pete went on, "imagine how the people would have reacted if they found out that there was an alien intelligence with technology so superior that the government could do nothing to protect them. There would be panic. In fact, there would be panic today if what you two saw this morning was ever made known to the general public. This is one time when the public cannot be told the facts," Pete insisted in his military tone.

After a pause he continued. "There are other craft that you may want to see. They're from other crashes. The latest ones are not round but are more triangular in shape."

"You have other craft!" Corey sat upright. "I think the triangular ones might be from a different race of aliens. Wendy, we should check them out. The markings may be different" Corey added. "The Earth may be swarming with aliens from all over the galaxy. Since we began nuclear testing, Earth may be the local 'hot spot.'" He turned and gave Wendy a sheepish smile, for his poor pun.

The beige phone rang. "Excuse me," Pete said, as he picked up the receiver and spoke softly. Neither Wendy nor Corey could make out what he was saying. After a few seconds, they heard him say, "Thank you."

Pete hung up. "I'm sorry. We'll have to end today's session." Pete turned to Wendy. "Wendy, did you understand all of what we have discussed?"

"Yes ... Well enough for now, thank you."

"Good. Before we break for today, I have to tell you the rest of my conversation with the President." Pete paused for a moment. "The general told the President that the reason he did not bring the device to this base, even though he was assigned here for four years, was for security reasons."

"Security reasons!" Corey looked puzzled. "This base has got to be the most secure base on this planet!"

"Secure from other humans, perhaps. But it is not secure from the aliens."

"Do you mean that the aliens might attack this base to get this thing back?" Wendy was alarmed now. Her heart was pounding.

Pete looked at both of them. "No, they won't attack. They don't have to. They're already here."

"What!" Wendy was struck with terror. "Does the base commander know?"

"I don't know. He would have no way of knowing. According to the general, the aliens that are here are hybrids who look just like us. He thinks they even have all the proper records so they can merge with human society without being detected. So, you see, we have to be particularly vigilant. Talk to *no one* about what we're doing."

Wendy and Corey sat in disbelief.

Pete looked at his watch. "I'm going to be gone until tomorrow morning." He looked at Wendy. "While I'm gone, I would like you and Corey to continue to work on getting that device turned on. You can have your supper in here."

"Pete, if I may, I'd like to take this back to my apartment."

"No. That would violate safety protocol," Pete said.

"It would be as secure there as it would be here. Also, if I stay here, where would I put it when I'm finished for the day? Do you expect me to sleep here?"

Pete thought for a moment. "Letting you take this out of this room goes against normal security procedures. My natural instincts tell me that allowing this to leave here is wrong. However, your points are well-taken."

"Also, all of my reference material is in my room," Wendy added.

Pete stroked his chin and mused. "Okay, but it must be in this case whenever you transport it." Pete placed the device back into the brief case and relocked it. "Here, take this key. Be sure to keep the device locked in this case when you're not working with it."

"I will," Wendy assured Pete. "Corey, does that sound good to you?"

"Sure. I agree, your apartment is as secure as this room and we would be more comfortable there."

"Make sure you keep you notes locked up." Pete looked again at his watch. "Okay then, that's it for today. See you both tomorrow at oh eight hundred hours. Bring your breakfast."

Chapter 12
Origin

Corey held the door open with his hip as Wendy led them into her apartment. She pointed toward her kitchen table. "Why don't we sit there?"

After unlocking the briefcase, Wendy withdrew the device. "Maybe if we put our heads together, we can make this thing work."

"Have you got any new ideas?"

"No, but I'm sure these depressions have to be part of the answer. I've tried pressing them in various combinations but nothing happens." Wendy flipped the device over several times, looking for signs of any small doors or compartments. "Maybe the battery is dead," she said jokingly. She handed the device over to Corey.

Corey examined the device again for any seams. "I looked earlier and couldn't find any place to connect power. I guess we have to assume the device is powered internally. There's no seam. It's completely smooth except for these eight depressions. I agree, they must be the keys. Maybe these hieroglyphs on the top surface would tell you how to work it," Corey said with a voice of desperation. He ran his fingers over the symbols. They were perfectly flush with the surface.

"I doubt it," Wendy said. "That would be like finding instructions printed on a telephone. Everyone knows how to use one. The only things printed on a phone are the numbers. No, I think those markings are involved in the use of this thing, but not the instructions, unfortunately. I'm sure the meaning of those symbols will become obvious, in time. Solutions to things like that seem to come in the middle of the night for me. For some reason, I often do my best and most creative work late at night."

"I know what you mean," Corey said. "I'm the same way." Corey continued fingering the device as he studied Wendy. She was the first woman he had felt any strong attractions toward since losing his fiancé. *She truly is attractive, and intelligent*, he thought. He wanted to know more about her. "What made you decide to take on this project?"

"I don't know." Wendy sensed Corey's interest in her. "I think I was intrigued by the importance of the project. If the President is involved, then it must be really important."

"That's true."

Wendy watched Corey as he tried different finger arrangements. "What made you get into astrophysics?"

"I don't know exactly," he answered. He flipped the device over and scrutinized the back. "I always liked science and in fact, when I was young, my parents thought I was going to be a doctor. I was always looking under rocks for bugs and snakes. When I was only thirteen, my friend and I were convinced we could do heart transplants." Corey laughed softly to himself. "Several dead frogs later and a heart-to-heart conversation with the high school biology teacher convinced me that I wasn't ready yet."

Wendy scrunched her nose. "You didn't really try to do heart transplants on frogs, did you?"

"Yes, but I discovered that the procedure was becoming commonplace and lost interest. I abandoned the field of heart transplants to become an astronaut. It wasn't until my early college years that I settled on physics and astronomy."

He looked at Wendy with a question in his eyes. "How is it you became a linguist and got into reading glyphs?"

Wendy shrugged her shoulders and cocked her head as she started to become self-conscious. "Technically, I'm a philologist, but most people call us linguists. Anyhow, the study of written languages came naturally to me just as physics did for you. I think it was something I was born to do. Ever since I was a young girl, languages have intrigued me. This may sound strange, but I can remember hearing voices talking to me in strange tongues when I was a little girl. I couldn't understand what they were saying but it got me interested. So, as long as I can remember, I've been translating. It seems I have this ability to look at writing, and after some time, it makes sense to me. I can't explain it; the answer just pops into my head."

"I know," said Corey. "I have the same experience sometimes when I'm working on a technical problem. I'll ponder and ponder and study all the facts I can find. Then, suddenly, like magic, the solution appears in my head!" Corey tapped his forehead with his fingers and then looked at Wendy with a far-away expression. "I find the intuitive process fascinating. In fact, I almost changed my major to psychology."

"What stopped you?"

"I don't know, exactly. I guess I felt more attracted to physics and astronomy. I had read a lot about flying saucers and became fascinated by that topic. It blew my mind to think there might be a life form of higher intelligence watching us. Even though I never saw a UFO, I found the logic for their existence too compelling to ignore. I kept searching for explanations for their observed behavior."

Corey brushed his fingers through his hair as he stretched. "In my senior year of college, I hit on the idea that they might be using gravity as a means for propulsion. From that time on, I began to focus on the study of gravity. The entire effort in my doctoral dissertation was on the interactions between gravity and electro magnetism." He looked at Wendy wistfully. "Some day, we might learn how to manipulate gravity the way the aliens do!"

"I'm not sure I understand what you mean," said Wendy. "I'm not sure I understand the significance of that. In fact, I had difficulty understanding your explanation of gravity drive you gave earlier today."

"When we go back for another look at the craft, I'll try to point out a few things about the alien craft that support my ideas about their drive system." Corey's frustration with the device continued to grow. It was still inactive. "Here, I give up, you try it." He laid it on the table and pushed it over toward Wendy.

She picked it up and began trying various finger arrangements. "I think it's time to start taking notes on the different combinations of keystrokes I try." She went over to her briefcase an extracted a note pad. As she returned to the table, she said, "You know, Corey, when I looked at that body and the alien craft this morning, I couldn't help but wonder where they might have come from. Do you think they come from Mars?"

"I'm not really sure. There are many who think they do. Perhaps they come from the planet Nibiru that you mentioned." Corey was serious. "Where ever they come from, I think it's within our galaxy."

"How far away do you think their home star might be?"

"I believe that the advanced civilizations in our galaxy probably have organized themselves into some kind of galactic federation."

"You mean like in Star Trek?" Wendy asked, as she held the device next to her ear and shook it.

"Yes. I know it sounds strange, but I think highly intelligent civilizations would do that. They have probably divvied up the galaxy so that each civilization has its own sector to oversee."

"How big do you think our sector is?"

"That depends on how many advanced civilizations there are. Many scientists believe that there may be anywhere from one thousand to one million advanced civilizations in our galaxy." He looked at Wendy with a believe-it-or-not smile. "I've actually done some calculations on the probable size of these 'Star Trek' sectors."

"You have?"

"Yes, and what I found out was, given the volume of space enclosed by the Galactic Habitable Zone, if that volume were divvied up by a million civilizations, our sector would be a cube that is about one hundred light years on each side. In that case, our alien friends may have to travel fifty to one hundred and fifty light years to get here."

"What if there are only a thousand advanced civilizations?"

"Then our sector would be a cube one thousand light years on a side and our visitors would need to travel five hundred to fifteen hundred light years to get here."

"But even if they could travel at one tenth the speed of light, it would take ten thousand years to reach us! Why would they do that?" Wendy asked. She set the device back into the open briefcase in frustration.

"I'm betting these beings are so advanced that they will have the technology to travel at near light speed."

"Maybe they travel much faster than the speed of light."

"Well, some think it's possible to exceed the speed of light but Einstein didn't, and I'll place my bet with him," Corey explained. "According to the Einstein, it would take an infinite amount of energy to travel that fast. However, there is a phenomenon known as time dilation that is also predicted by him. That saves the day."

"What do you mean by time dilation?" Wendy asked.

"It means, for a traveler going very near the speed of light, the traveler's clock and biological processes slow down as compared to a stationary observer. If I jumped into a spaceship and flew off at 99.99 percent the speed of light, to visit a planet that was fifty light years away, I could be there in a few weeks ... according to my clock." Corey pointed to Wendy. "According to your clock, it would take me fifty years. By the time I return, you would be dead."

"Why would these aliens want to travel all this way to visit us, only to return to their home planet and find all their friends and relatives dead?"

"They bring all their friends and relatives with them!" Corey answered with a smile, as he waited for Wendy's reaction.

"What?"

"Sure. A whole colony goes along, with no intention of ever returning to their home planet."

"Why would they do that?"

"Why not?" Corey parried. "What else do they have to do? Imagine what we will be doing thousands of years from now. Probably all the energy, food, and shelter we need will be plentiful. Computers and robots will be pervasive throughout our lives. Robots will do all of the work that needs to be done. So, what will we do with all of our spare time? After all, there are only so many movies to watch in this universe. We'll be bored out of our skull. So why not build a huge ship and go on safari with all your friends and relatives? You could even do time travel."

"Cool!" Wendy clasped her hands together. "So could we travel back in time and see the ancient civilizations?"

"No, that would create a paradox. But, we could travel forward in time. Just travel at near light speed out to a star system that is, say ... one thousand light years away, and when you return, you'll be in a world that is two thousand years in the future from when you left. For you, only a few weeks will have passed."

"Okay, so the aliens are here with their mother ship and they're watching us," Wendy said. "Now let me ask another question. Why haven't they made contact with us? We supposedly have all of these artifacts from various crashed UFOs but we have no direct communication with the aliens. Why?"

"I'm not sure. One theory is that we're too aggressive. It would be like us landing a helicopter in the middle of the tropical rain forest and finding ourselves surrounded by a primitive tribe of headhunters. We would probably avoid contact."

Corey got up and began to explore Wendy's lounge area as he continued to talk. "Perhaps, to the aliens, we may seem pretty uncivilized. Perhaps we're no more significant to them than, say, a termite colony. Another theory I heard is, they avoid contact so they don't 'contaminate' our culture and influence our natural development."

"That's a good point," Wendy said, as she nodded her head in agreement. "Anthropologists have shown that, throughout human history, whenever a more advanced society encounters a less advanced one, the less advanced society eventually dies out or is absorbed by the more advanced society."

Corey rubbed his temples as he thought for a moment. "I recall reading an article in *Science*, about searching for extraterrestrial civilizations."

Wendy's eyebrows rose. "That's a pretty prestigious periodical to publish something on ETs."

"Yes it is. Anyway, the writer postulated there is the real probability that if aliens with significantly superior technology made open contact with us and shared their technology with us, human technology would cease to develop. It would create a 'culture shock'."

"I guess the real question is not why *haven't* they made contact, but, why *would* they make contact," Wendy said.

"That's true, the same article discussed that question. Aliens would contact us if they were after some resource on this planet that they could not take covertly."

"Like what?"

"Perhaps it could be large quantities of minerals, water, human labor, or even human knowledge. Of course," Corey chuckled, "the latter would not occur until we had something to offer. Limited, covert contact could occur for the extraction of rare elements or even samples of biological or genetic materials."

Corey stood next to Wendy's piano and ran his fingers lightly over the keyboard she had mastered so well. He was having difficulty getting his mind off of her. "You really seem to love music. You play the piano like a professional."

"Thank you," she said, with an appreciative smile. "Yes, I do love music. I almost made music my chosen career. If my mother had been more persuasive, that's what I would be doing now. But, my father, in his engineering logic, was more persuasive and, here I am." Wendy rose and walked over to the piano and stood next to Corey.

He looked up from the keyboard and into her eyes. "So what did you tell your parents when you decided to come here?"

"They … they were both killed several years ago," Wendy said.

Corey winced. "Oh, I'm sorry. I didn't know. I'm really sorry."

"Oh, that's okay. I've adjusted," Wendy assured him with a smile. "We have to go on with our lives. I'm sure my parents would be telling me that if they were here."

Corey looked back down at the piano as he considered whether he was ready to share his inner feelings. "I … I had a tragic loss in my life too, so I know how hard it is to adjust," Corey said, as he fingered the piano.

"You lost your parents, too?" Wendy asked softly.

"No. My fiancé." Corey's voice quivered as he focused on his hands.

"I'm sorry. What happened? ... Oh ... you don't have to talk about it ... forget I asked." Wendy was embarrassed as she saw how much difficulty Corey was having. She reached up and stroked his shoulder.

Corey turned to look at her. With a gentle smile he said, "That's okay, sometimes talking about it helps." He looked back down at the piano. "She ... she drowned in a sailing accident. We were sailing off the coast of Cape Cod when a wind gust blew us over. I should have seen it coming. We both were dumped into the water. When I came up, I thought she had come up on the other side, but when I called her, she didn't answer. I panicked. I kept diving under the boat looking for her but she never came up. I kept looking but she never ... came up." He turned back toward Wendy. "I have a lot of sailing experience and should have recognized the signs of the wind gust on the water. I guess that just goes to show what happens when you let down your guard."

"You seem to be blaming yourself for her death," Wendy said as she tried to console him as she reached out and stroked his arm. "Sometimes things happen. We just have to deal with it and move on."

"I know." He looked at Wendy. "It's surprising how much time it takes to heal."

Corey wanted to change the subject. "I'll bet we're at Area 51." His face brightened.

Wendy blinked at the sudden change in subject. "Area 51? You mean that secret base the government is supposed to have somewhere in ... New Mexico, I think?"

"Yes, but it's in Nevada. Actually we're probably in area S4 next to Area 51, on Groom Lake. That's northwest of Las Vegas. You saw the way the mountain opened up for your plane when you arrived yesterday, didn't you?"

"Yes. Thank God it opened!"

"I've seen photographs of area S4 taken from a satellite. It has similar doors that are camouflaged just like the ones they have here," Corey explained.

Wendy smiled. "I think you might be right. This morning, after I got up, I turned on my TV and found the Weather Channel. Guess what, their local weather forecast was for Las Vegas."

"Interesting."

Wendy was ready to relax and let her mind get recharged with energy. She ran her hand over the top of the piano. "Would you like to hear some music?"

"You bet!" Corey replied, with a grin. "I'd love to hear you play."

Wendy sat down on the leather topped piano bench and began to play some of her favorite relaxing melodies, beginning with Franz Liszt's *Liebestraum no. 3.*

Corey moved over to the soft armchair, near the piano, so he could better appreciate her while she was in her realm.

Chapter 13
Crop Circles

After an hour, Wendy's fingers stilled on the keyboard. A thought occurred to her about the ways aliens might make contact if they chose to. *The answer to that question might help unlock the device*, she thought. She recalled SETI. When she looked over at Corey to ask him about SETI, he was dozing off.

"Corey?"

"Wha ... Yes." He sat up straight.

"I remember hearing of an organization called SETI (*Search for Extra-Terrestrial Intelligence*). Hasn't it been sending radio signals into space for years and listening for a reply in an attempt to make contact with aliens?"

"Yes, for years."

"Do you think that effort is futile?"

"Yes." Corey composed his thoughts. "I think, until the aliens decide *they* want to make contact by radio, SETI won't hear from them. But, I've often wondered why SETI isn't investigating the crop circles that have been showing up all over the planet. I think these are messages. I think the aliens are using these designs as a means of communicating with us. Either that, or they're trying to measure our intelligence."

Wendy looked at Corey with a questioning expression. "I'm surprised you mentioned that. I thought they were shown to be hoaxes. People have even confessed to making crop circles by using measuring strings and boards to push down the crop. I remember seeing that on the news years ago."

"There have been over ten thousand crop circles reported world-wide since the 1980's," Corey said. "There's no way they could all be hoaxes. Less than twenty percent are known to be hoaxes. The government likes to point to those as a way to dismiss crop circles as a non-issue."

"Another government cover-up?" Wendy leaned on the piano and smiled at Corey in disbelief.

"Yes. Of course. If the government were to admit that crop circles were produced by aliens, people would panic."

"I guess you're right. It would be like admitting that UFOs exist."

"Yes. Even though about twenty percent of the crop circles are manmade, the other eighty percent have been created with technology that we don't possess. Those are the 'real' ones. They could not have been faked."

"Now, I am curious. How can one tell whether or not a crop circle is manmade? It seems to me they all could be made by people," Wendy said.

"Those made by humans usually contain errors in their geometry. Real ones are perfect in their design and execution. All of the manmade crop circles take hours or days to make and are made by using some mechanical device like a lawn roller or wooden plank to lay the crop down. As a result, the stalks are broken and the soil under the laid-down-crop is compressed and shows evidence of being trampled. Also, there is usually a sign of an entry point where the perpetrators walked into the field with their equipment. They're almost always made under the cover of darkness over a period of hours or days."

"How are the real ones made?"

"The real crop designs are produced in minutes, often in broad daylight, without the use of any mechanical device to lay the crops down. The crops are simply bent over near the ground at 90 degrees, without any damage to the plants. Also, the soil under the laid-down plants is not compacted and there is no sign of entry into the fields."

Wendy felt like giving Corey a hard time. "I don't think it would be that difficult to construct some circles in a few minutes, if you had the right equipment."

Corey could see that this was not going to be an easy sell. "Okay, explain this one. On a Sunday afternoon in 1991 in Wiltshire, England, a complex design was made consisting of one hundred and fifty-one circles forming a curving spine design over nine hundred feet long and five hundred feet wide!" It was made in forty-five minutes and in broad daylight!"

Wendy had to think for a moment on this one. "Who witnessed it being constructed, if it was in daylight?"

[See back cover]

"It was made in a field directly across the highway that passes the famous Stonehenge. Planes are always flying over to take pictures. An aerial photo was taken right after the design was constructed. It was the same pilot who had flown over the field forty-five minutes earlier. On his first flyover, the field was empty. If you saw how complicated and perfect the design was, you would have to agree, it was not manmade."

"I always thought crop circles were just designs made by using a series of circles."

"They started off that way back in the eighties, but now they have gotten much more complicated. That's one reason I think the aliens may be testing our intelligence." Corey thought for a moment to collect his thoughts. "Another point I think you would appreciate. Even when a series of simple circles are formed, they often have rings around them." He looked into Wendy's eyes and smiled. "Listen to this. The ratio of the squares of the diameters of the circles and rings in crop circles, follow the same diatonic ratio as found in music. They follow the same intervals of the musical scale as the white keys of a piano!"

Wendy's eyes brightened and a smile appeared. "That's true, the octave scale is a diatonic ratio." She was beginning to formulate an idea. *Perhaps the device needs to be played like a music instrument*, she thought.

"Yes." Corey was ready with another intriguing fact. "Did you know that many of the Neolithic structures, such as Stonehenge, have rings around them that follow the same ratio?"

Wendy stared at Corey. "No, I didn't know that." *This is getting interesting*, she thought. "Has anyone ever seen the real crop circles being made?

"Yes, there are over fifty people world-wide who have witnessed the making of real crop designs. They report that the plants begin to sway and then suddenly spiral down to the ground. Many people report hearing a strange buzzing sound coming from the field in the area where the design appears."

"Have they seen what made them?"

"Many saw nothing. Some have seen strange lights over the fields. Some have seen columns or tubes of light shooting down onto the fields from a point in the sky, but no object seemed to be there. Very often, there were reports of UFO sightings, or strange lights, seen over the fields the night before the farmer discovered the crop design. There is an astounding videotape that actually caught UFOs in the act of making a crop design. It shows several balls of light flying in a pattern over a field. Within seconds, the crop fell down and a complex crop design appeared."

"A ball of light is not the craft we saw this morning."

"I know," Corey said. "Some think the balls of light are some sort of drone that is controlled by a UFO off in the distance."

"How do you think the aliens are making these crop designs? You can get technical with me if you want." Wendy winked at him.

"If you insist," he said, with a smile. "Researchers are beginning to get a handle on that. A famous and respected biophysicist has analyzed specimens taken from over two hundred and fifty crop circles around the world and has concluded that some electromagnetic vortex seems to be causing the crops to lie down. This vortex seems to generate microwave radiation that instantly heats the plants internally. In every case, the nodes near the top of the plants expanded by up to two hundred percent and are bent over by about thirty degrees. Near the base of the plant, where the stalk is more mature and more tuff, some nodes have exploded from the steam pressure generated inside. The soil under the plants has been dried out but not compacted, while the soil outside of the affected area is still moist."

"What causes the plants to lie down?"

"That's unclear, but there is no evidence of any pressure being applied to the soil under the plants."

"You must have worked out a technical explanation for all of this. How do you think the UFOs make the crop designs?" Wendy asked.

"I think that the UFOs somehow beam down narrow tubes of spiraling electromagnetic and gravitational fields to form their desired designs. Sometimes they remain cloaked, which is why many observers only see the column of electromagnetic radiation that is beamed down. This radiation is in a broad spectrum ranging from visible light to microwave radiation."

"Wait a minute," Wendy said, with a look of disbelief. "Cloaked? That sounds like Star Trek again!"

"I know it does and that's a whole other topic. I'll explain how they do that sometime when we visit the craft again. Anyway, the microwave energy causes the observed heating of the plants and the gravitational field is what causes the plants to sway and get knocked down. As water vapor is ionized by the electrical discharges, it creates the sounds that are often heard by witnesses. Another interesting fact is that the crop fields, under the designs, are altered electrically and magnetically. Animals often refuse to enter the crop circles and humans who enter, often experience strange psychological effects and even physiological effects, such as nausea."

Wendy stared into Corey's eyes as she mentally digested what he had just said. The only words she could come up with were, "That's very interesting."

"I think that might be an understatement," Corey said.

"How long has this crop circle phenomenon been going on?" Wendy asked.

"Crop circles have appeared since antiquity. Some researchers think that many of the Neolithic structures found around the world were made in response to sightings of crop circles. The circles may have been viewed as some religious phenomenon and the people of antiquity sought to capture them in stone, so-to-speak. Many of these famous Neolithic designs found in England are in the same concentrated areas as the crop designs have been appearing. What's really interesting is the dramatic increase in both the number and the complexity of designs that have appeared in the last ten years. It's as though we're being given a message that something is going to happen."

"Maybe something *is* about to happen and *soon*. Just as the general had told the President," Wendy said. "I think the Bible mentions there will be signs from heaven."

"Yes, well … some of these signs are becoming pretty clear. In 1991, a crop design was discovered in southern England that gave a message in Latin. I can't remember the exact words but they were something like: 'I oppose acts of craft and cunning.'

"In Latin? Now that is interesting," Wendy said, as she stroked her chin.

"That's just the beginning," Corey said. "Two more recent crop designs appeared, in England, and showed some amazing pictures. The first was a picture that was a copy of the 1974 binary transmission SETI sent out from our huge Arecibo radio telescope in Puerto Rico. The message we sent was about life on this planet. In a binary pictogram, it told about humans, their shape and size and the population of the Earth. It also showed the location of our planet relative to our sun and the other eight planets."

"Why would the aliens just copy that picture? Were they just trying to tell us that our message was received?"

"They didn't just copy the binary picture we sent, they modified it!"

"How so?"

"Their picture showed a being that is considerably shorter than us and with a larger head in proportion to the body. They gave their planet's population, but I can't remember what it was. I just remember that it was much larger than ours. They showed a picture of our solar system to indicate where they're from."

"They're from our solar system?" Wendy leaned toward Corey in anticipation.

"Their picture showed they are from Earth, Mars, and four of the moons of Jupiter!"

"Amazing!"

"You think that's amazing, listen to this." Corey leaned toward Wendy. "There's an astounding crop circle that appeared in 2002 in southern England. It's known as the Crabwood Farmhouse crop circle."

"What's astounding about it?"

"It was a rectangle that was about two hundred feet by three hundred feet. Inside, was an image of an alien face.

Intersecting the rectangle was a circle that was about one hundred feet in diameter."

"That's pretty amazing."

"No. Here's the amazing part. Spiraling out from the center of the disk was a message written in a binary code."

"A message! What did it say?"

Corey stood up and pulled out his wallet. "The message so intrigued me that I keep a copy of the translation in my wallet. The binary code was translated into our ASCII code."

"ASCII code. That's English ... Amazing!"

"Yes." Corey leafed through his wallet and found a small folded piece of paper. "Here it is." He unfolded the paper. "It says, 'Beware the bearers of FALSE gifts & their BROKEN PROMISES. Much PAIN but still time. Believe there is GOOD out there. We Oppose DECEPTION. Conduit CLOSING. Message continued.'. Here, Wendy, look at the message." Corey placed it on the piano keyboard.

She leaned over to it. "That's spooky. V-e-r-y spooky." Wendy felt a chill run down her spine. "What do you think it means? Why are some words all in caps?"

"No one knows the answer yet. I think the aliens are trying to tell us something. I don't know what it is. Perhaps the next message will enlighten us. You know, with all that's happening with crop designs, I'm surprised that you haven't been commissioned by SETI or the government to interpret what someone out there is trying to tell us."

"This whole topic of crop designs is intriguing," Wendy said. "Their use of musical relationships is something I'm definitely going to explore."

Corey glanced at his watch and noticed that it was past six o'clock. "Well, I don't know about you, but I'm getting hungry. Maybe if we take a dinner break, an idea may come to us that will help us activate that device." Corey pointed toward the briefcase on the table.

"We should be so lucky," Wendy said with a smile as she locked the device in the briefcase. "I am hungry though. Let's go!"

Chapter 14
I've Done It!

In less than twenty minutes, the two were back with their dinner. Corey had a chicken and biscuits dinner. Wendy had a tofu stir-fry with biscuits.

"I see you got extra honey for your biscuits," Corey observed. "I forgot to get some. Can I use some of yours?"

"Sure, I don't know why I got two packages. Usually, I just get one. I must have known you'd need some," she said with a laugh.

As they both began to eat their meals, Wendy resumed their earlier conversation. "How long do you think the aliens have been observing us?"

"Well, certainly since the end of World War II when we began exploding atom bombs and announced to the rest of the universe that we had entered the atomic age. Probably many different species have been here observing us for thousands, if not millions, of years. It seems that twelve thousand years ago was an active period in human history. Deep in the jungles of northern Brazil, near Guyana, there's a huge painted rock known as Pedra Pentada. This rock is over three hundred feet long, two hundred feet wide and one hundred and fifty feet high. It's covered with strange writings that are thought to be over twelve thousand years old. This was reported by Professor Homet, a famous anthropologist, in a book he published in 1963."

"Oh! Yes, I know of him and I read his book about the ancient rock. One member of my dissertation committee actually met him," Wendy said.

"Did you know that most of the strange symbols shown in his book also appeared in a book about UFOs written by George Adamski? He claimed to have been aboard an alien craft and was given the writings in the form of a photographic plate."

"Maybe he just copied Professor Homet's symbols into his book," Wendy suggested.

"I don't think so. Adamski's book was published ten years before Homet's," Corey responded.

As they ate, Wendy began to think about the connection Corey related between ancient writings and how they might be connected to aliens. "Corey, do you think the aliens had something to do with disappearance of some of the ancient civilizations such as the Mayan?"

"What about the Mayans?" Corey took a bite. "Weren't they exterminated by Cortez?"

"No. They disappeared hundreds of years before Cortez. In my studies, I found their writing not only interesting but also beautiful. Did you know that they were one of only two civilizations to develop the concept of zero? They had a number system that used a base of twenty instead of ten as we have."

"I guess they counted on their toes as well as their fingers," Corey laughed. "Come to think of it, I'll bet the aliens have a number system with a base of eight since they have only eight fingers."

"You might be right! Music is based on octaves. Maybe the aliens passed music on to us. Corey, I'm convinced the key to unlocking the device lies with some musical tune!"

"Did you see the movie *Close Encounters*?" Corey asked.

"Yes. I remember they communicated by using musical notes!" Wendy was excited now and rushed to unlock the briefcase. She removed the device from the briefcase and pushed her tray aside so she could place the object directly in front of her, as though she was playing a piano. She rapidly moved her fingers up and down on the depressions, as though she were running the scale. Nothing happened. She then tried various combinations of notes, similar to the ones she remembered in the movie. Still nothing happened. After ten minutes, her frustrations got the best of her and she returned the device to the briefcase. "Needs more thought," she said.

They chatted about their college years as they finished their suppers. Wendy was not up to trying a new round of experiments with the device. *Perhaps playing the piano will inspire me*, she thought, so she crossed over to the piano. "Would you like to hear some more music?"

"Sure, just don't play too soft or too slowly. I might doze off after that dinner," Corey said, as he moved over to the soft chair near the piano.

As Wendy began to play, Corey sank deeper into the chair as he began to relax. Her playing was hypnotic to him. As she played, Wendy lost all sense of time.

It was nearly two hours later when she looked toward Corey and found him asleep.

"Well, he warned me," she said softly to herself.

Wendy hated to wake him since he was sleeping so peacefully but it was after eight. *Pete wants us there by eight and I want to have some quiet time with the device*, she thought.

Wendy whispered softly into Corey's ear. "Corey, do you think we should call it a night?"

"W...What?" he said as he woke. "What time is it?"

"It's after eight, Pete wants us by eight tomorrow. Do you think we should call it a night?"

"Oh ... aaahhhh ... sure. I'm sorry, I fell asleep. Your music was so beautiful. Let me clean up my mess and then I'll go."

"Don't worry about that, I'll clean it up. It's no problem," Wendy insisted.

He protested and she shook her head.

"Never mind! It really is no problem, and I have to clean my mess anyway. You go and get some sleep. Keep thinking about how we can activate the device. Maybe the answer will come in your dreams!"

Wendy led him to the door.

"Okay. I'll see you tomorrow. Good night. Sweet dreams." Corey looked into her eyes. He couldn't resist. He pulled her towards him and kissed her with a long embrace. Wendy didn't resist. She savored the moment. The outside world ceased to exist for both of them as they embraced. Finally, Wendy pushed herself gently away from Corey and looked up at him.

"Let's call it a night ... Okay?"

"Okay," Corey said as he reluctantly opened her door. "Good night, again."

After Corey left, Wendy leaned against her door, marveling at how wonderful life was.

After several moments, she headed over to her table to pick up. In the process, she somehow managed to get honey all over her fingers. *What a mess. It seems almost impossible to eat honey without getting it on everything. My fingers are all sticky now,* she thought to herself.

The image of the alien hand with the suction cups on his finger tips, suddenly flashed into her mind, *That's it! That's why I can't get that thing to work! I've been pushing on those depressions. The aliens have suction cups on their finger tips. They must pull up on the depressions!*

Wendy was so excited she could hardly get the device out of the briefcase fast enough. She carefully set it on the table and immediately placed all of her sticky fingers into the depressions and began to pull. Nothing happened. There was no sign of life. She tried different combinations, but nothing. *Wait! Maybe they wouldn't pull up with their short finger. Perhaps the opposite finger would be used for leverage!* She cleaned the honey off her thumb and outside finger and tried again. This time she pushed down with her thumb and outside finger and pulled up with the two inside fingers. Suddenly the top surface of the device came alive with symbols! She screamed in surprise. "Wow! God! I've done it! I've done it!"

Chapter 15
Abducted

The clanging bell was becoming annoying as Wendy struggled to remember where she was. *Oh yeah*, she thought, *I'm in some secret base and that's my alarm clock*. As she struggled to open her eyes, she reached over toward the sound and found the button to silence the noise. It all began to come back to her. She had to meet Corey and Pete at eight and she'd set her alarm for seven.

It took her only ten minutes to shower and wash her hair. As she was blow-drying, she reconstructed the events from last night. *Wait until Pete and Corey find out!* She thought.

By twenty minutes of eight, Wendy was finished dressing and was preparing to leave for the cafeteria when she heard knocking at her door. *It must be Corey stopping by to walk me to breakfast.* "I'm coming." She smiled as she opened her door.

"Dr. Ahearn, I just stopped by to remind you of your meeting this morning."

It was Lieutenant Gibbs standing no more than a foot from the door and staring straight into her eyes.

"Yes, thank you, lieutenant. I was just getting ready to leave," Wendy said. A strange feeling came over her. It was as if every nerve cell in her brain and down her spine was being probed. In an instant Lieutenant Gibbs turned away from her and went down the hall, back toward her own room.

That was strange, Wendy thought. Her gaze followed Gibbs down the hall. *What a strange sensation. Oh ... it was nothing. Forget it.* She closed her door and turned back toward her dining area. "Oh my God!" she said to herself. "I forgot to put the device back into the briefcase." She was hoping that the lieutenant hadn't seen it sitting on the table.

After collecting her notes and placing the device, Wendy headed for the cafeteria.

"How was your dinner last night?" Pete asked as Wendy entered the conference room. Her breakfast tray was balanced on the briefcase. Corey was already there and patiently waiting to start his breakfast.

"Very good, thank you," Wendy said. "The cooks made an excellent tofu stir-fry for me."

"Yes, I agree," Corey echoed. "I tried some of Wendy's meal and it was very tasty. I think I could become a vegetarian without difficulty."

"I'm still a meat and potatoes man myself," Pete said. After a pause, he looked at Wendy. "Well, we need to get going again. This time I'll put you in the hot seat. How did you and Corey make out with the device last night?"

Wendy smiled. She could hardly keep her composure as she opened the briefcase and withdrew her notes and the device. "Let me show you." She opened a package of honey and put some on her middle two fingers. "Last night after you left, Corey, an idea struck me as I was cleaning up from our meals. The fingers of the aliens have little suction cups on their finger tips. So, I thought, maybe they pull up with some fingers and push down with the other fingers." As she was talking, Wendy set the device on the table between her and Pete and placed her fingers on the depressions along the top surface. "I think double-sided tape would work just as well as honey." She pulled up with the middle two fingers of each hand as she pushed down with the outer two fingers. Suddenly, the device came to life. The top surface began to display several columns of strange new symbols within the recessed rectangle, just above the depressions.

"Brilliant! Talk about serendipity!" exclaimed Pete as he glanced over to Corey.

"That's wonderful!" Corey beamed at Wendy. "Have you broken the code?"

"No. Unfortunately, that's as far as I've been able to get. I tried playing around with different key combinations after I got it activated, but I haven't figured out what the symbols mean yet. We need to revisit the alien craft and study the glyphs on the control panel and around the interior of the control room."

"Certainly! I'll make it happen." Pete immediately reached for the beige phone on the table.

Corey looked at Wendy and winked. "At least now we know the batteries aren't dead."

Wendy was a hero now so she thought she would try again. "I know I asked you this yesterday. Is it possible for me to take a pad and pencil so I can make notes?"

"No. I'm sorry, Wendy, *no notes*. No matter how good one's intentions are, somehow papers with notes get misplaced and fall into the wrong hands. I don't mind if you take notes here in the conference room or in your room but not outside of our area. If the secrecy of this project is compromised at all, then heads will roll." He looked sternly into Wendy's eyes. "Even if you survive with your life, you will be discredited. Your career, and mine, will be ruined. I hope to make brigadier general after this mission. No, you'll have to find another way."

"Okay. Can I take the device with me into the craft?" Wendy asked. "It's almost essential, if I'm to succeed."

Pete considered her request for a moment. "Yes, I'll allow that, but keep it in the briefcase except when you're using it."

"That's not a problem."

Pete finished dialing and within a few seconds, a voice answered on the other end of the line. Pete responded, "Colonel Andrews, this is Colonel Mitchell in Section G. I need access to Pathology G and Art C as soon as possible. Can you arrange that?" There was a pause. "Well, I need to have them leave. My team has top priority. How soon can they have their equipment out of there?" Pete turned to Wendy and asked softly, "How long do you need to be in there?"

"Probably a couple of hours will do for now."

"Colonel, we'll need those rooms for two hours. Can you get right back to me with a time-slot? Please apologize to the other group for any inconvenience. Call me in Conference Room G. Thanks." Pete hung up. "Wendy, I think I know the answer, but why do you need to go back to see the craft?"

"I'm hoping to learn more about the aliens and their writing. Normally, when I've translated written text in the past, I had some knowledge about the history and culture of the people who made the inscriptions. In this case I have almost nothing. Perhaps by comparing the symbols that come up on this device with those in the craft, I can begin to make some connections. Maybe I can determine if the writing is a form of pictograph, word signs, logograms, or simply an alphabet."

"What does all of that mean?" Corey asked.

"Well, very early—"

The beige phone rang. Pete answered, "Colonel Mitchell. Okay, eleven hundred hours then. That'll be good. No, we don't have to move any equipment in so we will be out by thirteen hundred hours. We may have to go back later today or tomorrow morning. I'll let you know as soon as I can. Probably the other group should hold off going back in until I get back to you. Thanks, colonel." Pete hung up the phone and turned to Wendy. "As you heard, we go in at eleven. Is that okay?"

"Sure. Well, to finish answering Corey's question, I was saying that primitive civilizations often used pictographic forms of writing. That form of writing has no linguistic reference. The pictographs simply convey an event or message though a series of drawings. Early hunting or fishing communities used this form of writing. The best examples of this are from the early Navaho Indians."

"Are the writings in the ancient Egyptian ruins another example?" Corey asked.

"Yes, to some extent, but they also used the next level of development, word-signs or logograms." Wendy looked at both men. "Perhaps if you tell me more about their interactions with humans, I can get a better understanding. Can you tell me about those abduction cases you mentioned? What did those people see and experienced."

"Yes," Corey said. "I've read quite a lot about that. One of the earliest reported cases. Perhaps you have heard about it since they made a movie about it. It was called, 'Interrupted Journey' and was about Betty and Barney Hill, a New Hampshire couple, who were abducted back in 1961."

"Yes, I think I have heard about that," Wendy said.

"Then you may remember that they were mesmerized by the beings and taken aboard the craft. There, they both underwent a physical exam and then released and taken back to their car. Their captors induced amnesia. The next thing they knew, they were arriving home with no recollection of where they had been, and what they had done for the last three hours. I've actually retraced their path to get a better understanding of the case."

"How did they find out they had been abducted if they had amnesia?" Wendy asked.

"Betty began having nightmares and Barney was troubled and uneasy and his health began to deteriorate. He couldn't sleep, and he developed ulcers. They were both advised to see a hypnotherapist since their regular doctor could not find any physical cause. It was from many sessions of hypnotic regression, that the couple discovered the truth about the missing time and what had happened."

"What did happen?" Wendy was engrossed. "Did the Hills find out why they were abducted?"

"As far as they knew, they were abducted simply to be examined by the aliens; much as a field biologist examines specimens he finds in the wild."

"What sort of exams did the aliens do?"

"Under hypnosis, Betty reported that ear wax, hair samples, and skin scrapings were taken, she was scanned by something the aliens told her was to study her nervous system. The most alarming thing was the long needle they inserted near her navel. They told her it was a pregnancy test. As you might imagine, this was quite painful to her. When she showed signs of discomfort, the aliens did not expect this. The leader said he was sorry and placed his hands over her eyes. The pain went away. Barney reported that they did an examination of his groin area."

Wendy was puzzled. "You say that they were told things. Did the aliens speak English?"

"The leader spoke a limited amount of English, with an accent. The examiner had poor English. She said, when the aliens talked to each other in their own language, it was a sing-song sound, almost like humming. Other people who have heard them, say they often speak in a clicking sound."

"How did they look?" Pete asked.

"The leader was taller than the rest of the crew and looked different; more like us. The crew members were smaller and never spoke. When Betty asked for something as evidence of her visit, the leader gave her a book. However, when she was to leave, the other aliens made her give it up."

"Did she see some of the writing in the book?"

"Yes, in her account of the event, she explained that the script was different from anything she had ever seen. It was very simple. The symbols went vertically instead of horizontally." Corey looked at Wendy. "Could that be a clue?"

"Perhaps. Ancient Chinese was written vertically from top to bottom and from right to left. Throughout human history, there have been a variety of approaches to writing."

Wendy looked at Corey. "So, back to the abductions. Did alien abductions begin with the Hill abductions?"

"I don't know about that," Corey said. "But this was the first case published. After reading the book, other people began to realize that they had experienced 'missing time.' Under hypnotic regression, they discovered that they had been abducted. Some people even discovered that they had a history of being abducted since childhood! They discovered that even their parents and children had a history of been abducted! There are now thousands of cases."

Pete turned to Wendy. "This is the pattern that the general, who found this device, was becoming concerned about. I've been reading everything I can find on abduction cases, ever since I was assigned this project. That's how I've been spending my evenings. I've been hoping to gain some clue about what the aliens are up to. I'd be glad to share as much of that as I can."

"Yes. I'd like that," Wendy said. "Are only certain individuals targeted for abduction?"

"No, people from all walks of life have been and are being abducted. Men and women, doctors, professors, artists, factory workers, engineers, and housewives have reported being abducted."

"How do we know these people are not just delusional?" Wendy asked.

"That's a good question. As you might expect, some people think there is that possibility. In fact, there are three possible reasons why people might report being abducted. First, they could simply be perpetrating a hoax. Most researchers into the abduction phenomena check each person's story for that possibility. Almost always, that is not the case. The stigma attached to people who report abductions is similar to that given to a rape victim.

"The second possibility is that these people are delusional. One investigator, who is highly respected in the field, went to the extreme of hiring a highly qualified psychologist to administer a full battery of psychological tests on nine people who had come to him for help. The psychologist was not told of the connection between the subjects and alien abductions. The tests performed by the psychologist revealed that all nine subjects were above average intelligence and had no major mental disorders such as schizophrenia or paranoia. After the psychologist submitted her report, the investigator explained the reason for having the tests performed on these subjects. Armed with this new information, the psychologist amended her report. She pointed out that the subjects exhibited a psychic scarring indicative of such a traumatic experience."

"So the psychologist confirmed that the subjects had been abducted?" Wendy asked.

"No, but she did show that these people were not delusional. However, all of this does lead to the final possibility."

"What's that?" Wendy asked.

"*People really are being abducted.*"

"How are these people abducted? Wendy asked.

"The method varies. Some have been abducted from their cars," Pete said.

"Much like Betty and Barney Hill, Wendy," Corey added.

"Yes, and some are abducted while out for a walk. Probably most are taken from their homes at night, while they're in their beds," Pete said.

"Do their spouses or other people in the house know it's happening?" Wendy asked.

"No, they're immobilized. They're placed in some form of suspended animation and have no memory of the event. Sometimes, other members of the household are also abducted at the same time."

"How do the aliens get their subjects out of the house?" Wendy asked.

"Usually, several aliens, known as grays, enter the room while the abductee is sleeping. They immobilize them and float them out of the house through a window to a waiting craft."

"Pete, when you say 'grays,' are you talking of the beings we saw yesterday in that tank?"

"Pete, do these people know they're being abducted?" asked Wendy.

"They usually begin to have a strange feeling when the craft is near. It may just be a sense of uneasiness. There's a case of a person who's had abduction experiences since childhood. She has become so sensitized to magnetism that she can now sense the presence of a strong magnet brought into the room. She begins to feel warm and tingly when she's near a magnetic field. Often she'll get this feeling before she sees a UFO or has an abduction experience."

"That's interesting!" Corey said. "It supports my theory that the aliens are using a strong magnetic field to create the gravitational field used to support and drive their craft."

"Corey, perhaps when we go back to see the craft, you can explain your theory to us," Pete said.

Wendy was anxious to continue exploring the abduction topic. "Are there ever witnesses to these abductions?"

"One investigator interviewed the neighbors of a woman who had been abducted from her back yard. Both neighbors saw flashes of lights, heard a loud noise, and their houses were severely shaken when the abduction occurred. Their houses shook so violently that they both thought there was an earthquake.

"Under hypnosis, one of the neighbors said that she had been cleaning the house and had her TV on at the time of the incident. There were flashes of light and a loud noise that shook the house. The dog became terrified. Her TV screen changed to a red color.

"When asked why she didn't call her neighbor, who was being abducted at that time, she said that when she turned to go to her phone, her body began to feel very warm and she just felt compelled *not* to make the call," Pete said.

"Compelled? Did she hear a voice or was it just a feeling?" Wendy asked.

"It's just a feeling."

Wendy cocked her head. "You would think that if people are being abducted in broad daylight, people would see."

"Usually, the abductees are directed, lured, or in some unexplained way made to go to a place out of sight. There have been cases where people have been abducted in front of witnesses but the witnesses were immobilized or placed in suspended animation while the abductee was taken away and tested. After the abductee was brought back, the witnesses were reactivated and given some form of amnesia so they wouldn't remember. Abductees were given the same amnesia. Sometimes it may be years before memories of the event begin to come back; usually in the form of flash-backs or disturbing nightmares.

"What happens to these people during their abductions?" Wendy asked.

"There seems to be a pattern during abductions. The abductees awake from a trance to find they're in some sort of large white room. They're on a cold, hard, table surrounded by some grays and one or two taller aliens. The 'patient' is immobilized and cannot move. The taller aliens are the ones in charge and conducting the tests. One of the tall aliens seems to be there to reassure the abductee that they will not be harmed and that these tests are necessary."

"So they talk to the abductee then?" Wendy asked.

"No," Corey replied. "They often do this by a staring procedure in which they bring their face right up to the abductee's face and stare directly into their eyes. With this, they are able to calm them and do a form of mind scan."

"That's right," Pete said. "During the tests, both men and women report samples taken of various body tissues and fluids. Often, scoops of flesh are taken from the lower leg. Also, their nervous systems are scanned by some type of device. Men often report sperm samples taken. Women have gynecological examinations. These involve the feeling of extreme pressure in the abdomen and are usually painful. Sometimes the examination includes the removal of eggs."

"That sounds terrible!" Wendy wrinkled her nose.

"Yes it is," Pete said, as he tried to determine Wendy's intestinal fortitude. "It gets much worse. Sometimes the examination may include the implantation of an embryo. The 'mother' is allowed to carry this fetus for about two trimesters. Then, they're abducted again, and the fetus is removed. You can imagine the trauma this produces."

Wendy shook her head in the affirmative as she quietly listened.

Pete continued. "At later abductions, these women are often shown, and allowed to hold, 'their' babies. When the 'mother' asks to take her baby home with her, she is told that, because the child is not completely human, it cannot survive in our world."

"Oh ... those poor women. I feel so sorry for them," Wendy said.

"Women often find, under hypnosis, that they have had numerous abductions beginning when they're very young, three to five years old, and continuing until they reach womanhood. Then, they are used as part of the 'breeding' experiments."

"That's absolutely shocking. How can any civilized beings do such a thing? If the aliens are so advanced ... well ... I just don't understand." Wendy was in shock. "When these women find themselves mysteriously pregnant and then, later, just as mysteriously not pregnant, what does their doctor say?"

"They usually don't have a good explanation," Pete said. "There have been a few cases when the woman has felt that the pregnancy was not 'right'. Also, they had no way to explain why they were pregnant. Often and mysteriously, a few days before a more extensive test by a doctor, the fetus disappears: taken during the night."

"It's almost as though the women were being watched by the aliens who know their every move," Wendy said.

"Yes," Pete added. "In fact there's considerable evidence that many abductees have had implants placed in their heads either through their nose, their ear, or sometimes through their eye sockets."

"Pete!" Wendy interrupted. "Are you trying to gross me out or *what*? That's terrible!"

"It's as if the person is being tagged," Pete continued, "much like we tag animals in the wild." He found Wendy's limits.

"That must really be terrifying and painful." Wendy grimaced at the thought.

"Yes, but the person has no choice. They're immobilized, as a long needle, tipped with a BB sized implant, is inserted. The aliens, through telepathy, tell them to relax and try to calm them as much as possible but, as you said, the procedure is painful and terrifying."

"Have any of these implants ever been removed?" Corey asked.

"Only a few. Almost every time an abductee tries to have it removed, it mysteriously disappears the night before the scheduled surgery."

"What do the implants look like? Have they been analyzed?"

"They're not very large. They measure about a half millimeter in diameter by only a few millimeters long. The analysis indicates that they're made of some metallic material that's not of this world. It's very hard and can't be cut with a scalpel. Also, they're encased by some foreign material that seems to prevent rejection."

"The aliens are always one jump ahead of us," Corey added.

"Yes, they seem to be able to do what they want, when they want, and we're powerless to stop them."

Wendy was shaking her head in disbelief. "Why are they doing this?"

"Ah, that's the reason we're here. We have to find out, *and soon*." He eyed them both. "The story gets stranger. Many abductees report that they're told they'll be allowed to remember their experience when the time is right. But for now they are *not* to remember. They're told that mankind is still being prepared and is not ready to have the presence of the aliens known to them.

"Meanwhile, most researchers agree, there seems to be some type of genetic alterations being performed to produce a hybrid human race."

Wendy did a double take. "Do you think they have the ability to do this?"

Pete was silent for a moment and then answered. "What I am about to tell you, would have been unbelievable back in the mid twentieth-century, when DNA was unknown. However, today we know that only five thousand genes separate humans from chimpanzees. Today, a couple can choose the sex of their baby for only $2,500. Today, experiments have been done where mice that glow in the dark have been produced by splicing in the genes from jellyfish. Today, doctors can use the gene analysis of a fetus to spot potential genetic diseases.

"Couples who have a high risk of having babies with a genetic disorder can now have several embryos started and then, after a gene scan for a particular disorder, allow only the healthy embryo to develop. Given *our* level of technology, I have no doubt that the aliens can produce human hybrids."

"How do you think they do this?" Wendy asked.

"From information gained through hypnotic regressions done on hundreds of abductees, the following scenario has evolved. These genetic alterations to the human species have been going on for generations. As any geneticists would tell you, it usually takes several generations of alterations to make the changes you want.

"The procedure used by the aliens is to take human sperm and fertilize a human egg that has been genetically altered to include alien genes. The fetus is then implanted into an abducted human surrogate to gestate up to a certain point."

"How long is that?" Wendy asked.

"About two to three months before full term. The surrogate is then abducted again and the fetus is taken. It's quickly placed into a special 'growing tank' filled with a special fluid. It seems important that the fetus not breathe any air during this procedure. As the fetus is placed into the tank, various tubes or wires are connected to its body to help it develop."

Wendy winced. "Do the babies look human?" She was visibly shaken.

"Well, from the information compiled thus far," Pete said, "these genetic experiments have been going on for several generations. The first generation of hybrids looks more like the aliens than humans. They have very large black eyes with no pupils, large heads, and small, slender bodies with no hair. They have only tiny mouths and ears. For them, food is not taken through their mouths but is absorbed through their skin in special feeding tanks. I guess you could call this transdermal feeding. They can't survive in our atmosphere. Also, they have no genitals so they're sterile."

"Just like a mule," Corey added.

Pete agreed. "Yes, that's a good analogy. Genetic material from these hybrids is then used to produce the next generation. The procedures are the same. These early hybrids are similar but slightly larger and have some whites in their eyes. They also are sterile.

"The genetic material from this second generation is then used to produce the third generation using the same procedures. The resulting hybrids look much more human but may lack eyelashes and eyebrows. Also, their eyes may often have too much black in their pupils. They also cannot reproduce.

"The process is repeated once again using the genetic material from the fourth generation. The result is now a hybrid that is so human looking that they would pass unnoticed by most of us." Wendy was at the edge of her seat now.

Pete noticed Wendy's reaction and her changing demeanor. He continued. "These late-stage hybrids have eyes that are nearly normal looking with, perhaps, a slightly enlarged pupil. Because many have blond hair and blue eyes, they're often referred to as the Nordics by researchers. They can live in our world, eat our food and reproduce with humans. Their most important alien attribute is extraordinary mental ability.

Wendy suddenly felt really strange. She began to pale. "What sort of extraordinary mental abilities?"

"They can do staring procedures and mind scans," Pete answered. "Imagine the advantage that would give a person."

Wendy felt nauseated. She wasn't sure why.

"What's wrong Wendy?" Pete asked. "You look pale. Are you going to be okay?

"Oh sure … I'm okay. I think it must just be something … I had for breakfast. I'll be okay."

"Would you like to take a break? I know this stuff is pretty gruesome," Pete asked.

Corey gave Wendy a thumbs-up and shot her an encouraging look.

Wendy recovered her composure. "Why do you think they're creating this race of super-humans?"

"I don't know, but I believe that these revelations are near," Pete answered.

"Do you think these aliens mean us harm?" Wendy asked in a more serious tone.

"I don't know, but General Douglas MacArthur gave a speech at West Point in which he said, in essence, the future people of the Earth would have to unite to defend themselves in a war with 'people' from other planets," Pete said.

"That sounds pretty ominous," Wendy said.

"I believe they have the technology to destroy us with ease," Pete said. "However, do I think they mean to harm us? No."

"If they have the technology to take over the Earth with ease, why don't they?" Wendy asked.

"Wendy," Corey said, "I believe I have an answer to that. My feeling is the aliens have evolved away from aggressive behavior. I believe this is a natural outcome for any society that has all their food, shelter, and energy needs provided for thousands or perhaps millions of years. I believe they are here simply to observe us." Corey hesitated. "At least … that's my hope."

The beige phone rang. "Colonel Mitchell here. They are? Great, then we can go in now? Okay, thanks for your help, Colonel." Pete smiled as he hung up the phone. "Okay, we're cleared to go in now," he said as he glanced at his watch. "It's now ten-fifty. We have until thirteen hundred hours to examine the body and craft. Let's get ready to go in."

Wendy put the device into the briefcase and started to put in her notes. "Don't put your notes away," Pete said. "Take those back to your apartment and put them in safe keeping; out of sight." Pete glanced at his watch. "Let's plan to meet back here at eleven hundred hours."

Chapter 16
Kazaam!

It was 11:02 by the time everyone was gathered at the conference room door leading out to ART C and PATHOLOGY C. Pete entered the code numbers into the door keypad and within seconds the red light over the keys switched to green. Two minutes later they were in PATHOLOGY C and standing in front of the specimen tank containing the alien.

"Are you ready?" Pete asked.

"Yes," Wendy answered. Corey and Wendy exchanged glances and nodded.

Pete pressed the button on the side of the tank and suddenly the tank lit up exposing the alien, floating in the bluish green liquid. Both Wendy and Corey gasped and stepped back. It was still too unreal for them. To be looking at a creature that was perhaps hundreds of thousands of years more advanced than humans, was unnerving to both of them.

"So, this is what abductees call 'grays'?" Wendy asked.

"Yes, as near as I can determine, these are the ones who do all of the menial tasks such as fetching the victims and getting them ready for the examinations. They seem to report to a different form of alien, though. The leaders are often described as very tall and reptilian in appearance. The reptilians are the ones who actually perform the tests and operations. These grays seem to fill the function of 'worker bee' in the alien society."

Wendy studied the alien's hands. "Those suction cups on their finger tips give them another degree of freedom in manipulating the controls; they can push or pull." She got close to the tank for a closer look of the hands. "That's strange," she said. "I didn't notice before that they have a slight webbing between their fingers. Also, there is a slightly mottled look to their skin."

"Yes, it almost reminds me of a frog's skin," Corey said.

Wendy's attention was drawn to the alien's head. The eyes were overpowering. Wendy became mesmerized by the eyes, even though the alien was dead. She drew closer. They seemed to be staring straight through her and probing her brain.

"WATCH OUT!" Corey shouted as he jerked Wendy back, away from the tank. He began to laugh.

"Very funny," Wendy said as she turned to sock Corey in the arm.

"I'm sorry, but you looked like you were about to climb into the tank after that thing."

"No, I wasn't. I was just fascinated by those big eyes. It seemed to still be alive."

"I think that after over fifty years, the alien is dead; if he ever was truly alive," Pete said. "I've often pondered what it means to be alive or to be human, for that matter." Pete said rhetorically. "What is it that sets us apart from all the other species on this planet?" He turned to Wendy. "What do you think makes us human?"

"That's not an easy question," she replied. "I think it was Ben Franklin who coined the phrase 'Man the Toolmaker.' For centuries, that was used as the definition that separated humans from other species. We were the only animals that fashioned tools. It was only in the last half of the 20th century that Dr. Jane Goodall overturned that definition by observing chimpanzees fashioning twigs to fish termites out of their mounds. Since then many other examples of tool-making by other species have been observed."

"What about the ability to communicate via a spoken language?" Corey asked.

"That was another test that did not survive. It has been observed that whales and dolphins also have the ability to communicate through complex sound patterns. Another test that some invoke is self-awareness. However, there is some evidence that chimps exhibit self awareness when placed in front of a mirror."

"So what's left?" Pete asked.

"Well, my favorite definition for being human is the ability to record our history and pass that knowledge on to our descendents. That allows our species to grow intellectually and technically," Wendy said. "There's no evidence that any other species can do that."

"I take exception to that definition," Corey responded. "What would you call a little gray man with bug eyes who steps out of a flying saucer and says 'Take me to your leader'?"

"Good point. I guess I wouldn't call him human even though he probably does have the ability to record history and certainly is way ahead of us technically. I guess, in the final analysis, there is no action that humans perform that makes them unique. Perhaps the only test for humanism is in the genetic code."

The tank light went out. "Do you want me to turn it back on?" Pete asked.

"No, I think I've seen enough, thank you. What about you, Corey?" Wendy asked.

"No, I'm good." Corey was chomping at the bit to get into the next room. "We can go on to the craft now."

"Okay, let's go," Pete said as he led them over to the door to ART C.

After entering the small hangar-type room, they all went over to the craft, still suspended as they had last seen it.

"Corey, you were going to explain how you think they generate their gravity drive using a magnetic field," Wendy said.

"Sure. Come over here to the gash in the ship's edge," Corey said as he led them over to the jagged edge. "If you look inside, you can see the top surface of those three spheres that extend through the bottom of the craft. I *think* those are the gravity generators. Their location makes sense to me."

"How does the magnetic field come into the picture? You said earlier that they generated a huge magnetic field." Pete questioned.

"Yes, good question." Corey pointed back toward the spheres. "Technically, those are magnetic field generators, I think. The magnetic fields they produce, interacts with the ship's metal skin. The electric current flowing in the skin, reacts with the magnetic field to create a gravitational field." Corey rubbed his hand over the metal surface of the craft. "I'm not quite sure of the physics yet. My project at GraviDyne is to prototype a system like this." Corey looked at Wendy with a grin. "Now that I've told you that, I have to ask Pete to shoot you.

"Funny, Corey," Wendy said, as she jabbed him in his ribs.

Corey continued with his explanation. "I think they sequence the magnetic generators to create a rotating magnetic field. That creates the torque in the field necessary to generate the gravitational field. It also gives the craft stability."

"Is that what causes the crafts to wobble when they're landing?" Pete asked.

"It might. Both the magnetic fields and the electrical currents in the ship's skin are immense. They need to be in order to create any significant gravitational field. That's why I think the craft's skin is a superconductor."

Wendy gave Corey a questioning look. "If gravity drive is this simple, why don't we have one now?"

"Wendy, if you time-traveled back to the Wright brothers' time and handed them the blueprints for a stealth fighter, do you think they could have built one?" Corey said.

"Probably not," she said.

"Right," Corey said, "because they would not have the manufacturing technology required to build one. And, that's our problem in trying to duplicate this. We don't know how to make high temperature superconductors yet or how to join component together like you see here."

Pete had been studying the craft's skin as Corey was giving Wendy his explanations. "Corey, what causes the crafts to glow? Most people report seeing the craft glow different colors. How is all of that radiation produced by a magnetic field?"

"I believe that's caused by two effects," Corey answered. "I believe the skin is made of a superconducting material that allows for extremely high electrical currents. The extremely strong electric field in the skin creates a corona discharge; like what you could see in bug zappers at night. The second cause is synchrotron radiation. As I said, extremely strong magnetic fields pass through the surface of the craft. This causes the free electrons flowing around the skin of the craft to fall into extremely tight orbits. As you may recall, when electrons pass through a magnetic field, their paths are curved. The stronger the magnetic field, the smaller the radius of curvature. As electrons move in a curved path, they are actually accelerating towards the center of curvature. It's this acceleration that causes the electrons to shed photons. The whole spectrum of radiation is produced, from radio waves to gamma rays. The maximum intensity occurs at a wavelength that depends on the strength of the magnetic field and the energy level of the electrons. If the UFO is changing the strength of the magnetic field in order to maneuver, the color of the craft's glow will shift, perhaps even into a wavelength that is not visible. A significant amount of x-rays and gamma rays could be produced which would make it very hazardous. That's why you don't want to be too close for too long when these things are working."

Wendy stared at Corey with her mouth open and a blank expression. "If you say so, Corey."

Corey chuckled. "Did you see the movie *Close Encounters* where Richard Dreyfuss got a sunburn when he looked up at the UFO as it passed over his truck? That was from the UV radiation the craft was emitting. The producers of that movie did their homework."

"Corey, some people who have seen UFOs say that sometimes they appear in one place, 'wink out', and suddenly reappear in another place. How do you explain that?" Pete was still awed by Corey's explanation of the drive system.

"That's right," Wendy added. "When you and I were in my apartment, you mentioned that these craft can cloak themselves. Is that the same thing as winking out? How do they do that?"

"Excellent questions." Corey gave Wendy a special smile. "One possibility is that the synchrotron radiation jumps to a wavelength that we cannot detect with our eyes; extreme ultraviolet, for instance. The other possibility is that they use a cloaking device, created by a magnetic field they generate."

"You mean a cloaking device like in *Star Wars*?" Pete asked, with a smile.

"Yes." Corey smiled because he knew how that sounded.

"Okay, professor, I give up. How do they cloak themselves with a magnetic field?" Pete asked.

"There was an amazing paper published in *Nature* magazine, by Professor Thomas Erber. I think it was a 1961 issue. I remember his name because the paper was that significant. In that paper, he developed an equation that tied light refraction to magnetic field strength. It turns out that light, passing through a very strong magnetic field, is refracted."

"I've never noticed that," Wendy said.

"Neither have I," Pete said.

"Even at the strongest magnetic fields that we've been able to produce so far, the effect is insignificant. It takes an extremely strong field to have a noticeable effect. Such a field strength is presently beyond our ability to produce. But, theoretically, at extremely strong magnetic fields, light passing from behind the craft could be refracted around the craft so that the craft becomes invisible to an observer in front. It's sort of like a lens effect."

"So they do cloak themselves!" Wendy exclaimed.

"Exactly ... neat, isn't it?" Corey said, in a chipper voice.

"I read accounts where a chase plane would go after a UFO and see it, but the ground radar could not. Why is that?" Pete asked.

"That's because the amount of refraction is dependent on the frequency of the radiation passing through the field. Radar waves have a different wavelength from visible light. Sometimes, radar observers have reported seeing the craft but the chase pilot couldn't."

Pete glanced at his watch. "Okay, you both need to get inside this craft so Wendy can begin to decipher the writing on the device."

"We can't all fit up there in the control room, so Wendy, you and Corey climb up and I'll hand you the briefcase."

Wendy knew she could have climbed up by herself but she was thinking it might be more enjoyable to have Corey help her. She let Corey go first. He squeezed through the gaping hole in the craft and eased himself up into the control room.

"Grab my hand," he called down to her.

She crawled through the hole and reached up to his waiting hand. He pulled her up.

"I feel uneasy in here," Wendy commented, after getting settled onto the deck. "This place gives me the creeps!"

"Yeah," he said. "It's like stepping into another world."

"Yes, except that we had to *crawl* into this one." She turned back and looked down at Pete who was standing by. "You can pass the briefcase up now."

"Okay, pass it back down after you extract the device. That will give you more working space."

After pulling up the briefcase, Wendy took out the device, some packets of honey, and packets of moist towelettes she brought from the cafeteria. She closed the briefcase and passed it back to Pete."

"Let me know when you're done and I'll send it back up," he said.

Wendy opened one of the packets of honey and put some on her fingers. "Here, do you want some, Corey?"

"Sure, that's a good idea, I'll see if it works on the craft's control panel."

Wendy put honey on her fingers and, after a few seconds, got the device to activate again. As she watched the symbols scroll in columns up the screen, Corey got his fingers sticky with honey. He began fingering the craft's control panel, placing his fingers into the small depressions and trying combinations of pressing and pulling motions. "This doesn't seem to be working." Suddenly, the surface of the control panel came alive with symbols! "Wow, look! After over fifty years, this thing still has power!"

She brought the device over to where Corey was keying the controls and began to compare symbols. "You don't suppose you're going to accidentally make this thing take off do you?" Wendy was half serious.

"That would be neat, but I don't think so. The cable connecting the control panel to the gravity generators is severed. Look at what I discovered, though. If you pull on the depressions, you get one result and if you push on the depressions, you get a different result."

"That means that each depression can have three values; zero, plus, and negative," Wendy said, as she recalled some of her Computer 101 class.

"Now you're beginning to sound like a computer programmer."

Wendy watched as Corey fingered the various depressions. "Look at those three symbols that are laid out in a triangular pattern. As you fingered the depressions near them, the symbols lit up."

"Yes, I think those symbols represent the three gravity generators. I must be trying to turn them on. It's a good thing the cable's severed." Corey repeatedly tapped one of the buttons near the top gravity drive symbol. "Look, as I keep keying this button, the symbol next to that gravity generator symbol keeps changing. Those changing symbols must be indicating the level of power to that drive unit."

"Yes, I see. Can you get that drive symbol to go off and then tap that button just once to bring it back on?"

"I'll try," Corey said as he pulled up in a succession of strokes. "There, it's off. Now, I'll tap it once." As he did, a symbol appeared next to the drive symbol.

Wendy studied the symbol. "Okay, now tap the button once more." As Corey did, another symbol appeared. "Okay, now tap it slowly seven more times." Corey obeyed. As he did, different symbols appeared for the next six taps but then on the seventh tap the symbol appeared that had first appeared. "That's it!" Wendy exclaimed, "Only eight different symbols appear and then they begin to repeat."

They looked at each other, smiled and said simultaneously, "Octal code!"

"Based on the fact that the aliens have only eight fingers and the fact that there is a set of only eight different symbols, I think those symbols are probably numbers in the octal numbering system; just as we suspected. We're making progress!" Wendy grinned.

"I heard that," Pete yelled up. "Keep up the good work."

Wendy turned to her handheld device and began keying. As the symbols scrolled by, she noticed that occasionally she could see some of the same symbols appear as had appeared on the console. She experimented with different key patterns. Before long, a satisfied look appeared on her face. "Look, Corey, I now know how to make any one of the eight numbers appear on the device."

"Great! Look at this." Corey pointed toward the right side of the columns of symbols he had been working. "As I adjust the power levels of the gravity generators," he motioned, "this column of symbols changes. If I make the power levels all the same, I get this square pattern. If I increase the power of the top generator above the other two, I get this triangular pattern that points up. If I increase the power of one of the other two generators, I get a triangle which points either to the right or to the left. I think the triangle probably points in the direction we would move."

"Yes, I think you're right."

"The symbol to the right of that symbol hasn't changed. It might display the actual direction we would be going, if we were moving. Not all of those symbols on the first column appear to be numbers though. The top two symbols don't look like the numbers we saw; only the bottom four take on the symbols of numbers. What do you suppose the top symbols are?"

"I don't know," Wendy said. "I'll see if I can get those symbols to appear on this device."

The two continued to experiment with different patterns.

"How are you coming?" Pete called up to them. "It's nearly thirteen hundred hours."

"Is it that late already?" Wendy asked as she glanced at her watch. "I guess my brain is at the saturation point for now. It would be good to have some time to write this stuff down."

"I agree," Corey nodded.

"Have you figured out how to shut down the control panel?" Wendy asked.

"I think so. At one point, while trying different button combinations, I accidentally shut it down. Let me try a few things here," Corey said, as he tried a few different key stroke combinations. "There, I got it."

"Good, here, take some of these handy wipes and clean up," Wendy said as she opened a pack of wipe-ups. She turned and called out, "I'm ready for the briefcase now, Pete."

After locking the device into the briefcase, Wendy and Corey climbed down and returned back to the conference room with Pete.

Chapter 17
Explanations

"Have a seat," Pete said as they entered the room. "Tell me how you made out. It sounded like you were making progress."

"Yes," Wendy said, as she filled him in on their discoveries.

"Great," Pete said, after she had finished. "That'll allow you to experiment with the device while you're in your apartment."

"Yes, and something else," she said. "As Corey was making changes on the control panel, it seemed that some of the same symbols that were appearing on the control panel, also appeared on the device; as though they were communicating with each other. The strange thing was that there was a two to three second delay between the two. What do you make of that?"

"I don't know," Pete said. "Corey, do you have any ideas?"

"Well, I suspect that, with the technology the aliens have, the delay is not computer processing time. The response is as though the console and the device are separated by a large distance. Since they're not, there must be a distant relay station somewhere." He did a quick calculation in his head. "With a three second delay, the relay station must be over a quarter million miles away."

"That's about how far the moon is from Earth," Pete said. "Perhaps the aliens have a relay station somewhere on the moon. What else did you discover? Do you know yet how to read their symbols?"

"Only the numbers, but I'm pretty sure that their writing is a form of alphabet that has some phonetic value. From what you and Corey have told me, they not only communicate with each other by mental telepathy, but also use singsong sounds, clicking and chirping. I don't have the pattern down yet. Perhaps if I can have this afternoon to myself, I can make some progress."

"So, I take it that you don't want to go back to the craft any more today? What about you, Corey?" Pete asked.

"Yes. I'd love to tinker some more with that craft," Corey said. "If it's okay, I'd like to go back."

"Sure, and I think I'll go back with you. Let me call and let the base commander know our plans. Corey, why don't you meet me here at fourteen hundred hours and we'll go back in. What time do you want to go back in tomorrow, Wendy?"

"How about ten o'clock in the morning. That will give me a couple of hours to brief you both on what I accomplish this afternoon."

"Good, it's now thirteen-ten, why don't you two go on to lunch. Wendy, I'll see you here tomorrow morning at oh eight hundred hours."

"Okay, see you tomorrow," Wendy said as she took the briefcase and left with Corey for the cafeteria.

Within ten minutes they were in Wendy's apartment and enjoying their lunches as they reviewed their findings from this morning.

As Corey finished his, he asked, "What's your plan for this afternoon?"

"Well, I want to try to learn how to get symbols, other than numbers, to appear on the device. Once I have control, then I can bring up combination of symbols and perhaps develop a relationship between them."

"That sounds ambitious," Corey stated as he placed his empty dishes back on the tray and stood up to leave. "I'll leave you so you can get started. Give me your tray and I'll return it to the cafeteria."

"I'm not done yet, thanks, just take yours. I'll take mine back later."

"How about a date for supper? My treat."

"That sounds great. When you return your tray to the cafeteria, why don't you put in an order for some pizza for tonight? I have a sudden craving for a vegetarian pizza."

"Okay, that sounds great! What time do you want to eat?"

"I'm sure that I'll be ready for a break by six."

"Well, I'm off to see the wizard, or at least what the wizard built," Corey said with a smile. Corey gazed at Wendy for a moment and then bent down and kissed her. Wendy reached her hand around his neck and held him close.

They embraced for what seemed like minutes. Finally, Corey gently pulled away and brushed his hair back.

"Well, that was an enjoyable surprise," Wendy said as she stared up into Corey's eyes.

"Yes it was. We'll have to try that again, later. Pete's going to be waiting for me so I better run now. I'll see you later. Have fun playing with that thing," Corey said as he pointed to the briefcase.

After Corey left, Wendy sat for a moment to finish her lunch and then prepared to continue her research. She began trying various keystroke combinations. Note taking was awkward with sticky fingers so she searched the apartment and found some double-sided tape and placed it in the depressions on the device.

For several hours, she tried various key combinations, writing down the results and repeating the process until she felt she was able to call up various symbols at will. As she worked, images began to appear in her head. Voices began talking to her in a strange tongue. *Fatigue is beginning to set in,* she thought. *It's time for a break.* Wendy moved over to the piano. *Perhaps I can get my mind into a more relaxed and creative mood,* she thought as she began to play.

It seemed like only a few minutes had passed when Wendy heard a knock at the door. "Just a second," she called out as she went back to the table and placed the device, with her notes, back into the briefcase. She glanced at her watch. *It's only four-twenty, Corey shouldn't be back this early.* After locking the briefcase, she went over and opened the door.

It was Lieutenant Gibbs.

"Doctor Ahearn, I heard the music, so I thought this might be a good time for me to clean your room. Besides, I enjoy your music," Gibbs said as she entered the room and closed the door. She stepped closer to Wendy; closer than Wendy felt comfortable with.

"You know, I'm really kind of busy now, Lieutenant. Perhaps we should make it another time." Wendy was beginning to feel uneasy near Gibbs.

"Well, I thought that if you were playing the piano, you wouldn't mind me cleaning up," Gibbs said as she came even closer to Wendy.

Wendy couldn't avoid making eye contact. *Oh God! It's happening again!* She felt like her brain was under attack! As Gibbs continued to stare into Wendy's eyes,

Wendy lost all will to resist. *Perhaps it is okay for Gibbs to be here. Yes, I think it is okay.* "Yes, I guess you're right," she murmured. "This is a good time for us to talk."

"Good, because I have some important things to tell you," Gibbs said as she led Wendy over to the couch.

Corey and Pete stood next to the UFO.

"Corey, as you were talking to Wendy earlier, about the *Close Encounters* movie, I was remembering the scene in the movie where Richard Dreyfuss was sitting in his truck at a stop sign when a UFO passed closely overhead. The stop sign started flapping wildly back and forth. Do you remember that?"

"Yes, that was caused by the strong magnetic field. That same effect has been described by a number of people who have reported a close encounter. I'm not sure what to think about the TV screen turning red in that one lady's house. Probably, that is also the result of a strong magnetic field."

"What led you to make the connection between magnetic fields and gravitational fields?" Pete asked.

Corey leaned against the UFO with his left hand as he stroked his chin with his right. "At the turn of the 20th century, Einstein predicted that a strong gravitational field, like our sun, could deflect a beam of light. He predicted that a star near the edge of the sun's disc would have an apparent shift in position from where it was known to be. His theory was proven in 1919 during observations of a solar eclipse. This shift was only about three degrees, but it was almost exactly what he predicted.

"What does the distortion of light have to do with gravity drive?"

Corey held both hands out to his sides as though to balance them. "Well, to me it means that if light, which is a form of electro-magnetic radiation, can be distorted by gravity," he raised his right hand slightly, "then maybe the reverse is true and gravity can be distorted by manipulating electro-magnetic fields," Corey replied as he raised his left hand slightly to indicate a balance. "We haven't done it yet because we don't have the technology. I think we will have to produce extremely strong magnetic and electric fields to make the process work. This will take the development of high temperature super conductivity as well as a tremendous source of power such as fusion power."

"What makes you think that you would need a strong magnetic field and not just a strong electrical field?" Pete asked.

"People who have close encounters with UFOs experience electrical malfunctions in their car's electrical system, as the UFOs get close. Most gasoline engines use a spark ignition system. A strong magnetic field interferes with that."

"Does that mean diesel powered engines are not affected?"

"That's right. Also, it has been observed that when a UFO passes over metal structures such as road signs, the signs begin waving wildly from what seems to be a rotating magnetic field from the craft." Corey flapped his right hand in the air. "Upon later investigation, the signs are found to have some residual magnetism."

"Does the strong magnetic field harm any of the people who may be near by?" Pete bent down and studied the three spherical shapes projecting from the bottom of the craft.

"No. The magnetic field doesn't harm them but, as I said before, the synchrotron radiation does. People who have gotten too close to UFOs when they were maneuvering, have experienced the feeling of heat from the infrared radiation, sunburn from the ultraviolet radiation, and after the event, have suffered nausea and other symptoms associated with excess exposure to gamma radiation."

Pete stood up. "I have another phenomenon that I would like explained. I've read that UFO witnesses have reported seeing large blimp-shaped craft, sometimes referred to as leviathans, traveling silently at thousands of miles per hours. Even pilots have reported this. These craft create no shock wave or sonic booms!"

"It sounds like you've been reading up on UFOs."

"Yes, I have done a lot of reading lately. So what about my question? Why don't they make shock waves?" Pete asked.

"I think there are two factors are at play," Corey answered. "First, the ionic charge in the corona that surrounds the surface of the craft may be part of the reason. Second, they may be able to project a negative gravitational field ahead of their craft."

"Can you explain that? I'm not sure I understand."

"Yes. As you recall from your aeronautical engineering classes, the reason we experience shock waves at high speeds is because the air molecules ahead of the craft are pushed aside by the pressure wave created in front of the craft. As the craft approaches the speed of sound, the pressure waves, which are limited to the speed of sound, can no longer fore-warn the air molecules that the craft is coming. Suddenly the craft is upon them before they can get out of the way. This collision produces a huge pressure spike at the leading edge causing a shock wave. It's this shock wave that creates the sonic boom."

"How does the ionized layer around the craft help reduce the shock wave?"

"Well, either the electric field in the ionized gases or the negative gravity field can be projected ahead of the craft at the speed of light. So the electric field can act as an advanced warning, if you will, to tell the air molecules that the craft is approaching. This will allow the molecules more time to move aside. If a negative gravitational field can be projected ahead of the craft, it will have the same effect. The end result is what you aerodynamicists call potential flow or loss free flow."

"Excellent! That's the best explanation I've ever heard. I know that some research is being done to reduce drag by applying an electric charge on the nose of aircraft." Pete ran his hands along the underside of the craft. "Now I have another question. What about the cooling effect that has been observed?"

"What do you mean?"

"Witnesses have reported that after a saucer has departed, the area where the saucer had rested was frozen. Can you explain that?"

"No I can't, but one theory is that the negative gravity under the craft as it hovers, expels the air underneath, causing a vacuum. This causes the moisture to evaporate and produce a refrigeration effect that freezes the water. However, that doesn't explain the cooling effect noticed by an eye witness at the UFO crash in the Plains of St Agustin, in New Mexico. When interviewed in 1990, the witness stated that he was at the site with his father, brother and uncle. He said that as he walked under the exposed portion of the craft that was protruding from the side of an arroyo, the air was much cooler. When he touched the underside of the craft, it felt very cold." Corey looked at Pete. "I can't explain that, yet."

"Okay, one final question. With such advanced technology, why do these things crash?"

"I have been asking myself the same question. Lightning strikes perhaps. The Roswell and the Aztec crashes in New Mexico in the late forties could be a result of intense radar beams disrupting the craft's propulsion system. The 1988 crash west of Gulf Breeze, Florida could have been caused by the electromagnetic pulse beam weapon at nearby Eglin Air Force Base. Who knows?"

Pete smiled in agreement and motioned for Corey to follow him as he began to circle the craft. "Let's check this thing out and 'kick some tires and light some fires.'"

Chapter 18
Awesome

"Sit down, Wendy, I have to talk to you."

Wendy sat down on the couch and Gibbs sat down next to her. "We really aren't supposed to have any conversations," Wendy wanted to say, but somehow, it seemed okay to be talking to Gibbs. "What is it you want to talk about?"

"I know why you're here and I know what's in that briefcase over there," Gibbs declared matter-of-factly as she pointed towards the dining table.

"How do you know about that?" Wendy was in a daze. "Pete said you didn't know what we were doing here."

"I know a lot. Let's just say that I am well-connected."

"I guess you are. I thought that even the base commander doesn't know what we're doing here. How is it that you do?"

"I have a story that will explain everything."

Gibbs paused to organize her thoughts. Everything she had to tell Wendy was stored in her mind as a recording. "I need to go back in time to about two years ago. I was still attending West Point, and some classmates and I made a weekend hiking trip to the White Mountain area of New Hampshire. We were camping near a forest and for some strange reason, I felt compelled to leave the campsite and explore the forest. No one wanted to join me since it was overcast and about to snow. I wandered for about an hour and a half and became lost."

"You got lost!" Wendy said, "I thought military people were not supposed to get lost."

"That's true, but since I wasn't an upperclassman yet, I hadn't had my survival training. Anyway ... the sky was overcast, and I lost track of which way was north. As I tried to get my bearings and find my way out, I heard a voice calling my name.

"Sandra, Sandra, come this way," the voice said. I thought it must be someone from a rescue party. Who else would know my name? I followed the sound and finally came to a clearing. There, standing in the clearing, was the most beautiful young man I had ever seen. He almost seemed to have a glow about him. I decided this glow was from the diffused daylight shinning down on him through the clearing.

"Sandra, I've been looking for you," the young man said, in a most gentle voice.

As Gibbs looked into Wendy's eyes, Wendy began to visualize Gibbs's story as though she, herself, were living it.

"Are you part of a rescue party?" I asked.

"Yes, your friends are very worried about you because the temperature is dropping and it's about to snow. Follow me," he said as he motioned for me to follow.

"What's your name?"

"Jomar."

"Well, Mr. Jomar, I guess I'm lucky you found me?" I said as I followed him through the forest.

"Yes you are. But, my name is Jomar, not Mr. Jomar."

Soon, we came to another clearing and as he stepped aside, I could see this strange, disk-shaped craft, about thirty feet in diameter, sitting in the clearing. He turned to me and saw that I was beginning to panic.

"Sandra, look at me," he said as he came closer and stared into my eyes. "You have nothing to fear from this craft ... or me. Follow me into the craft and I'll take you to safety."

Initially, my mind was telling me not to go, but soon I accepted whatever was to happen. It was like I didn't care what was happening. I had complete trust in Jomar. He was in control and I followed him into the craft. After we entered the craft, it took off and flew into space. I don't know how far. We traveled for nearly an hour. All during that time, I was in a stupor, just sitting in the seat he had led me to.

A light began flashing on the consol.

"We're here," he said, and took me over to a window. He pointed to an object in the distance. "Sandra, can you see that small object over there? That's our destination. We are only thirty miles from it now and we have to approach slowly."

It was just a speck in the blackness of space and difficult to see. As we got closer I began see that it was a huge, dark gray cylinder with hemispherical ends. I mean, it was huge!

"Sandra, we are still five miles out but soon we'll be so close you won't be able to see its entirety. It's over eight miles long and two miles in diameter. Our ship is now under the control of that craft. They're guiding us into that large hangar door over there." He pointed to an immense door in the side of the craft. It was opening like a giant clamshell.

"See, it just opened."

As we drifted towards the large opening, the ship loomed larger. The surface was covered with thousands of windows and transparent domes. There were hundreds of projections off of the surface that reminded me of the masts on the old sailing ships.

Soon we were inside the hangar and the door closed. I could hear a hiss as it sealed behind us.

"In just a few minutes, the pressure will be high enough in the hangar so we can safely exit our craft."

"Why did you bring me here, Jomar?"

"I brought you here to meet the ones who seek you. They will meet with us very soon. For now, we have some time for a tour of this craft. I can see from your eyes that you are interested in such things. Follow me and I'll take you to the lowest level to start our tour."

Jomar led me to what looked like a large glass tube that came through the ceiling and passed through the floor. As we approached, an opening appeared in the tube. It was an elevator.

"Step in," he said.

Each floor flashed by as we descended. Finally, we came to a stop and I followed Jomar out of the elevator into a hallway. As I followed him, I noticed that I was tending to bounce a little.

Jomar glanced back at me and smiled. "It will take a little while for you to get used to this reduced gravity."

"How reduced is it?"

"The gravitational pull here is about two thirds of that on Earth. We spend considerable time on Earth, and having the gravity on this craft similar to Earth's makes it easier to adjust."

"Why don't you just use zero gravity like our astronauts experience when they're in orbit?" I said.

"Zero gravity is bad for the body, just as it is for yours, over extended periods. Being in zero gravity for extended periods has harmful effects on our heart and other organs as well as our skeletal system. Our body's skeletal system, just like yours, will lose calcium. The bones will become weak and brittle. It is important that we spend only a few days in zero gravity. That's why we produce our own gravity."

"Why not make it equal to Earth's?"

"Well, that is a good question. You see ... it's a compromise. More gravity means more internal pressure would be required to make a balance."

"What do you mean by balance?"

"Follow me and I'll show you."

Jomar took me into a side room. The floor in this room had many large round windows set into the floor. These viewing panels were about six feet in diameter and about three inches thick. He pointed down to the one in front of me. "It's okay, you can stand on them. Go ahead...step on it and look down...it's safe...see." He stepped onto one.

Looking down, I could see to the other side of the huge cavern that formed the interior of this craft.

"What you see down there is actually the other side of the inner chamber. That's about two miles in diameter," Jomar said. "Think of this as a huge transparent balloon and we are looking through to the other side. Actually, it is a lot like a balloon."

The inner surface of this balloon-like craft was covered with thousands of round windows like the one I was standing on. Running though the center of this cylinder was what looked like a small wire. It extended from one domed end to the other.

"What's that wire for?" I asked.

"That small wire-like thing running the length of the cylinder at its axis is actually a tube that's about ninety feet in diameter. Inside the entire length of that tube is the gravity generator that pulls the outer cylinders, like the one we're standing on, towards the center. That creates the gravity you feel."

"What keeps this thing from collapsing?" I said.

"Pressure. Inside this cylinder we're standing on is enough pressure to keep the whole craft from imploding. The more gravity we want, the more pressure we have to have inside. So, it's really a balance between internal pressure and gravity. The Director felt that two thirds of the Earth's gravity was enough and since it only requires two thirds as much internal pressure, there is less risk."

"How much pressure is inside this cylinder?"

"Surprisingly little. The gas is only pressurized to four pounds per square inch. If you entered that space, you would need an oxygen mask to keep from suffocating. Not only is the pressure low but also, there's no oxygen. It's filled with pure nitrogen gas."

"Why not use a combination of gases like our Earth's atmosphere; then it could be breathed."

"There's less risk of fire by using pure nitrogen. Also, the materials used to make this craft would deteriorate if there were oxygen mixed with the gas. No one goes inside, anyway. It's too dangerous."

"Why is it dangerous?"

"As you get closer to the gravity generator, the gravitational force increases exponentially. If you tried to walk on the surface of that ninety foot diameter tube, you would be crushed by the force. When repairs are required, we send in special robots that can withstand the force."

"So, if I understand what you said, we're standing on the outside surface of the pressurized inner cylinder of this space station."

"That's correct."

"How many shells or layers are there above us?"

"There are seventeen concentric shells that form the sixteen levels on this craft." Jomar pointed upward. "The lower eight levels, like the one we are in now, are used as living and working space. The next seven decks above those are used for manufacturing and storage. The top level is where space docks and craft hangers are located. Also, at various locations around the outer surface, there are observatories. The large tubes you may have seen running along the craft on the outside are more gravity generators. They are aimed outward and generate a negative gravity field around the outside of the craft."

"What's that for?"

"To deflect any space debris that might strike the craft. You may not have noticed. As we approached the craft, our ship had to pause so the negative gravity field could be turned off. Otherwise, we could not get near the craft."

"That sound like the shields that the *Enterprise* uses in *Star Trek*."

"I don't know about this *Star Trek*, but it is a form of shield."

"That tube at the craft's center not only generates gravity, but it also generates a magnetic field that surrounds the craft. That field gives protection against radiation from space. Much like the Earth's magnetic field does."

"Why are the living and working quarters located toward the interior?"

"That arrangement gives the maximum protection from radiation and meteorite impacts from space in the event something gets through the shield."

"I'm amazed by how well all of the surfaces on this craft blend together. There are no seams. The wall joins the floor and ceiling seamlessly with a smooth radius. How did you build this thing?" I asked.

"We have very advanced construction methods. We build at a molecular level. It would appear to you as though this craft was grown."

"How many people live here?"

"There are about thirty-two thousand entities here at any one time."

"What do you mean by entities?"

"Follow me and you'll understand. I'm going to take you up to level seven," he said as we left the inner viewing room and returned to the elevator.

In less than a minute, we were at level seven and in a large room filled with tanks. In the tanks were creatures that looked like giant red lobsters. At the tips of their eyestalks, were huge black eyes about the size of tennis balls.

"Is this were you grow your food?"

"No ... heavens no. We do not *eat* living beings. We grow these animals because of their unique feature. They can regenerate lost body parts, in particular, their eyes. We periodically harvest their eyes. One at a time of course. They eventually grow a replacement."

"Why do you want their eyes?"

"They're for our workers. The workers' eyes are sensitive to ultraviolet radiation and must be surgically replaced from time to time."

"Why is that?"

"The light from your sun damages their eyes when they are on the Earth. Also, when they land

and are working around the outside of their scout craft, the ultraviolet radiation that is given off, damages their eyes."

"Have I seen any of your workers yet?"

"Not yet, even though there are over thirty-one thousand on this craft, we aren't in an area where they usually work."

"What do they look like?"

"They're very short; only about four feet tall. They have gray skin and have large eyes. That's their most distinctive feature, their eyes."

"What do they do around here?"

"They do just about everything. They do whatever we wish them to do. They act under our direction."

"Are they your slaves?"

"Not really. They were made to perform work for us. We grow them. They're not really alive in the sense that they have a soul or any feelings. Think of them simply as organic robots. That's why I said we have thirty-two thousand entities here. Only about one thousand inhabitants are living in the sense that they have feelings and a soul."

"So are you a member of the ruling class then? Are you alive?"

"Yes, I'm alive." Jomar smiled. "But no, I'm not a ruler, I'm just a citizen here. We each have different responsibilities. All of us here are in a constant state of learning and developing."

"What do you mean by the word, developing?"

"Oh, I mean that as we live, we are constantly developing our spirit, our soul. We always seek perfection in our spirit."

"How do you achieve that?"

"We achieve that by striving toward unconditional love. I'm surprised you do not know that. Is that not what Jesus taught you?"

"Well ... yes. I guess so."

"The ones you will soon meet are very advanced in spirit and learning. Speaking of them, I think it's time we go down to level twelve and meet the ones who sent for you."

Chapter 19
Revelations

"Wendy, are you still listening?"

"Yes."

"Good. I have much more to tell you about my journey. I want you to listen closely now as I continue my story."

Within five minutes we were at level twelve and entering a spacious conference room with a large oval table surrounded by twenty-six chairs. This room, as with every room I was in, had an ethereal glow that seemed to come from the ceiling and the walls. The walls glowed in various pastel colors that changed from time to time. It truly was beautiful.

Shortly after we arrived in the conference room, three other people, as beautiful as Jomar, entered the room. They had beautiful gowns that seemed to have a white glow. Their heads also had a golden glow about them; almost an aura.

"I want to introduce you to three of our directors," Jomar said. "This is Enlil, the Chief Director of our craft."

A very handsome, middle-aged man, with snow white hair came forward and shook my hand.

"It's nice to see you again. I've have been anxious to see you, ever since you became a woman."

"I'm honored to meet you." *That's strange,* I thought, *I don't recall ever meeting him before.*

"And this is Nintu, our Science Director," Enlil said, as he took me over to a very attractive, middle-aged woman. She also had snow-white hair.

"I am pleased to see you again," Nintu said.

Now I'm starting to freak out.

"Over here, is Enki, our anthropologist," Enlil said, as he took me over to a middle-aged man with blond hair.

"I'm pleased to meet you," Enki said, as he shook my hand.

"Let's all have a seat," Enlil said as he directed us to all take seats near one end of the table. As I sat down, I noticed that each person was wearing a beautiful plain gold band around their foreheads. Even Jomar was now wearing one. I'm sure he wasn't wearing one before.

"Those headbands are beautiful. What do they signify?" I said.

"Thank you," said Enlil, "They do look nice but they signify nothing. We all wear them for their function."

"What's that?"

"They allow us to communicate with the ship's computer. Any question we have in our mind is answered by the computer."

"Does the computer speak to you through those headbands?"

"In a way. Actually, the answers to our questions appear in our minds."

"If you can communicate with your ship's computer through thought, then is seems that you can then communicate with each other by thought through the computer. Is that true?"

"You're very perceptive, Sandra," said Enlil. "What you say is true. However, we do not need these headbands to communicate with each other by thought. We can do that naturally. We are all wearing these headbands now because we anticipate that you will have questions of us for which we may need to consult the ship's library of information."

After a pause, Enlil said, "I suspect that your first question is why Jomar brought you here."

"Yes, I am very curious about that. I'm also curious to know who you are and why you are here."

"Yes, I can imagine. Well, we are Sernon and come from a star that is much like your sun but it takes nearly one thousand of your Earth years for its light to reach Earth. That is where we originated, but none of us has been back there for a very long time. We have all been here since we were assigned this star system by the Federation."

"What federation?"

"We are part of a federation that extends throughout our galaxy. There are thousands of advanced civilizations within our galaxy who are members of the Federation. We happen to be the closest to your solar system so we were assigned this zone. We have established bases on various planets and moons within this star system, but have spent most of our time developing Earth."

"Hmmm… Do you have bases on Mars?"

"Yes."

"Why haven't our astronomers seen them?"

"Our bases are buried deep underground for protection."

"Protection? From what?"

"Because of Mars' smaller size, it had less gravity to hold its atmosphere. And, because it cooled so quickly, its iron core solidified and it lost its magnetic field."

"Why is the magnetic field important?"

"The charged particles thrown out by your sun are very hazardous to life. The Earth's magnetic field shields it from these particles. When Mars lost its magnetic field, the surface became bombarded. Also, since there was no magnetic field to divert the particles around the planet, the atmosphere was stripped away. Because of Mars' small size, this happened relatively quickly."

"So," I said. "You have bases on Mars but are concentrating on developing Earth. Why?"

"Within your solar system, Earth has the most diverse environment and forms of life. It has the best conditions for developing an advanced civilization."

"So, you've come here to take over the Earth!"

"Oh no." Enlil smiled. "We can't do that. The Federation will not allow one planet to take over another. Disputes would arise and peace would be lost. That would bring disharmony within the Federation.

"Your Earth is a very beautiful planet, rich in a variety of natural resources. Not all members of the Federation are as benevolent as we are, and would exploit this planet. It is the Federation Law that protects this planet. It is forbidden for any member to take over any planet, populated or not. If we want to extract any resources for commercial purposes, we are only allowed to act in a cooperative way with the dominant species."

"So, you came here to set up a relationship with us?"

"Yes and no. When we came here, humans did not exist, so there was no life form with which we could form any alliance. The surface temperature and other conditions were very good here. Earlier visitors from the Federation planted life on this planet when conditions were suitable. With time, these primitive life forms evolved into a great diversity of life.

"We had been informed by scout ships that, because of the diversity of life and the vast amount of liquid water, the Earth looked like a good prospect for the development of an advanced species which we could work with in the future. An advanced biped similar to us had already evolved."

"Are you talking about *Homo erectus*?"

"I think that is what you call them. They had one of the characteristics required for making advances in technology."

"What characteristic is that?" I asked.

"They had fingers with an opposing thumb necessary for making things and had the potential to become highly advanced. Another reason for choosing them was they had excellent adaptability and could survive the dramatic climatic changes that we knew would lie ahead. Your planet is unique in that it goes through periods of extensive glaciations every twenty-two thousand years or so. Also, periodic shifts in the Earth's crust causes dramatic changes from time to time. Both of these effects have dramatic effects on *animal* and plant life. Adaptability is the key to survival."

"Are you telling me that you recognized the potential of *Homo erectus* and waited for them to evolve into us so you would have someone to do commerce with?" I said.

"No. We are patient, but not that patient. It took millions of years for *Homo erectus* to evolve to their present state. We did not want to wait for more millions of years until their brain developed sufficiently, if it ever would." Enlil paused.

"Because of *Homo erectus'* similarity to us, both Nintu and Enki felt sure that with some simple modifications, these creatures could be altered to have vastly increased intelligence. They felt we could make what you would call a 'quantum jump,' in the development of this species. *Home erectus* already had a relatively large brain mass because of their protein rich diet. Nintu was able to genetically alter the existing species to create what you call *Homo sapiens*, or humans. She enhanced their brain functions and their larynx to allow speech and cognitive thinking. Recordkeeping and communication skills are very important if a species is to advance. The resulting humans, as you can see, are very similar in appearance to us."

"Yes. Remarkably so," I said.

"Enki has been monitoring the progress of humans ever since."

"How long have you been here?"

"The three of us, along with all of the crew, were assigned the task of bringing this craft here and setting up this outpost about four hundred and fifty thousand years ago."

"Do you mind if I ask how old you are?"

"I don't really know," Enlil said. "Age has no meaning for us. We have learned how to control the aging process. It is rare that we become ill but if we do, and need a new organ, we can replace the diseased one. There is no reason to die unless we're in an accident. We're very good at predicting events. For us, accidents don't happen, or at least they are extremely rare. We live as long as we wish to."

"What happens if you do die?" I asked.

"If we die by accident, or choice, our souls continue on, just as yours does."

"So I take it that you believe we have an immortal soul. Do you believe there is a Heaven and God?" I asked.

"No, we don't think…*we know*."

"How do you know that?"

"Our scientists proved the existence of an immortal soul over five million years ago. Before that, they proved that the universe is so finely and beautifully tuned that it could not be by chance. The ratio of various important elements and the mix of various sub-atomic particles is in a perfect balance for the universe, and indeed life itself, to exist. There had to be a Creator," Nintu said.

"It is the life force from The One that gives us all life and keeps us alive," Enki added. "We can neither create nor destroy a spirit. Only The One can do that."

"You are fortunate to have found the proof. For most humans, our belief is based only upon faith," I said.

"Yes."

"So, you created humans in your likeness and have been here ever since?'

"Yes, and Enki has been monitoring your progress ever since.

"I guess that means, not only are you our creator, but you are also our guardian angels," I said.

"I guess you could say that," Enlil said. He looked at Enki. "Why don't you tell her about what you have been doing?"

"Yes, I would be glad to," Enki said. "We have constantly monitored the progress of human development. From time to time, we had to intercede to correct your course but we were very careful to do that sparingly and covertly. We were careful not to interact with humans directly."

"Why? What harm would that do?" I asked.

"Humankind would become too dependent on us and not develop properly. Had we interacted with humans directly, in an official capacity, we would have disturbed the natural development and stifled your progress. Also, the Federation discourages that. It was very important that humans develop naturally."

"So you just stood back and watched, so to speak," I said.

"Not exactly. We did occasionally implant some key ideas in some of your most brilliant humans in order to accelerate your development. Otherwise, you would still be simple herdsmen living in straw huts. We had to interact indirectly, through your priests, so that we could remain hidden and would be thought of as Gods."

"You don't strike me as having a big ego. Why did you want us to think of you as Gods?"

"That way, we could lead you in the direction we wanted by proclaiming laws for you to live by. We would pass down some important knowledge through your priests. This was knowledge required for civilization; writing, laws, and mathematics, for example. From time to time, we would instill in certain individuals, the notions for inventions in technology. They believed that the ideas came from their own minds."

"When the deluge came, we tried to save some humans."

"Are you talking about Noah's flood? Did you cause that?"

"No, we, that is Enki, knew the flood was about to happen but we did not cause it. Enki's scientists had been monitoring the ice sheets at the Earth's southern pole and knew it was about to shift away from the pole. We knew that when it slid into the ocean, it would raise the level of the ocean by several hundred feet and cause massive flooding. At most risk were the human settlement north of the area you now call the Persian Gulf. At that time that area was a freshwater lake and marsh lands. A natural land bridge that was holding back the sea was going to be breached by the ensuing tidal waves. We knew there was no way to prevent this so we warned some humans to prepare."

"Why didn't you evacuate all of them?"

"There were too many to evacuate in the time we had. Also, we felt that most had become corrupt. So we decided to let nature take its course and we would save only the most worthy. But, we did not cause the flood; it was a natural event.

"That was not the only natural disaster humankind has faced. In some cases, they completely obliterated entire civilizations. Several times, we had to build new civilizations again."

"What were these other natural disasters?"

"Most were the result of the Earth's crust shifting suddenly and dramatically, causing great earthquakes and volcanoes. Parts of the Earth's surface that had been near the equator were moved closer to the poles and polar areas were moved to more temperate climates. Many land areas became covered by water and new land areas appeared from the oceans. These changes happened so fast that many species had no time to respond. They just perished. Many civilizations suddenly disappeared below the oceans."

"What caused the Earth's crust to shift?"

"An imbalance caused by the thick ice sheets near the poles. The center of their mass did not coincide with the location of the poles and this created a torque on the crust. Eventually it became great enough to move the crust. This placed the center of the ice mass even further from the poles. The process accelerated causing the dramatic effects I just mentioned."

Enki went on to explain the many ways they had watched over humankind and nurtured its development.

"I'm curious, why did you allow us to war upon each other and slaughter millions of people?"

"We found those phases of your development very repulsive, but it was your natural course. We felt, and hoped, that eventually you would grow beyond your need for violence. It has been hard for us.

"You must know that even human parents, who are trying to raise their children, often find it necessary to let them argue with each other and battle it out. They have to make their own mistakes. This is painful to the parents, but the children learn from their mistakes and grow."

"Yes, I know what you mean. My parents have told me the same thing."

Enki looked at the others. They nodded and he continued. "What we did find intolerable was your development of nuclear power as a destructive force. Unfortunately, you are developing faster technologically than you are spiritually and socially. You are becoming a threat.

"Your technology has advanced to the point where you are destroying the Earth's environment faster than you realize. The chemicals that humans are now releasing into the environment are beginning to affect your ability to reproduce. Human males are becoming sterile. Soon, if we don't intercede, you will be faced with extinction. Now, you are beginning to explore space, and it will only be a matter of time before you discover you're not alone in the universe.

"Worse yet, you may bring nuclear weapons into space with you. We cannot allow that. We feel that time is running out and we must now take action to correct these problems."

"That's why you are here, Sandra," Enlil said.

"What can I do?"

"We have found humans to be very emotional beings. You're emotions are much more diverse than ours. In fact, your emotions are much more diverse than any other species we have ever encountered. Within your species, you range from benevolent to evil. Very few other species in our galaxy have that range. For almost all the other advanced species, the range of goodness is very narrow. You are one of the most emotional species we have ever encountered. For us, emotions are a hindrance to social development.

"You may have observed that we all act much more alike. You will learn that we act much more in unison, more in tune with our society, more in harmony. Your leaders must be less concerned about their own welfare and more concerned about the welfare of humanity and your planet. These leaders must be in tune with our minds — our plan. To make that happen, over the years, we have been developing hybrids who are less emotional and have a greater insight into our way of thinking. They are more in tune with the good of our society rather than the good of the individual. These hybrids are connected to us mentally and spiritually."

"How have you created these hybrids?"

"We combined human sperm with human eggs that are genetically altered to contain some of our genes," Enlil said. The parents are not aware that this process is occurring. They do not realize that they are bearing offspring that are not completely human. These children have a normal childhood with the exception of being periodically brought here so we can check on their development and give them education. They do not remember being taken. In fact, almost all of the thousands of hybrids living on Earth do not know they are hybrids. Their parents do not suspect their children are any different from others. Nevertheless, they are different. They have the skills we want."

"How do you plan to use these hybrids? I asked.

"When the time is right, we will activate them. Meanwhile, they are moving into positions of responsibility. Eventually, they will take over the leadership roles in human society. To prepare humankind for that day, we have begun to place signs on the Earth for all to see. Eventually all people will understand these signs and know we are coming to show the way."

"I still don't understand, what is my part in this?" I asked.

Enlil rose from his chair and came over to me. He stared into my eyes. "It's okay for you to remember now. Don't you remember? You have been here many times for your education. Today, you are being activated for a special mission."

I was at a loss for words. As I stared at them in amazement, this place was becoming familiar to me. *I remember now, the glowing walls, with all their beauty. Yes, I remember them now. I remember the training room where they had me manipulate the panel that spoke to me in a strange language. No, it actually isn't strange; not now. I remember it! I understand it all now!*

Wendy was beginning to hyperventilate.

Gibbs, sensing Wendy's mental state, touched her cheek to compel her gaze. "Relax now. Everything is okay. You should not be concerned."

Wendy began to feel more relaxed and her breathing became more normal.

"Take slow, easy breaths. That's it. Slow and easy," Gibbs said in a calming voice.

After Wendy regained her composure and was breathing normally, Gibbs continued. "I'm sorry I made you see all of that, but I thought it would help you understand if you could see it in your own mind. Do not be concerned. You must know that their mission here is to help humankind."

"Why?" Wendy questioned. Every bone in her body said no one does something for nothing.

"They love humans. They always have. They created us!"

"So they've been waiting patiently for half a million years until we develop? That's really hard to believe."

"Dr. Ahearn, you forget, time has no meaning for them. They're patient and have been willing to interact with humans from time to time to nurture our development until we are ready; until we have the required level of technology."

"Required level of technology for what?" Wendy asked

"To be brought into the Federation."

"How will that be good for us?" Wendy asked.

Gibbs went on to explain the advantages humankind will have after a formal relationship is established with the Sernons.

"It sounds too good to be true," Wendy said.

"It is true."

"What role will humans play in this new order of things?" Wendy asked.

"Humans will benefit as they fall in line behind their new leaders and begin to follow their plan."

"So, they want us to become trading partners?" Wendy asked.

"I think so." Gibbs paused and stared over at the table with the briefcase sitting on it. She turned and stared into Wendy's eyes. "Wendy, open the briefcase now and show me the device, please. I want to see it."

Wendy hesitated. Her resistance was gone. She took Gibbs to the table, unlocked the briefcase, and opened it. "This is it," she said, as she extracted the device from the case. "Isn't it beautiful?"

"Yes it is," Gibbs said. "You must be very careful with that. The Sernons told me that it has access to all the knowledge they possess. If the knowledge is misused by mankind, it could destroy the Earth."

"How do they know that I have this device?" Wendy asked.

"Over the years, they have lost craft and their pilots. They know these remains are now in the hands of humans and are being studied. They have not been concerned because they know humans haven't evolved technically far enough to unlock their secrets."

"If the Sernons are so perfect, why do their craft crash?"

"Some of their small scout craft have been lost because their pilots, the grays, have taken the craft into areas with very high electromagnetic fields such as lightning strikes. Also you have struck our craft with intense beams of microwaves. These have disrupted the maneuvering systems and caused the crafts to crash."

Gibbs looked at the device and then back at Wendy. "The Sernons warned me about *this* device. If humankind ever discovers how to make it work, it gives them access to too much information, too soon. I was positioned at this base to watch for any signs that the device has been activated." Gibbs looked at Wendy. "I sense that it has been." Gibbs paused and looked into Wendy's eyes. "Can you make it work yet?"

"Yes, I am making progress, but have not yet deciphered their language."

"Why do you want to decipher their language?"

"Our mission is to find out why the Sernons are here. We are hoping that this device is a key."

"Dr. Ahearn, you don't need to do that now, I've told you why they're here. You must pass that knowledge on to the other members of your team. I will make sure that you retain enough memory of our meeting this afternoon so that you can explain the Sernons' mission. After I leave, you will believe that you got this information from the device." Gibbs led Wendy back to the couch. "You will remember that I was only here to clean your apartment. We did not talk. Do you understand?"

"I understand," Wendy said.

"Good. It's time to sleep now. You've worked very hard today and now you are very sleepy."

As Gibbs said those words, Wendy's eyelids became heavy and she fell into a deep sleep.

"Wendy, are you there?"

"Wha …Who … is it," Wendy answered as she awoke. She had not heard Corey knocking at the door.

"It's me, Corey. You said you wanted to have supper together. Remember?"

"Oh … aaahhhhh … sure. Hold on." Wendy went over and opened the door.

"Hi…Were you asleep? I kept knocking and knocking but you didn't answer. I almost went on to the cafeteria to look for you. It's after six. Are you all right? You look terrible."

"Oh, I'm okay. I guess I just worked too hard. I'm famished."

"Good. I turned in our order for pizza right after lunch. Let's go get it."

"Okay. Let's eat." Wendy gave Corey an apologetic look. "I'm sorry, but if you don't mind, after we eat I want to hit the sack. I'm exhausted."

03:30 AM:

The crew-chief saluted the plane as the Lockheed F-117A Nighthawk Stealth Fighter taxied out of the mountain and onto the taxiway. Thirty seconds later, the large hanger door closed behind. Within minutes, the plane was climbing toward its assigned cruise altitude of Flight Level 310 on a heading of 335 degrees. The pilot's face had a smile of contentment as his mission was nearing completion.

Chapter 20
The Answers

Corey entered the conference room at 8:02 AM carrying his breakfast tray. Pete was already there enjoying his breakfast.

"Good morning, Pete," Corey said. "Wendy isn't here yet?"

"No, I figured you two would be coming in together. She must be right behind you."

"No, I didn't see her in the cafeteria, maybe she overslept. She looked terrible last night. I'm worried about her. Last night, she just sat, picking at her food and not saying much of anything. She seemed tense and ill at ease about something but all she would say was that she was tired. Something about the device is getting to her."

"Well, if she doesn't show up in five minutes, I'll give her room a call," Pete said.

Just then the door opened and Wendy entered the conference room carrying her breakfast tray. "Good morning, I'm sorry I'm late. I overslept," Wendy said as she set her tray down on the conference table.

"Good morning," the men said in unison. Both were alarmed at Wendy's appearance; she looked like she hadn't slept at all.

"How are you feeling today?" Pete asked, with a tone of concern in his voice.

"Oh, I'm fine. I'm just tired. I think I must have put too much time into the project yesterday. I didn't sleep well, either."

Pete studied Wendy carefully. "Maybe we should have a short day today. I have another appointment after lunch. We can quit then. While you eat, Corey and I can bring you up to date on what we did yesterday."

"That would be fine," Wendy said listlessly.

Pete glanced at Corey. "Do you want to start?"

"Sure." Corey eyed Wendy for a moment. "We learned a lot more about the technology they use in building the craft."

"Oh, I see," Wendy said, casually.

Corey was exuberant. "Wendy, I think if we can splice that control cable back together, maybe we can make that thing work!"

Pete shot Corey a glance. "Corey, don't forget, there was a reason that thing crashed. What about the gaping hole?"

Corey and Pete spent the next hour telling Wendy of their discoveries as she picked at her breakfast. Corey was like a little boy explaining all the neat toys he saw at a new toy store. Despite Corey's enthusiasm, Wendy seemed to be only half interested as her mind wandered in and out of the conversation.

"So, Wendy," Pete said, "It's your turn. Tell us how you made out yesterday. Have you 'broken the code,' so to speak?"

Wendy sat up straight as she was brought back into the conversation. "No I haven't yet, not completely. But, I do have some results to report. I'm not sure if I mentioned this before, but as I work with the device more and more, it becomes more intuitive to me. Perhaps intuitive isn't the right word. It's hard to explain. I don't want to say that it speaks to me but it is something like that. With other translations I have done, after I have studied the written script a while, the translation suddenly appears in my mind. I think artists have the same feeling when they suddenly see in their mind's eye what they are about to paint. Well, when I'm working with the device, images begin to appear in my mind."

"What sort of things have you learned from these images?" Pete asked. He was still concerned by Wendy's demeanor; she seemed frazzled.

"There is information in there about our future encounter with the aliens and the day they will reveal themselves to us officially."

"That's good! That's exactly what we want to find out. When is this encounter going to occur?" Pete leaned toward Wendy so as not to miss a word.

"I don't know," Wendy answered, "but I sense the encounter is near."

"So you think the end is near?" Corey asked.

"I'm not sure that the word *end* is the correct word," Wendy countered. "I think that we are approaching a time when dramatic changes will be occurring in the way we live. The Mayans were aware of that. They had great skills in predicting astronomical events. Did you know that over a thousand years ago, they predicted the exact time and date of the total solar eclipse that occurred in Mexico City in 1999. They also predicted the date when our lives will change dramatically."

"When did they think that would occur?" Corey asked.

"December 24th, 2012," Wendy answered.

"That's pretty specific!" Pete said.

"Yes," Wendy said. After a pause she continued. "I've learned other things."

"Like what?" Pete prompted.

"Many things. I'm convinced that device really is connected to the alien knowledgebase." Wendy went on to explain what she had learned. She confirmed that the grays were merely sophisticated robots. She described how they were grown and how their eyes required replacement from time to time.

Pete glanced at Corey and then looked at Wendy strangely. "How did you know that?"

"From the device. I think. I don't know." Wendy suddenly became aware that she had not heard either Pete or Corey mention that fact. She just knew! A sense of panic began to come over her.

"Are you alright?" Corey asked with concern. Wendy had turned pale.

"Oh yes, I'm alright. At times I amaze myself by what I've learned from the device. It's like ... bang ... the information is in my head and I don't even know how it got there. I don't recall seeing these things written or displayed on the device. I just became aware of certain facts. It's beginning to scare me."

"Wendy, if you want to take a break, I'm sure Pete will understand," Corey said.

"That's right," Pete said, "if you want to break now, we can."

"No, I want to go on."

"Well, if you're up to it, let's go on," Pete said. "What else have you found out?"

Wendy went on to describe what she had learned aboard the alien ship as she was mind-melded with Gibbs. But, in Wendy's mind, she had learned all of this from the device.

The two men sat in amazement as she told her story. When she started to describe them as reptilian, Pete interrupted again.

"Reptilian! I thought you could see them in their glowing white robes?" Pete said.

"That's true," Wendy said. She was puzzled. *Why did I say they were reptilian? How strange.* "Yes, I did. That's strange... I don't know why I thought they were reptilian in form."

"It's stranger than you think," said Pete. "Many people, who have been abducted, report that the aliens in charge are very tall and seem to have a reptilian form." Pete thought for a moment. "Do you know where they're from?"

"Yes, I do. They came from a planet they call Sernon."

"Where is that?" asked Corey.

"Beyond the star system of Zeta Reticuli," Wendy said.

"Do you know where that is?" Corey asked.

"No." Wendy looked at Corey and shook her head. "I haven't the foggiest idea."

"Then, how did you know where that star is?" Pete asked.

"I don't know. I just know that they're from there," Wendy said. She was beginning to become unnerved again as her voice took on a tone of panic.

"Okay ... relax, Wendy. I'm not trying to argue with you. I am just puzzled as to how you know these things. Let's continue. Why do you think they created us?"

Wendy went on to describe their need for commerce. She described how the Federation rules required the aliens to create the human species and how they did that.

"Hold on," said Pete. "You're going too fast. It seems strange that they would create us and then hang around for one or two hundred thousand years while we develop. They're pretty patient!"

"Yes, they are. Time has no meaning to them," Wendy said.

"How long do they live?" Corey asked.

"I don't know, but the same aliens who created us are still here; alive and well. Barring an accident, I think they can live as long as they want."

"Where is here?" Pete asked, as he glanced with an expression of disbelief over to Corey.

"Their main base is a craft that orbits our sun in a region far enough away to be undetected by us. Their craft is huge and easy for us to see with our telescopes if they keep it too close to Earth. So, they keep it out beyond Mars. I think it's in the asteroid belt. Does that make sense, Corey?"

"Well, that's pretty far out. How big is their craft?"

"It's a cylinder two miles in diameter and eight miles long," Wendy said, surprised that she knew that.

"How do you know all of this?" Pete continued to be amazed with her knowledge.

"I told you I don't know! The device seems to have put all of this information into my head somehow. It seems to communicate with me through some form of telepathy. I'm not aware when it's doing it. I don't know what combination of keystrokes makes it do that. It just happens!"

Pete could see that Wendy was becoming agitated again. "I'm sorry, Wendy. I don't mean to keep asking, but it all seems so difficult to believe," Pete said, apologetically. "Please try to calm yourself. I won't question your answers again."

"That's okay, I understand. My answers amaze me too."

Pete looked at Corey. "Would our technology allow us to see a craft that big if it was hidden in the asteroid belt?"

"Probably not. I think even the Hubble telescope may not be able to detect it unless we knew exactly where to look."

"Wendy, you said the main base is out there. Are you saying they have other bases?" Pete asked.

"Yes, they have bases on Mars and Earth that have been here nearly as long as they have. Today they have bases underground at several locations in the United States and at several locations under both the Atlantic and the Pacific oceans."

"Exactly where are these bases, Wendy?" Pete asked.

"I don't know."

"Do you know why the aliens have been abducting people?" Pete asked.

Wendy looked at the device for a moment while she collected her thoughts. "Yes. They've become concerned that our advancement in technology is outpacing our advancement spiritually. Things are out of balance. The Sernons feel they must step in now and make corrections before we destroy all that they have accomplished. We became a threat to the planet and to the Federation when we developed the atomic bomb. They became extremely alarmed. This is especially true now that we're beginning to explore beyond our planet."

Pete looked at Corey and then turned to Wendy with a questioning expression. "Why are they performing the abductions?"

"Let me continue. They feel we're not ready for direct contact by them. So, that's why they haven't landed and made contact. They feel that if they were to make their presence known at this time, there would be panic and chaos. It would destroy all of the various religious fabrics that exist today.

"They feel that we, as a species, are much too emotional to deal with their direct intervention. Before they meet with us, we must have a new leadership; one with people who are much less emotional. Also, they feel that many of the problems we have today were brought about by leaders who have been self-seeking. They feel we need leaders who will lead us based on what is good for humankind. We need leaders who will make decisions that are for the good of our society and the Federation: decisions that are not based on emotions."

"So, they're genetically altering us to remove our emotional side. Is that it?" Corey asked.

"They are making genetic alterations to create the leaders of the future who will lead, not on emotion or self-interests but based on what's best for society," Wendy said defensively. "These leaders will be 'tuned in' to *their* thinking and more in harmony with the rest of the Federation. These new leaders will think as one and be able to communicate directly with the aliens; through their minds. When the new leaders are in place, then the aliens will make their appearance and share their technology with us."

"So, they're creating hybrids to lead us. Do these hybrids know what their mission is?" Pete asked.

"Almost all of them don't even realize they're hybrids; not yet anyway. When the time is right, they will be 'awakened,'" Wendy said. "By then they will be in leadership positions and their awakening will simply 'tune them in' to the higher authority of the Federation. They will understand what they have to do to unify the planet under one leadership whose goal is peace and cooperation between all nations on the Earth and with the Federation. When humanity is united under this leadership, the aliens will make their appearance and officially welcome us into the Federation. It will be wonderful! They will share fantastic technology with us!"

"What sort of technology?" Corey asked.

"Corey, you'll be shown how they propel their crafts by gravity. With this technology, we will be able to travel into space easily and visit other stars quickly. They will show us how to build power generators that we've not even dreamed of yet. We'll have all of the power we will ever need, and it will not destroy the environment!"

"I don't think there is a way to generate power without having a bad effect on the environment," Corey said.

"But they know how to harness the power of the Earth itself, through the pyramids," Wendy countered.

"The pyramids?" Pete asked.

"That could be true." Corey looked at Pete. "I have heard of that before. There are some researchers who think the Great Pyramid was a MASER power generator."

"I've always thought that the pyramids were Egyptian tombs," Pete said.

"That's a myth perpetuated by the media," Corey said. "The real tombs are many miles from the pyramids. Egyptologists don't really know what the pyramids were built for."

Wendy continued. "Unlimited power is not all the aliens will give us. They'll show us how to repair the damage we've done to the environment. Medical technology will be given to us that will eliminate all diseases. Our lives will be long and healthy ones. Drudgery will be eliminated because they'll show us how to grow worker clones like the grays. We will be free to enjoy life. We will be given new methods of transportation. We will finally be able to explore the galaxy and become part of the Federation. It will be wonderful! The Sernon's coming will truly be a miracle! We must watch the signs!"

Pete shot an incredulous look over to Corey. "What signs, Wendy?"

"The signs on the Earth. They will tell us when the time is right."

"Do you mean the crop designs?" Corey asked.

"Yes, the signs on the Earth," Wendy repeated.

"Wendy, when the aliens arrive, what will be our role in this new society?" asked Pete.

"In the advanced society of the Sernon's all members work together for the common good; just as bees all work for the common good of the hive. Our role will simply be to work in unison under their leadership. To act otherwise will not be allowed. Each member will have their place, their assignments, and their responsibilities."

"Won't this mean giving up our individual freedoms?"

"True, this will require the sacrifice of individualism, but everyone will benefit from this. It will be for the good of all humanity to act in unison and to obey the *higher* order. Can you see that?"

Pete shot a glance over toward Corey and then looked at Wendy. "I think I am beginning to get the picture. Our life will be wonderful as long as we don't rock the boat and try to have independent thought. Is that correct?"

"You make it sound like they're going to exercise some draconian rule over us."

"What you just told us seems to fit that model," Pete said.

"No, that's not true! They *love* us. They just want to temper our emotions so we'll be more stable; more civilized. That will be necessary so we can be trusted with all of the wonderful technology they'll be giving us. Right now, our range of emotions is far too great. We must become more like *them*; much less emotional. They all work and think in unison. So must we."

"So the free-spirited and free-thinking people will have to go. There will be no place for them in the new order of things. Is that true?" Pete asked.

"Pete, the only other choice for us is to continue down our present path of destroying the Earth and ourselves. Do you think that's better?" Wendy asked impatiently.

"Well, it seems to me that there must be a better way," Pete responded. "Though," Pete shook his head, "I have to confess, I don't know what it is."

Pete took a deep breath. "Perhaps this is a good time for a break. Please bring the device back with you when you and Corey return. I'd like to see what you do that allows you to know so much about the aliens. Also, I want to try to tap into their main computer."

Pete checked his watch. "Let's get back together in fifteen minutes."

Chapter 21
It's Gone!

When Wendy and Corey returned, Pete was already back, anxious to get started again. The prospect of gaining access to the alien's main computer excited him to no end. Corey set their two teas down as Wendy placed the briefcase on the table in front of her and unlocked it with the key she kept hung around her neck.

"Would you like to work with the device now, Pete?" she asked.

"You bet. Do you think you can access the alien's main computer now?"

"Well, I'll try, but as I said earlier, I don't know exactly how the information gets into my head," she said as she opened the briefcase.

The blood drained from Wendy's face as she stared into the briefcase in disbelief. "It's gone!"

"What do you mean, it's gone?" Pete barked. His heart began to race.

"I'm sure I placed it back into this case last night before going to bed!"

"The briefcase was always closed whenever I saw you last night," Corey said.

"Let me run back to my room and see if I left it on the table." She was embarrassed to think she could have been so careless with something so important. *What must Pete think?*

"Go ahead." Pete looked at Corey. "Go with her."

"Sure," Corey said. He could see that Pete was upset. "Let's go, Wendy. We'll be back in a few minutes, Pete." He and Wendy left the room carrying the empty briefcase.

It was nearly ten minutes before Corey returned. "Pete, you'd better come, quickly! Wendy's flipping out! We both searched her apartment and can't find the device. She's in a panic. She feels terrible."

"It can't be gone!" Pete was in denial. His worst fears had come true. Corey led him back to Wendy's apartment where she was sitting on her couch, sobbing.

"Pete, I'm sorry," Wendy said. Her eyes were pleading for mercy. "We've looked everywhere. It isn't here! I don't understand how it could have been taken. No one has been in my room in the last twenty-four hours except Corey and me, and Corey was here for only half an hour for supper."

"We'll find it," Pete said. He was trying to rationalize a tragic situation. "There's no way it can leave this base. It's more secure than the White House." He shot her a look. "Are you sure you've checked everywhere in your apartment?"

"Yes, Corey and I have turned this place upside down. It isn't here!"

"Okay. Let's calm down. Follow me back to the conference room and we'll work this out."

As soon as they had reached the conference room, Pete lifted the beige phone and dialed. Within a few seconds, a voice answered. Pete responded, "This is Colonel Mitchell in section G. I am reporting a CODE RED situation and am asking for a base lockdown. Also, I need access to the surveillance tapes of this section. Pipe those through to the main display here in my conference room. The extension is 2334. Thanks," Pete said as he replaced the phone.

Within seconds, the intercom throughout the base sounded a shrill horn sound followed by a female sounding voice repeating the verbal message with a drone, "WARNING, THE BASE IS NOW IN A CODE RED. ALL PERSONNEL MUST STAY IN THEIR SECTIONS." This notice was repeated every two minutes.

"What do we do now?" Corey asked.

"As soon as the surveillance tape is piped through, we'll scan it for any activity in and out of Wendy's apartment." He looked at Wendy. "When was the last time you know for sure you had the device in your possession?"

"I remember seeing the briefcase on my table last night at eight when Corey came to get me for supper. The briefcase was closed," she insisted.

"That's right, I remember seeing it on your table when you came to the door to let me in and it was closed," Corey confirmed.

"But was the device in the briefcase at that time?" Pete's voice was tense now. He tried not to let his sense of panic show.

"I think so," Wendy said. "I'm pretty sure that I placed it in the case just before taking a nap. I can't be positive though. It all seems hazy in my mind. I was really tired. I must have—" Wendy's voice fell off.

"Okay, the monitor is flashing now so the tape must be up," Pete said as he pressed a few buttons on the keyboard. Suddenly, the large screen at the end of the room lit up and a menu presented itself on the screen. Pete moved the cursor to the item listed as HALLWAY G. He clicked on that and another menu appeared asking for his password.

He entered his password and the next menu asked for the date requested, beginning at midnight. Pete clicked today's date and the hallway scene began to play forward at normal speed. A box inset in the lower left of the screen showed the time advancing from 00:00:00. Pete pressed fast-forward and the tape advanced at seven-times-normal rate. Nothing was happening. Pete pressed a button and the clock began to advance much faster, on super-fast-forward, at a rate of forty-eight times normal. Every ten seconds, Pete resumed normal speed, checking for movement in the hallway. There was no movement in the hallway until 07:22:10 when the back of Pete appeared, walking towards the cafeteria. Pete slowed the tape down to fast-forward. Because of the speed, he looked like a character in an old time silent movie running down the hall towards the cafeteria. At 07:26:22 Lieutenant Gibbs appeared from her room and walked, as quickly as Pete, towards the cafeteria. At 07:32:20, Pete came out of the cafeteria, carrying his tray and went into the conference room door. At 07:35:03 lieutenant Gibbs came out of the cafeteria with her tray and took it back to her room. At 07:47:06, Corey left his room and went to the cafeteria only to reappear at 07:58:03, carrying his tray to the conference room. At 07:59:34, Wendy left her room for the cafeteria and emerged at 08:09:18 with her tray and went to the conference room. At 08:12:03, Lieutenant Riley left his room, went to the cafeteria and, within ten minutes, emerged with a tray which he took to his room. Pete put the tape on super-fast-forward again, slowing to normal speed every ten seconds to check. There was no action until Wendy and Corey appeared from the conference room. Pete slowed the tape to fast-forward. Wendy and Corey went to the cafeteria and emerged shortly with drinks and went into Wendy's room at 10:02:34. At 10:16:02, Corey left Wendy's room and ran over to the conference room. At 10:16:44, Corey and Pete went from the conference room over to Wendy's room. Pete stopped the tape.

"WARNING, THE BASE IS NOW IN A CODE RED. ALL PERSONNEL MUST STAY IN THEIR SECTIONS."

"I can't see how the device could have been removed from your room today. Let me try yesterday's tape," Pete said. He went back one menu and selected yesterday's date. The clock was at 00:00:00. "When was the last time you know you had your hands on the device?"

"Well … Corey left my room right after lunch to join you here for another tour of the craft. That was about one. I worked on the device for a few hours and then took a break to play the piano, to relax. And then … oh yeah, I remember now. At shortly after four, I put the device away because Gibbs came to clean my room. I remember the time because when she knocked on the door I thought it was Corey and checked my watch. It was around four-twenty or four-thirty."

"Good! I think we're beginning to narrow the timeframe." Pete wanted to restore Wendy's confidence. "I'll key in fifteen hundred hours as our starting point. As he did, the clock showed 15:00:00. He set the speed for fast-forward. There was no action until 15:23:03, when both lieutenants left their rooms and went to the cafeteria. At 15:31:00, they both left the cafeteria and went to Gibbs's room. At 16:05:04 Riley left Gibbs's room with two trays and went to the cafeteria. At 16:06:34, he left the cafeteria and went back to his room. At 16:10:24, Gibbs came over to Wendy's door, stopped and put her ear near the door, and then turned and returned to her room. At 16:21:02, Lieutenant Gibbs left her room and went over to Wendy's door and knocked. Wendy's door opened at 16:21:52, and Gibbs went in. At 17:32:43, Gibbs left Wendy's room carrying something. Pete stopped the tape, backed it up and replayed it at real-time speed. "What's that she's carrying?" He stopped the tape on freeze-frame.

"It looks like my dinner tray," Wendy says. "Yes, I think it is. She took that after cleaning my room."

"Where was the device while she cleaned your room?" Pete asked.

"I put it in the briefcase before answering the door. In fact that was the last time I saw it because, after she left, I took a nap. Then Corey came to get me for supper and you know the rest."

Pete resumed the tape at normal speed. Gibbs carried what looks like a tray back to the cafeteria. At 17: 39:02, Gibbs left the cafeteria carrying what looks like a tray with food and takes it back to her room. Pete sped the tape back up to seven to one. At 17:44:03, Corey left the conference room and goes to his room. At 17:46:12, Pete left the conference room and went to the cafeteria. At 17:55:06, Pete left the cafeteria and walked past the camera with a tray of food. At 17:59:53, Corey left his apartment and went to Wendy's door and knocked. Pete switched to normal speed. At 18:01:03, the door opened and Corey went in. At 18:03:45, Wendy and Corey both left her apartment and went to the cafeteria. Pete went back to fast-forward. At 18:14:12, they both returned to Wendy's room with trays of food. At 18:29:12, Corey left Wendy's apartment and went back to his own. Pete stopped the tape there.

"Wendy, it seems that Lieutenant Gibbs was in your room for over an hour. That seems long to me. What was she doing?" Pete asked.

Wendy hesitated. "She… came to clean my room."

"What did you do while she was there?"

"I don't remember… I think I… relaxed. No… I think I played the piano. Yes… that's it… I played the piano. Gibbs said she enjoyed my playing."

"Was the device locked in the briefcase?"

"Yes, I always lock it in the briefcase before I ever open the door for anyone."

"Did she ask you any questions?"

"No...she just cleaned. Then, after she left, I took a nap."

"Are you sure the briefcase was locked?" Pete asked.

"I think so," Wendy responded, with a degree of uncertainty.

"She left your room with something that could have been a tray of dishes but she could have hidden the device under the napkins and then transferred it to her tray and taken it back to her room," Pete mused.

"WARNING, THE BASE IS NOW IN A CODE RED. ALL PERSONNEL MUST STAY IN THEIR SECTIONS."

Pete lifted the beige phone and dialed a number. Within three rings a voice answered. "Lieutenant Gibbs, could you come to the conference room right away, please. Thanks," Pete said as he returned the phone. Within a minute, Gibbs entered the room.

"Sir, what's the alarm all about?" Gibbs said as she took the seat Pete pointed to.

"Something important to our project has disappeared from Dr. Ahearn's suite, so I ordered the CODE RED."

"How can I help, sir?" Gibbs said.

"I just need to question you," Pete said. "You and Dr. Newton are the only other people to have entered Dr. Ahearn's suite since the article was last seen yesterday afternoon."

"Yes, I was in her room yesterday afternoon. It was just before supper because I remember taking her empty trays back to the cafeteria after I cleaned her place. I got my supper while I was in the cafeteria. Dr. Ahearn was in her room all the while I was there. I followed procedures, sir. She was playing the piano. In fact, when I walked by her door and heard the piano, I knew she was there and I thought that would be a good time to clean. What does the thing look like that's missing?"

"I'm sorry, but I can't tell you. Given the seriousness of our problem here, I'm afraid I must ask you to let us inspect your room, right now. I apologize, but I must do a thorough check of everyone's room. Dr. Newton, I will have to inspect your room too."

"Yes, I understand," he said.

Gibbs was becoming flustered. "Colonel, I must protest. Even though I have nothing to hide, my integrity has never been questioned before; by anyone."

"I'm sorry, but we must check your room. Let's go. You can be present as we check," Pete said.

As the four entered Gibbs's apartment, Pete took a quick walk-through. "Lieutenant, I must compliment you, your quarters are in immaculate condition."

"Thank you, Colonel," Gibbs said.

"Lieutenant, as Dr. Newton and I check the less personal areas of your suite, you can accompany Dr. Ahearn as she goes through your personal items."

"WARNING, THE BASE IS NOW IN A CODE RED. ALL PERSONNEL MUST STAY IN THEIR SECTIONS."

After nearly an hour, nothing was found. "Well Colonel, are you satisfied that I am not a thief?" Gibbs said. "I hope this will not go in my record."

"There will be no mention of this, Lieutenant. Again, I apologize, but this was necessary. May I please use your phone? I need to contact the base commander."

"Yes, sir. You aren't going to tell him that you suspected me of stealing are you?"

"No, Lieutenant, I need to advise him of our situation here so I can involve him in a broader sweep of the base," Pete said, as he keyed in the commander's number. "Hello, this is Colonel Mitchell in G section. May I speak with Colonel Andrews? ... He's not? ... Well this is very important, would you page him please. ... You can't? ...

Why not? ... Did you say he's left the base?" Pete's face became pale as he stared at the blank wall.

Behind him, a smile, ever so subtle, began to appear on Gibbs's face.

Chapter 22
The Chase

        Within minutes, Pete, Wendy and Corey were
back in the conference room trying to sort out what had
happened.   In the background, the calm female voice
repeated the CODE RED message every two minutes.
        "I felt bad about putting Gibbs through all that but she
was my prime suspect," Pete said.
        "She understands," Wendy said. "She certainly sensed
the severity of the situation and probably would have done
the same if she were in your position."
        "Maybe so," Pete mused. He was beginning to wonder
why Colonel Andrews left the base. He clicked on the wall
monitor.   "We never reviewed the tape much beyond
eighteen-thirty hours so let's see what's on the rest." He
pressed the play button and the tape began where it left off
at 18:29:15. Corey had just walked passed the camera and
nothing was in his hands. Pete pressed the super-fast-
forward button. Again, he slowed the tape to normal speed
every ten seconds to check activity. He continued until the
tape stopped automatically at 23:45:00. At that point the
tape went blank and snow appeared on the screen.

"What the heck?" Pete picked up the beige phone and made a call. Within seconds there was a voice on the other end.

"Hello, this is Colonel Mitchell in G section. I have been reviewing the security tape you piped over to me and it has stopped at twenty-three forty-five hours. Can you explain why it stopped fifteen minutes before midnight? ... I see. ... Earlier, you told me that Colonel Andrews left the base. What time did he leave? ... I see. How did he leave? ... Did he file a flight plan? ... He did? ... He's missing! ... How long can he stay up without refueling? ... Call me as soon as you locate him. ... Okay, thanks." Pete hung up.

"So, what's happening?" Corey got the gist of the conversation and could sense Pete's concern.

"Well, here's the story, as I see it," Pete began. "The tape has the last fifteen minutes missing because Colonel Andrews ordered it pulled at fifteen minutes before midnight so the tape heads could be cleaned. He left the base this morning at just past oh-three-thirty in a stealth fighter. His flight plan was to fly to the Boeing Air Field south of Seattle with a scheduled arrival at oh five hundred this morning. Forty-five minutes after departing, he began to descend and turned off his IFF transponder. Radar lost him shortly after. He never reported in at Seattle. They think he went down between here and Seattle and have sent out search and rescue crews."

"So what do you think happened, Pete?" Wendy leaned toward Pete anxiously.

"I think Colonel Andrews took advantage of the fifteen minute gap in the taping process, entered your room last night and took the device. He then left for Seattle to give or sell the device to someone. Either he crashed or he went below radar to change his course. We'll know soon. By now, he is out of fuel and has landed or crashed somewhere. If he landed somewhere we'll know. That kind of plane attracts a lot of attention. Regardless, with a crash alert out for a downed stealth fighter, everyone will be looking for it."

Pete's military training was now driving him. He checked his watch. He said, in military precision, "It's now eleven-oh-five. I want to contact Base Ops and arrange for fast transportation to where ever he has come down. If he has crashed, I want to keep the search-and-rescue people away from the site until we get there. I'll want both of you to go with me to help with the recovery of the device. No one but us three must see that device. We'll have to move quickly."

"Pete, do you think that Colonel Andrews is out to sell the device to some other country?" Wendy asked.

"I don't know, but it is possible. Right now I have to contact the President and bring him up to date," Pete said with a quiver in his voice. He was seeing his military career disintegrate by the minute.

Pete picked up the red phone to make his report. This was not going to be pleasant, he knew. Within seconds after he picked up the red phone a voice answered, "This is the White House, Colonel Mitchell. Do you wish to talk to the President?"

"Yes, and I need to have him on his private line, please." Pete's voice was tense.

"Please hold while I patch you through to him."

Within a minute, Pete heard the voice of the President. "Colonel Mitchell, this is the President speaking and I am alone and on a secure phone, so you can speak freely."

"Thank you Mr. President. I have news to report about the project. Doctors Ahearn and Newton are with me in our conference room so I'm going to put them on the speakerphone." Pete pressed a button on the phone and nodded toward Wendy to speak.

"Good morning Mr. President, this is Dr. Ahearn. Can you hear me okay?" Wendy's voice quivered as she realized that *she* was talking to the President of the United States!

"Yes, Dr. Ahearn, I can hear you fine. Actually, it's afternoon in my part of the country." The President paused. "Dr. Newton, how are you?"

"I'm fine, Mr. President," Corey answered in awe.

"So, Colonel Mitchell, how are you making out? I am very anxious to hear your results."

"Sir, I feel that we have made significant progress. Dr. Ahearn has been able to activate the device and has begun to learn a considerable amount."

"Wonderful! You have gone quite far in such a short time. I figured that you would still be wrestling with how to turn the damn thing on. But, it sounds like you're well past that stage. What have you learned about why the aliens are here?"

Pete felt an urge to cut right to the bad news immediately but his gut told him he should give the President a summary of their finding first. Then perhaps the President would receive the bad news better. He quickly gave the President his summary and took a deep breath.

The President jumped in, "Hold on, Colonel, that's a lot of info for me to digest in a few sentences! Slow down! I feel comfortable and relieved to hear that the aliens are our guardian angels but what do you mean by intercede?"

Pete went on to fill in those details and then it was time for the bad news. Pete took another deep breath. His heart was pounding. "Mr. President, there is much more that we will share with you later, but right now I feel that I must skip to the real reason I called you."

"Colonel Mitchell, I must say that I am extremely impressed with your findings thus far and hope to hear the rest soon." The President paused. "What is the *real* reason you called?"

"It's bad news, sir. The General was right about his concern for security at our base; we have been compromised. The device has been taken."

There was an eternity of silence. Pete waited. Then it came.

"Taken!" The President was silent again for a long moment. "Do you know who took it?" He regained his composure.

"I ... I am quite sure it was taken by Colonel Andrews, the Base Commander. As near as I can tell, the device was taken from Dr. Ahearn's quarters last night, just before midnight, while she was sleeping. The colonel left the base around oh-three-thirty hours in a stealth fighter headed for Seattle. Forty-five minutes after he took off, he took evasive measures and disappeared."

"I see ... that does sound suspicious. Yes, I agree with your assessment. It seems that the colonel is most likely our man. You must catch him and get it back!"

"Yes, sir, I will do my best." Pete paused, "Sir, I'll need your help. I need the Pentagon to assist me in taking whatever measures required in tracking down Colonel Andrews."

"You've got it! I'll call the Chairman of the Joint Chiefs right away and ask him to clear the way for you."

"Thank you, Mr. President." Pete thought he would sweeten the pot. "I need to tell you that we have discovered a most important aspect of the device; one I'm sure you will appreciate. This device is *much* more important than we originally thought."

"In what way, Colonel?"

"I'll let Dr. Ahearn explain, sir."

Wendy leaned closer to the phone. "Mr. President, we think it is more than just a ship's log. It seems that it can communicate directly to the alien's main computer. I have not completely encrypted their language yet but I think that when I do, we may be able to tap into their knowledge base and learn much more than we had thought. We may gain access to their higher technology."

The President did not speak immediately as he considered the implications. "Dr. Ahearn, that *is* astounding news. Colonel Mitchell, we *must* get it back, and soon, before Colonel Andrews has a chance to sell it to some other world power."

"Yes, sir, I agree."

"Colonel Mitchell, I want to commend you on a superb job thus far. Also, I want you to know that I will help you any way I can. I will bring the full power of my office to bear to remove any obstacles you encounter in getting the device back. Please, do not hesitate to call me for *any* help you need."

"Thank, you sir. With your help, we *will* get it back."

"Thank you, Colonel, and good hunting!" The line went dead and Pete hung up.

Pete shot Wendy and Corey a glance. "I thought the President took that quite well. Don't you agree?"

Wendy and Corey both nodded in agreement.

Pete stood up to leave. "I would like both of you to wait here for a few minutes while I run over to Base Operations to get the latest information on the whereabouts of Colonel Andrews."

Within minutes Pete was at Base Operations. As he entered the room, a colonel approach him. "Colonel Mitchell, I am Colonel Weir, Acting Base Commander. I was just contacted by the Pentagon and instructed to assist you in any way I can."

"Thank you, Colonel. Right now I just want to find out where Colonel Andrews went. After that, I'll want the fastest transportation you have to get me to him."

"Yes, we're as concerned about him as you," Colonel Weir responded. A sergeant handed him a note. The colonel looked at it and then Pete. "Well, I think we know where he is. An F-16, out of Luke Air Force Base, was on a cross country mission to Nellis when he spotted a downed F-117 stealth fighter at about eleven-fifteen this morning. He is in orbit over the site now."

"Can you get me into voice contact with the F-16 pilot?"

"Certainly. Stand by while I have my men patch you through." Colonel Weir went over to a sergeant near the radio consol. Within seconds Pete was handed a headset with a microphone attached. "Go ahead, the pilot, Captain Garner, is on the line," Colonel Weir said.

"Captain Garner, this is Colonel Mitchell. How do you read? Over."

A voice came back on the headset. "Five by five, Colonel. Over."

"Captain, can you tell me where the wreckage is located? Over."

"Yes sir. The plane is about twenty-five miles northwest of Kingman Arizona. It's sitting at the southeast corner of a dry lake. I think it's called Red Lake. I tagged my GPS as I did a close flyby to see if the pilot was still in the plane. The exact co-ordinates are: north 35 degrees, 33 minutes, 31 seconds and west 114 degrees, 3 minutes, 33 seconds. Over."

"Is he in the plane? Over," Pete's voice quivered.

"No, sir, the plane appears to have crash-landed but it's sitting, intact, with the canopy open. No sign of the pilot though. Judging from the skid marks, it looks like he was heading for the Kingman Airport when he came down. He did a hell of a great job landing that thing. Over."

"Thanks, Captain. You can stand down and continue on to Nellis. We'll take over the recovery from here. Over."

"Roger and out." The headset went silent.

"Sergeant, did you record those co-ordinates?" Pete said as he gave the headphones back.

"Yes, sir, I have them. Here's a map of the local area, Colonel," he said a he handed Pete a map and a note with the co-ordinates.

"What do you want me to do?" Colonel Weir asked.

"Please arrange for a chopper to take me and two members of my team to the site as quickly as possible. I want only the chopper pilot with us: no crew. Also, I want you to instruct all search-and-rescue teams to stay clear of the site until after I've had time to inspect the plane. Do *not* try to recover the plane or the pilot until I give the all clear. Do you understand?"

Colonel Weir gave Pete a strange look as he thought, *This is a strange request but this man has the Pentagon behind him.* "Yes, sir," he snapped back, sensing the urgency of the situation. "The chopper will be fueled and ready in fifteen minutes."

"Thank you, Colonel," Pete said, as he rushed out of Base Ops back to his office in G section.

Wendy and Corey were waiting in the conference room when Pete returned through his office door, wearing his flight jacket.

"Good news!" Pete said. "They've found the plane. We're going to move out in a few minutes."

"Did he land in Seattle?" Wendy asked.

"No, he landed in a dry lake near Kingman, Arizona."

"Is Colonel Andrews still with the plane?" Corey asked.

"No, there was no sign of him," Pete said as he unfolded the map he was given and placed it on the conference table. He studied the map and checked the location of the coordinates given by the F-16 pilot. "The plane is right here," Pete said as he pointed to the map.

Wendy and Corey stood next to Pete and studied the map.

"The plane is sitting right here in Red Lake. The F-16 pilot said it touched down here near the northwest corner and came to rest here at the southeast corner of the lake." Pete stroked his finger over the map.

Wendy bent down so she could read the markings. "It looks like he was heading toward the Kingman Airport over here," she said. "How far is that from where he landed?"

"About twenty-five miles."

"What time do you think he landed?" Corey asked as he began mentally calculating how long it would take to walk twenty-five miles.

"He would not have attempted such a landing until daybreak. That would be oh-five-thirty, at the earliest. He took off at about oh-three-thirty and could only fly about two to two-and-a-half hours without refueling. That would make him land at oh-six hundred at the latest."

"So, if he landed at daybreak, he has been on foot for about six hours," Corey mused aloud. "How far do you think he could walk in seven hours, Pete?"

Pete looked at the map again. "The terrain is hilly and given the colonel's age and condition, I would say he could travel about ten to fifteen miles." Pete's eyes widened as he traced the path between the plane and the Kingman Airport. "I'll be dammed," he said, almost in a whisper.

"What is it, Pete," Wendy asked as she saw his expression change.

"If the colonel continues along this line, he'll pass directly over the spot where the alien craft was recovered in 1953. That's ten miles from Kingman airport,"

"Do you think the crash site is his real target?" Wendy asked.

"I was wondering that myself. But why go there?" Corey added.

"That's a good question," Pete answered. "If that's his intention, we don't have much time. Let's get going!"

They were all on the flight line in less than five minutes. The Huey UH-1N helicopter was fueled and waiting. Two minutes later, they lifted off and headed southeast on a heading of 140 degrees at maximum speed.

In slightly under an hour, the chopper put down in a cloud of dust, one hundred yards from the stealth fighter. The plane seemed out of place, sitting in the middle of nowhere, with its canopy open. Just as the F-16 pilot had reported; no sign of Colonel Andrews. The plane had only moderate damage. Its nose-wheel was sheared off and the fuselage was resting in a nose-down attitude. Its nose pointed to the southeast; toward Kingman. Pete was impressed with the skill it must have taken to land in one piece on this terrain. He glanced at Wendy and Corey. "I want you two to follow me." He looked over to the pilot. "Captain, I want you to stay in the chopper while we examine the plane."

"Roger," the pilot said.

"Let's go," Pete said, pointing toward the plane as he jumped out of the chopper and began running in a crouched position. With the plane's nose resting on the ground, it was easy to see into the cockpit. As Pete stared in, Corey drew up next to him. "Corey, can you see the device in there?"

"No, I don't see it. Is there a storage compartment where he might have stashed it?"

Pete reached into the cockpit and opened a small compartment. "There's a small one but it's empty. I didn't expect to find it here," he said. "I'm sure he has it with him." He pointed to the floor at the base of the ejection seat. "There's a lot of blood here. Colonel Andrews must have been hurt in the landing. The blood trails over this side of the craft so I think this is where he exited." Pete's eyes scanned the ground. "Look, there's more blood over there in that direction ... heading toward the UFO crash site and Kingman."

Wendy had just arrived and turned away at the sight of the blood in the cockpit. "Do you think he is hurt badly?"

"It's hard to say," Pete answered, "but I'm sure he is not going to be traveling very fast. Perhaps that will buy us some time. We need to head out *now*," he said as he began to run back to the Huey.

As Wendy and Corey re-boarded the chopper, Pete spoke to the pilot. "Captain, I want you to take us over to the Kingman Airport at maximum speed. Then, I want you to turn and head back toward this location at thirty knots so we can look for the downed pilot." Pete had not briefed the chopper pilot and knew he assumed they were on a routine rescue mission. He wanted him to continue believing that.

Ten minutes later they were over the airport and turning back toward the downed plane. All eyes were pointed down as the chopper dropped down to five hundred feet and cruised northwest at only thirty knots.

Pete leaned forward and spoke to the pilot, showing him the map. "Captain, if we don't spot the pilot soon, I want you to set us down about one mile from this location," he said as he pointed to a spot on the map, one mile from the coordinated of the UFO crash site. "The terrain is pretty rough, so you'll need to find a level area. After we exit your craft, I want you to return to the Kingman Airport and wait for further orders. I'll call you on my radio when I want you to pick us up. Do you understand?"

"Yes, sir," the pilot snapped back.

As they approached the designated landing site, there was a flat area in the terrain fifty yards to the north. The chopper landed amidst a cloud of sand and dust. Pete jumped out and motioned for Wendy and Corey to follow. All three ran away, in a crouching position, to an area one hundred feet to the north of the chopper. They found refuge behind a large boulder.

The Huey departed with a roar and a cloud of dust. Soon the flapping sound of the rotors began to fade as the chopper disappeared over a ridge.

Pete spoke first as he pulled out his map and handheld Global Positioning System. He waited for the GPS to acquire several satellites and then took his reading. After looking at the map he said, "We need to head in that direction," and waived his hand in a pointing motion. "I want to be waiting at the UFO crash site when the colonel arrives. We need to catch him off guard to avoid any shooting."

"Do you think he's armed?" Wendy's face was drawn.

"Yes, he probably has a service revolver just like mine." Pete opened his flight jacket to reveal his pistol. "Let's head out now. Try to be as quiet as you can in case he's already there."

Pete's radio crackled, "Colonel, this is Captain Herber, I've landed at the airport and awaiting your call, over."

"Good, we may be here awhile. Over," Pete said softly into his radio.

"Roger and out," Captain Herber responded.

For twenty-five minutes the three worked their way up the mile-long slope strewn with rocks and boulders as large as cars. Periodically, Pete stopped to check his GPS before moving forward. Finally, "This is it," he whispered as he checked the map. "The UFO came down over there in that small plateau." He pointed ahead and to the left. "You two wait behind this boulder as I scout ahead for signs of the colonel." His voice was soft but tense.

Pete worked his way forward, staying under cover of the many boulders until he came to a crest in the hill. There, he could see down the other side for nearly a mile as the hill sloped gently downward to the west. Suddenly, there was a flash of light as the noon sun reflected off of something shiny in the distance. Another flash! *It's moving!* Pete thought to himself as he quickly crouched down behind a small boulder. *It's him! He's coming this way!* Pete surveyed the surroundings to find the best place for an ambush. *Down the hill. I'll move back down the hill so I can catch him in a pincer move between me and Corey and Wendy. They aren't armed but the colonel doesn't know that. If he tries to retreat, he has to move uphill.* Pete quickly moved back to where the others were waiting.

"He's coming!" Pete said in an excited whisper. "You two wait behind this boulder for Colonel Andrews to show. I'll take up a position on that high point over there," Pete said as he pointed to a prominent hill to his left. "I'll get behind that large boulder on the other side of this small ravine. After he passes my position, I'll expose myself and challenge him. Corey, when I tell him to lay down his weapon, you repeat that order so he thinks he's surrounded. I'll let him see me with my weapon drawn. You stay behind this boulder so he won't know you're not armed."

"Sounds like a good plan but what makes you think he'll show up here?" Corey asked.

"It looks like he's going to come up over the crest up there where this wash begins." Pete pointed up the crest where he had seen the colonel. "His easiest path down is through the wash between our two positions." He shot a glance at Wendy and Corey. "Okay, let's take our positions now!"

With that, they dispersed to their respective positions to wait.

No sooner had Pete reached his position when he caught a glimpse of a reflection at the crest of the hill. Colonel Andrews suddenly appeared and staggered into an open area of the wash just five hundred feet up the hill from where the three were crouched in-waiting. He was carrying a duffel bag in one hand and something else in the other. He paused, looked at the device in his hand, and headed down the hill, following the wash, just as Pete had guessed. Twice, as he approached the trio, he fell to the ground with a groan. The second time, as he slowly got back to his feet, he was only fifty feet from where Pete was hiding and was now between Pete's position and Wendy and Corey's.

Pete pulled out his sidearm, stepped out from behind his boulder, and shouted in a commanding voice, "Stop right there, Colonel, and drop that duffel bag. Keep your hands up where we can see them. You are surrounded."

From behind the large boulder on the other side of the wash, Corey called out on cue, "Drop your weapon. You are surrounded."

Colonel Andrews, caught by surprise and not knowing how many other people were there, followed orders and dropped the bag as he raised his hands. As the three made their way toward him, they could see that his right leg was wounded. His lower right pant-leg was torn and soaked in blood. Staggering, he fell to the ground just as they got to him. Pete picked up the bag and inspected its contents.

"How did you get this and where were you going with it, Colonel?" Pete asked.

"You know how I got it." He scowled at Pete. "Where I'm going is none of your business." He was struggling to keep from passing out.

"Did you have our section bugged?"

"It doesn't matter how ... how I knew what you had, I just ... just knew that you shouldn't have it. We ... we have no right to keep it. It's ... very dangerous for us to keep it."

"Dangerous for whom? Them or us?" Corey asked.

"Dangerous for ... for everyone. Too ... too much technology ... too fast. The human race is not ready yet. We'll ... we'll destroy ourselves if we have their technology. We're ... not ready ... yet." With that, he passed out.

"Is he dead!" Wendy said with alarm.

Pete bent down and felt his carotid artery. "No, he's just fainted." He looked down at the colonel's leg. "Looks like he cut his leg during the landing. He needs a tourniquet." Pete looked into the duffel bag and pulled out a cloth in which the colonel had wrapped the device. "Here, Corey, make this into a tourniquet and wrap it around his leg, just below his knee. We need to get him medical attention soon, before he goes into shock."

Pete pulled out his field phone and flipped it on. "Captain Herber, this is Colonel Mitchell. Over."

"Yes Colonel, I hear you loud and clear. Over," a voice crackled back.

"We're ready to be picked up now. We're located one mile northwest of where you dropped us off. We have the pilot and he will need medical attention after we return to base. He has a bad cut on his leg but we have the bleeding under control now. Radio the base and tell them we have the pilot and that they can retrieve the downed fighter now. Over."

"Roger, Colonel. My ETA to you is six minutes. Out."

Turning off the field phone, Pete turned to Wendy and Corey, "Are you two ready to get back to work? We have much to do."

"Pete, what will happen to Colonel Andrews?" Wendy asked.

"That's for the President to decide." He looked down at the colonel. "We have to return to base and continue extracting information from the device."

"Is it safe to go back there?" Corey asked.

"We have no choice. I think we need to be where the other artifacts are located in order to optimize our efforts. Vigilance will be the watchword for round two."

REFERENCES

For the reader whose curiosity is piqued by this book, I have included a list of references that will be helpful for doing more research. They are organized by chapter and in the approximate order their material was used.

Chapter 1
1. Randle, K., *A History of UFO Crashes,* Avon Books, New York, 1995

2. Randles, J., *UFO Retrievals: The Recovery of Alien Space craft,* Sterling Publishing, New York, 1995

3.Randles, J., *Alien Contact: The First Fifty Years,* Barnes & Noble Books, New York, 1997

4. Spighesi, S.J., *The UFO Book of Lists,* Kensington Publishing, New York, 2000

5. Stevens, Wendelle, www.ufophotoarchives.org

Chapter 6
5. Chaisson,G. and McMillan,S. *Astronomy, A Beginning Guide To The Universe.* Prentice Hall, New Jersey, 1995

6. Barrow,J. *The Origin of The Universe,* Basic Books, New York, 1994

7. Rees,M. *Before the Beginning, Our Universe and Others,* Perseus Books, 1997

8. Bennett,J.,Donahue,M.,Schneider,N.,Voit,M. *The Solar System, The Cosmic Perspective.* Addison Wesley, California, 2002

9. Darling,D. *Life Everywhere: The Maverick Science of Astrobiology,* Basic Books, New York, 2001

Chapter 7
10. Corse, P.J. and Birnes, W., *The Day After Roswell,* Pocket Books, New York, 1997

11. Hesemann, M. and Mantle, P., *Beyond Roswell: The Alien Autopsy Film, Area 51, & the U.S. Government Coverup of UFOs.*, Marlowe & Company, New York, 1997

Chapter 9
12. Kramer,S.N. *The Sumerians, Their History, Culture, and Character*, The University of Chicago Press, Chicago, 1963

13. Woolley,C.L. *The Sumerians,* W.W.Norton & Company, New York, 1965

14. Sitchin, J. *The 12th Planet,* Avon Books, New York, 1976

15. Sitchin, Z. *Genesis Revisited,* Avon Books, New York, 1990

16. Leakey,R. *The Origin of Humankind,* Basic Books, New York, 1994

17. Berger, L. with Hilton-Barber,B., *In The Footsteps of Eve: The Mystery of Human Origins,* National Geogaphic Adventure Press, Washington, 2000

Chapter 11
18. Brunswick, R., *UFO,* Goliath, Frankfurt, 1999

19. Berlitz, C. and Moore, W., *The Roswell Incident: The Classic Study of UFO Contact,* Berkley Books, New York, 1988

Chapter 12
20. Einstein, A. *The Meaning of Relativity*, Princeton University Press, New Jersey, 1956

21. Einstein, A. *Relativity, The Special and The General Theory,* Three Rivers Press, New York, 1961

22. Einstein,A. *Sidelights on Relativity ,*Dover Publications, New York 1983

23. Saussure, F. de, *Course in General Linguistics,* Open Court, Illinois, 1996

24. Walker, C.B.F., *Reading the Past Cuneiform,* University of California Press, California, 1987

25. Jean, G., *Writing The Story of Alphabets and Scripts,* Harry N. Abrams, 1992

26. Morley, S.G., *An Introduction to the Study of the Maya Hieroglyphs,* Dover Publications, New York, 1975

27. Coe, M.D., *The Maya,* Thames and Hudson, Ltd, London, 1997

28. Lewels, J., *The God Hypothesis,* Wild Flower Press, North Carolina, 1997

Chapter 13
29. Davies,P. *Are We Alone?,* Basic Books, New York, 1995

30. Silva, F., *Secrets in The Fields : The Science and Mysticism of Crop Circles,* Hampton Roads Publishing, Virginia, 2002

31. Thomas, A., *Swirled Harvest: Views from the Crop Circle Frontline,* Vital Signs Publishing and S B Publishing, England, 2003

32. Howe, L.M., *Mysterious Lights and Crop Circles*, Paper Chase Press, Louisiana, 2000

33. Pringle, L., *Crop Circles: The Greatest Mystery of Modern Times,* HarperCollins Publishers, London, 1999

34. Thomas, A., *Vital Signs: A Complete Guide to the Crop Circle Mystery and Why It Is Not a Hoax,* Frog Ltd., California, 2002

Chapter 14
35. Adamski, G., *Inside The Spaceships,* The George Adamski Foundation, California, 1955

36. Adamski, G. and Leslie, D., *Flying Saucers Have Landed,* The British Book Centre, New York, 1953

37. Homet, Marcel F., *Sons of the Sun*, Neville Spearman, London MCMLXIII
Chapter 15
38. Fuller, J.G., *The Interrupted Journey,* Berkley Paperback, California, 1966

39. Hopkins, B., *Missing Time,* Ballantine Books, New York, 1988

40. Strieber, W., *Communion: A True Story,* Avon Books, New York, 1988

41. Fowler, R.E., *The Watchers ,*Bantam Books, New York, 1991

42. Fowler, R.E., *The Allagash Abductions,* Wild Flower Press, Oregon, 1993

43. Jordan, D. and Mitchell, K., *Abducted!,* Dell Books, New York, 1994

44. Mack, J.E., *Abduction: Human Encounters with Aliens,* Ballantine Books, New York, 1994

45. Hill, B., *A Common Sense Approach to UFOs,* Betty Hill, New Hampshire, 1995

46. Walton, T., *Fire In The Sky,* Marlowe & Company, New York, 1996

47. Fowler, R.E., *The Andreasson Legacy,* Marlowe & Company, New York, 1997

48. Hopkins, B., *Witnessed: The True Story of the Brooklyn Bridge UFO Abductions,* Pocket Books, New York, 1997

49. Jacobs, D.M., *The Threat,* Simon & Schuster, New York, 1998

50. Boulay, R.A., *Flying Serpents and Dragons: The Story of Mankind's Reptilian Past,* The Book Tree, California, 1999

51. Leir, R., *Casebook: Alien Implants,* Dell Publishing, New York, 2000

Chapter 16
52. Erber, Thomas, <u>The Velocity of Light in a Magnetic Field</u>, *Nature*, April 1, 1961

Chapter 17
53. Hill, P., *Unconventional Flying Objects: A Scientific Analysis,* Hampton Roads Publishing, Virginia, 1995

54. Watts, A., *UFO Quest: In Search of The Mystery Machines,* Sterling Publishing, New York, *1994*

Chapter 19
55. Downing, B., *The Bible and Flying Saucers,* Marlowe & Company, New York, 1968

56. Ross, Hugh; *The Creator and the Cosmos: How the Greatest Scientific Discoveries of the Century Reveal God,* NavPress Publishing Group, Colorado Springs, CO, 1993

57. Turnage, C.L., *New Evidence That The Holy Bible Is An Extraterrestrial Transmission,* Timeless Voyager Press, California, 1998

58. Hapgood, Charles H., *Earth's Shifting Crust (foreward by Albert Einstein),* Pantheon Books Inc., 333 Sixth Ave., New York, NY., 1958

59. Hapgood, Charles H., *Maps of The Ancient Sea Kings,* Adventures Unlimited Press, Kempton, Illinois, 1966

60. Hapgood, Charles H., *Path of The Pole,* Adventures Unlimited Press, Kempton, Illinois, 1999

61. Allegre, Claude; *The Behavior of The Earth,* Harvard University Press, 1988

62. Imbrie, John and Katherine; *Ice Ages, Solving The Mystery,* Harvard University Press, 1979

63. Ryan, W., & Pitman, W., *Noah's Flood,* Simon & Schuster, 1998

Chapter 20
64. Bauval,R. and Gilbert,A. *The Orion Mystery,* Three Rivers Press, New York, 1994

65. Dunn,C. *The Giza Power Plant: Technologies of Ancient Egypt,* Bear & Company, Vermont, 1998

66. Brennan, H. *The Secret History of Ancient Egypt,* Berkley Publishing Group, New York, 2000

67. Mehler,S. *The Land of Osiris,* Adventures Unlimited Press, Illinois, 2001

68. Vallee, J., *Revelations: Alien Contact and Human Deception,* Ballantine Books, *New York, 1993*

69. Crystall, E., *Silent Invasion,* St. Martin's Press, New York, 1996

70. Walden, J.L., *The Ultimate Alien Agenda,* Llewellyn Publications, Minnesota, 1998

71. Krapf, P.H., *The Contact has Begun,* Hay House, Inc., California, 1999

72. Cannon, D., *The Custodians "Beyond Abduction",* Ozark Mountain Publishers, Arkansas, 2001

73. Dennett, P., *Extraterrestrial Visitations,* Llewellyn Publications, Minnessota, 2001

74. Summers, M.V., *The Allies of Humanity: An Urgent Message about the Extraterrestrial Presence in the World Today,* The Society For The Greater Community Way of Knowledge, Colorado, 2001

75. Good, T., *Unearthly Disclosure,* Arrow Books, London, 2001

THE AUTHOR

Dr. Farrell has been involved in technology most of his adult life. He holds a B.Sc. in Mechanical Engineering, a Masters Degree in Business Administration, and a Doctor of Engineering. For twenty years, he worked in industry, designing plastics processing machinery. For fifteen years, before retiring, he was a Professor of Engineering, preparing students for the plastics industry.

During his entire professional career, Dr. Farrell has been fascinated by the UFO phenomenon and has done extensive research through the literature to formulate his view on the topic.

This book is the result of that effort. He would greatly appreciate any feedback you are willing to give him as he prepares to write a sequel to this story.

He can be reached through: author@alienlog.com